THE
BABY-SITTERS CLUB
CLUB

LOGAN LIKES MARY ANNE!

DON'T MISS THE OTHER BABY-SITTERS CLUB GRAPHIC NOVELS!

KRISTY'S GREAT IDEA

THE TRUTH ABOUT STACEY

MARY ANNE SAVES THE DAY

CLAUDIA AND MEAN JANINE

DAWN AND THE IMPOSSIBLE THREE

KRISTY'S BIG DAY

BOY-CRAZY STACEY

ANN M. MARTIN

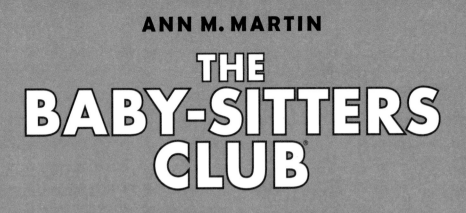

THE BABY-SITTERS CLUB

LOGAN LIKES MARY ANNE!

A GRAPHIC NOVEL BY
GALE GALLIGAN
WITH COLOR BY BRADEN LAMB

graphix

An Imprint of
SCHOLASTIC

All rights reserved. Published by Graphix, an imprint of
Scholastic Inc., *Publishers since 1920.* SCHOLASTIC, GRAPHIX,
THE BABY-SITTERS CLUB, and associated logos are trademarks
and/or registered trademarks of Scholastic Inc.

Library of Congress Control Number: 2019950319

ISBN 978-1-338-30455-8 (hardcover)
ISBN 978-1-338-30454-1 (paperback)

10 9 8 7 6 5 4 3 2 1   20 21 22 23 24

Printed in the U.S.A.   88
First edition, September 2020

Color assistants: Shelli Paroline, Sam Bennett,
Alenna Smith Boeker, and Jase Dale Boeker.

Edited by Cassandra Pelham Fulton and David Levithan
Book design by Phil Falco
Publisher: David Saylor

This book is for my old
baby-sitters, Maura and Peggy
A. M. M.

For Patrick, and the full minute we spent
laughing at a weird face Dipper made.

And for you! I'm so glad we got
to spend this time together.
G. G.

KRISTY THOMAS
PRESIDENT

CLAUDIA KISHI
VICE PRESIDENT

MARY ANNE SPIER
SECRETARY

STACEY MCGILL
TREASURER

DAWN SCHAFER
ALTERNATE OFFICER

MALLORY PIKE
JUNIOR OFFICER

CHAPTER 1

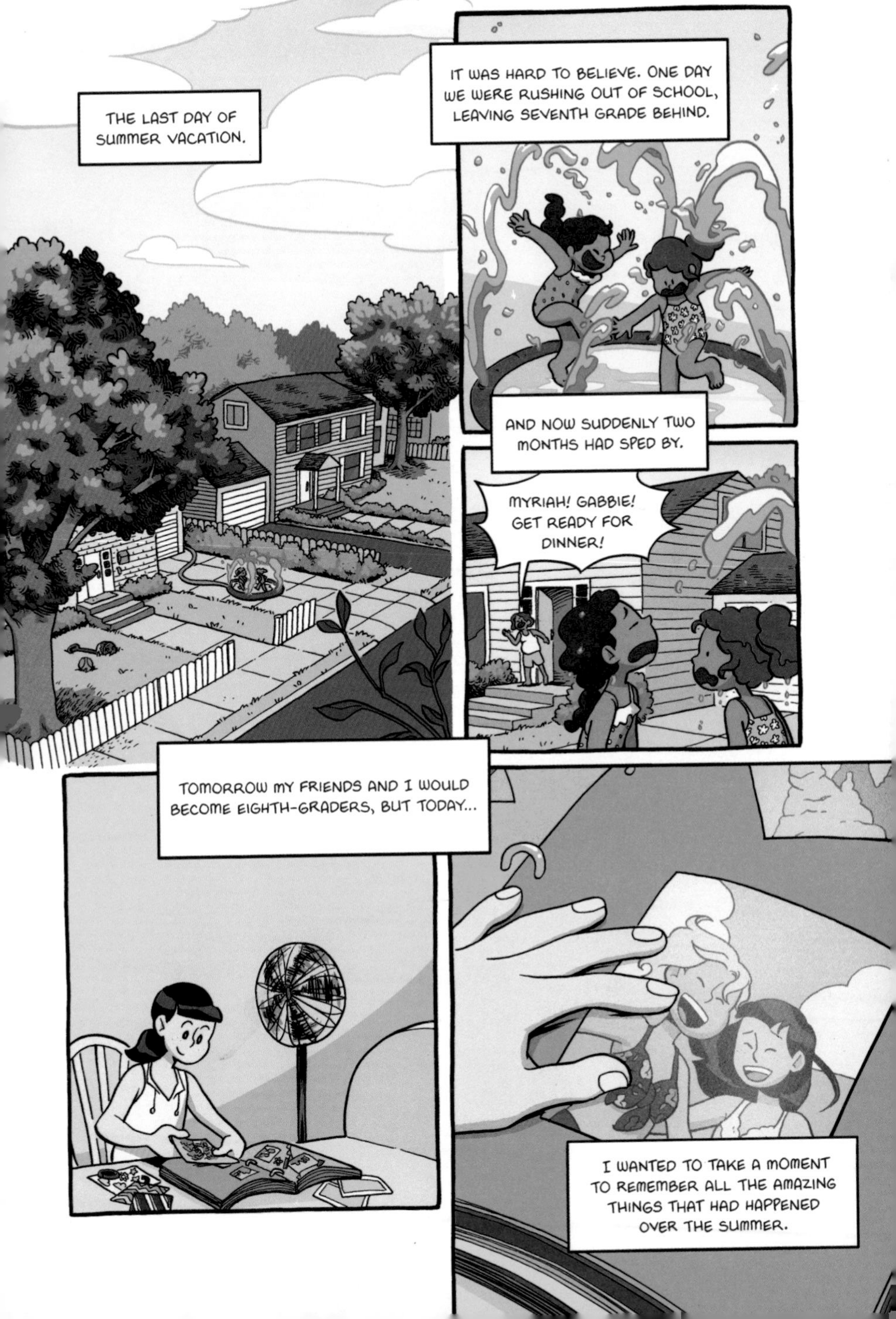
THE LAST DAY OF SUMMER VACATION.
IT WAS HARD TO BELIEVE. ONE DAY WE WERE RUSHING OUT OF SCHOOL, LEAVING SEVENTH GRADE BEHIND.
AND NOW SUDDENLY TWO MONTHS HAD SPED BY.
MYRIAH! GABBIE! GET READY FOR DINNER!
TOMORROW MY FRIENDS AND I WOULD BECOME EIGHTH-GRADERS, BUT TODAY...
I WANTED TO TAKE A MOMENT TO REMEMBER ALL THE AMAZING THINGS THAT HAD HAPPENED OVER THE SUMMER.

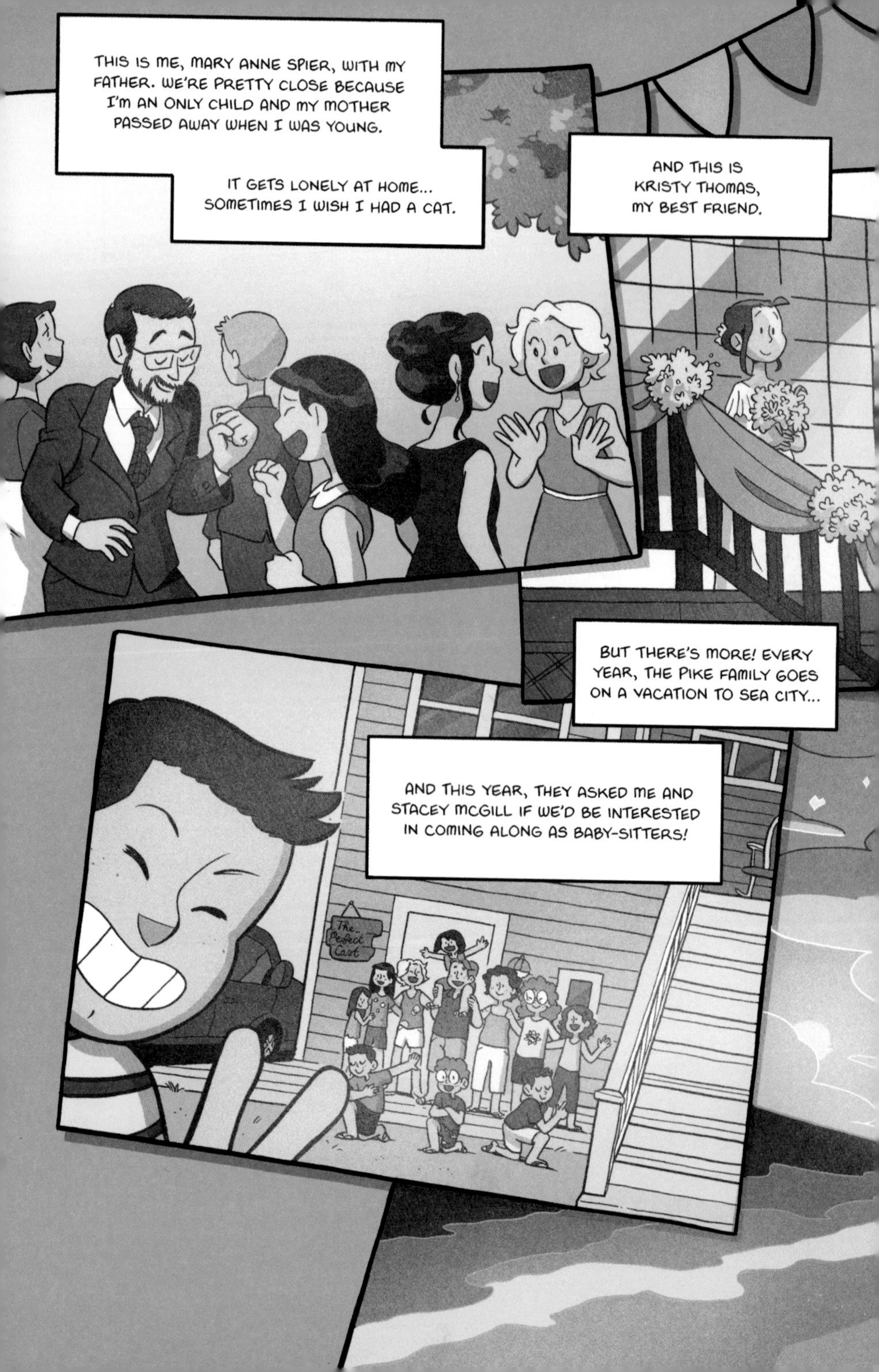
THIS IS ME, MARY ANNE SPIER, WITH MY FATHER. WE'RE PRETTY CLOSE BECAUSE I'M AN ONLY CHILD AND MY MOTHER PASSED AWAY WHEN I WAS YOUNG.
IT GETS LONELY AT HOME... SOMETIMES I WISH I HAD A CAT.
AND THIS IS KRISTY THOMAS, MY BEST FRIEND.
BUT THERE'S MORE! EVERY YEAR, THE PIKE FAMILY GOES ON A VACATION TO SEA CITY...
AND THIS YEAR, THEY ASKED ME AND STACEY MCGILL IF WE'D BE INTERESTED IN COMING ALONG AS BABY-SITTERS!
The Perfect Cast

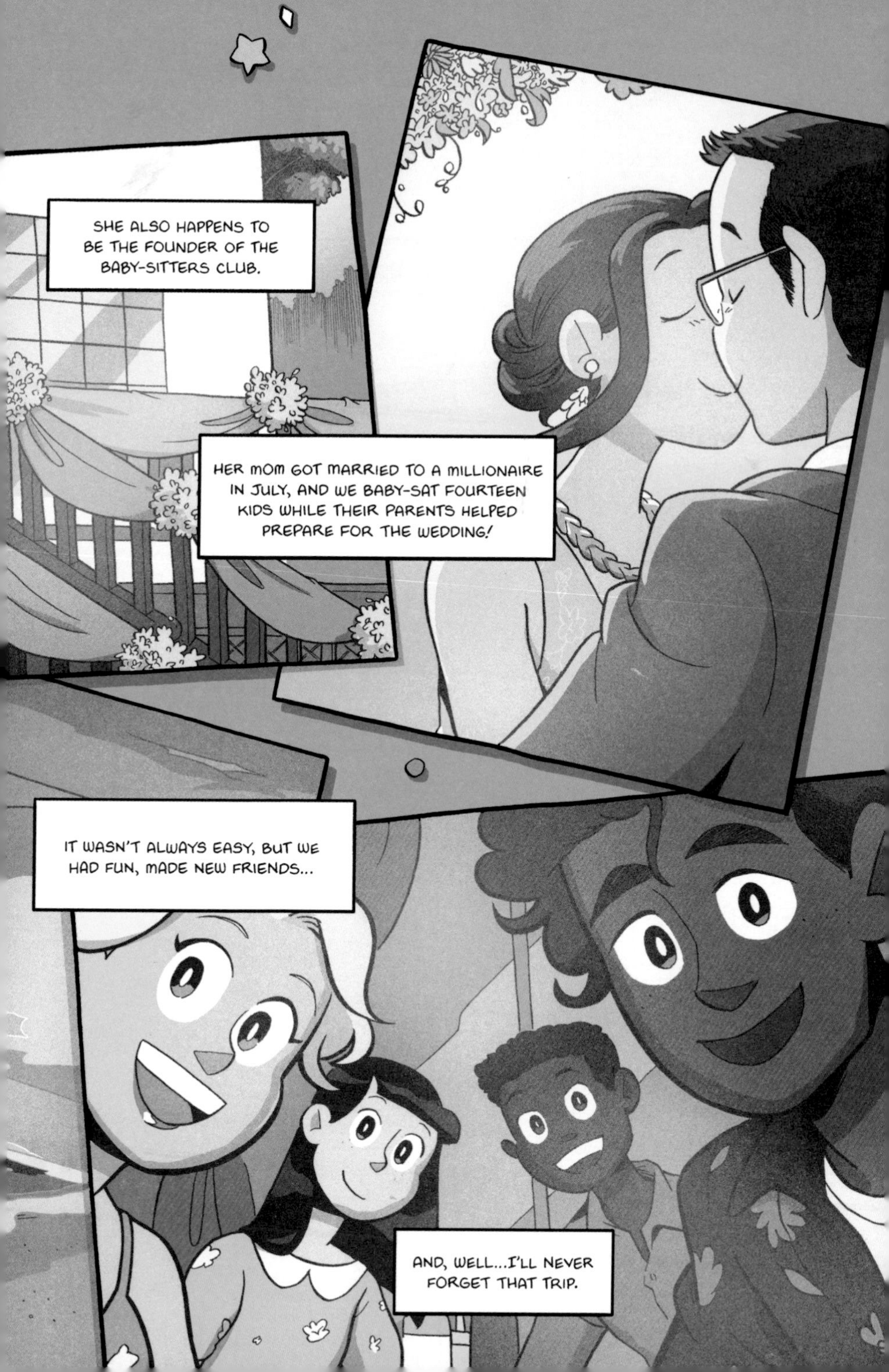
SHE ALSO HAPPENS TO BE THE FOUNDER OF THE BABY-SITTERS CLUB.
HER MOM GOT MARRIED TO A MILLIONAIRE IN JULY, AND WE BABY-SAT FOURTEEN KIDS WHILE THEIR PARENTS HELPED PREPARE FOR THE WEDDING!
IT WASN'T ALWAYS EASY, BUT WE HAD FUN, MADE NEW FRIENDS...
AND, WELL...I'LL NEVER FORGET THAT TRIP.

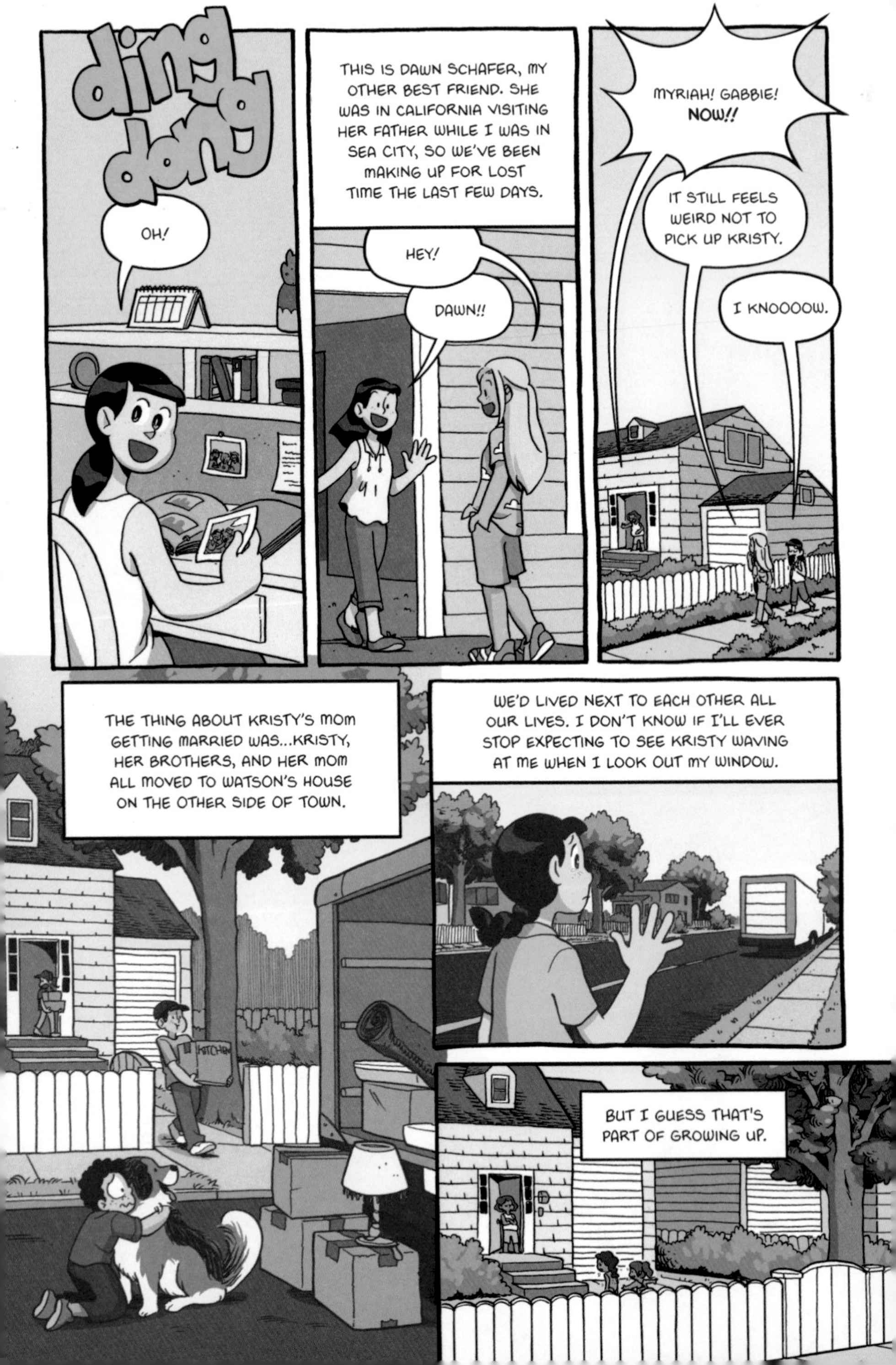
ding dong
OH!
THIS IS DAWN SCHAFER, MY OTHER BEST FRIEND. SHE WAS IN CALIFORNIA VISITING HER FATHER WHILE I WAS IN SEA CITY, SO WE'VE BEEN MAKING UP FOR LOST TIME THE LAST FEW DAYS.
HEY!
DAWN!!
MYRIAH! GABBIE! **NOW!!**
IT STILL FEELS WEIRD NOT TO PICK UP KRISTY.
I KNOOOOW.
THE THING ABOUT KRISTY'S MOM GETTING MARRIED WAS...KRISTY, HER BROTHERS, AND HER MOM ALL MOVED TO WATSON'S HOUSE ON THE OTHER SIDE OF TOWN.
KITCHEN
WE'D LIVED NEXT TO EACH OTHER ALL OUR LIVES. I DON'T KNOW IF I'LL EVER STOP EXPECTING TO SEE KRISTY WAVING AT ME WHEN I LOOK OUT MY WINDOW.
BUT I GUESS THAT'S PART OF GROWING UP.

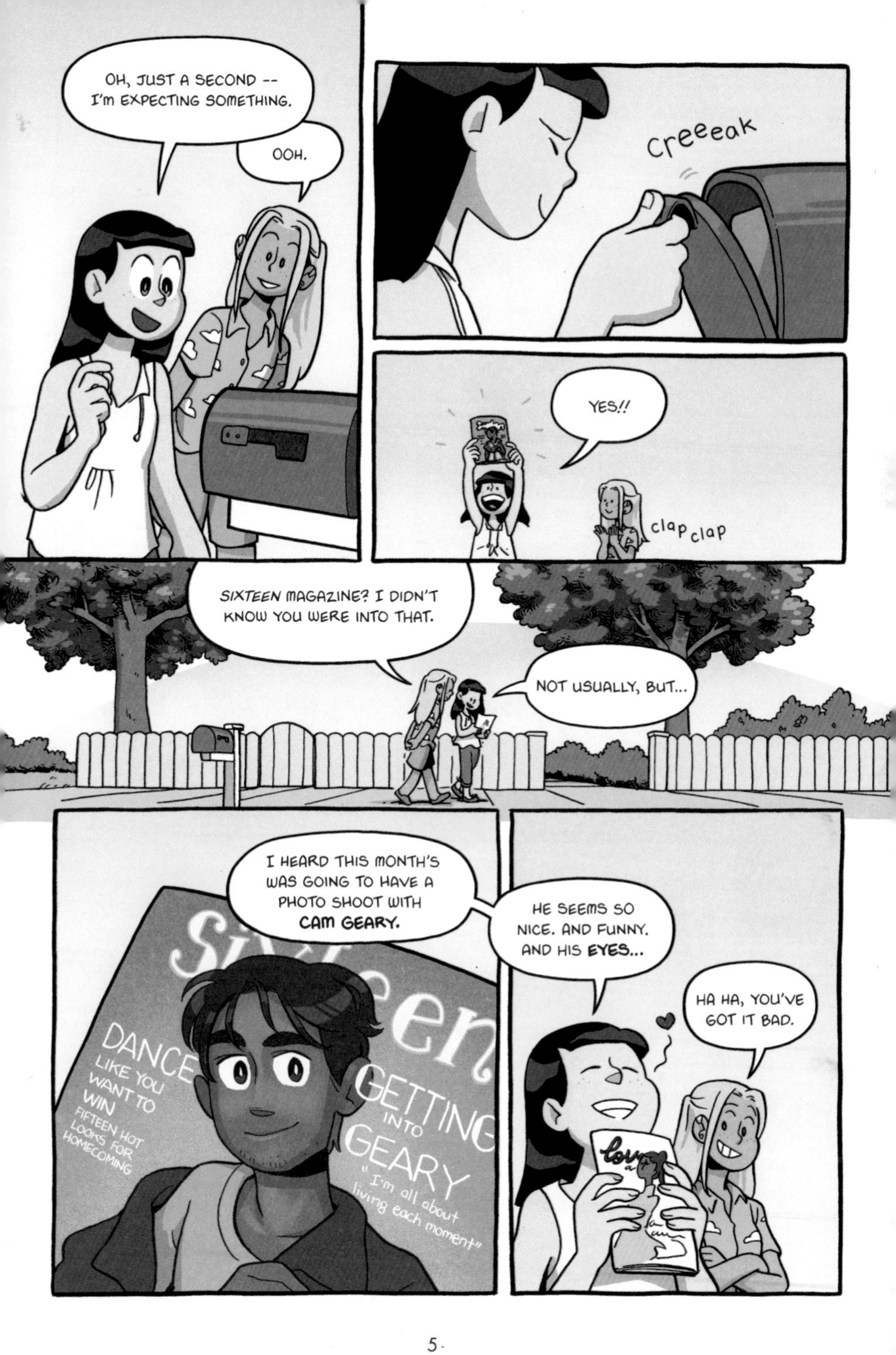

OH, JUST A SECOND -- I'M EXPECTING SOMETHING.
OOH.
creeeak
YES!!
clap clap
SIXTEEN MAGAZINE? I DIDN'T KNOW YOU WERE INTO THAT.
NOT USUALLY, BUT...
I HEARD THIS MONTH'S WAS GOING TO HAVE A PHOTO SHOOT WITH CAM GEARY.
Sixteen
DANCE LIKE YOU WANT TO WIN
FIFTEEN HOT LOOKS FOR HOMECOMING
GETTING INTO GEARY
"I'm all about living each moment"
HE SEEMS SO NICE. AND FUNNY. AND HIS EYES...
HA HA, YOU'VE GOT IT BAD.

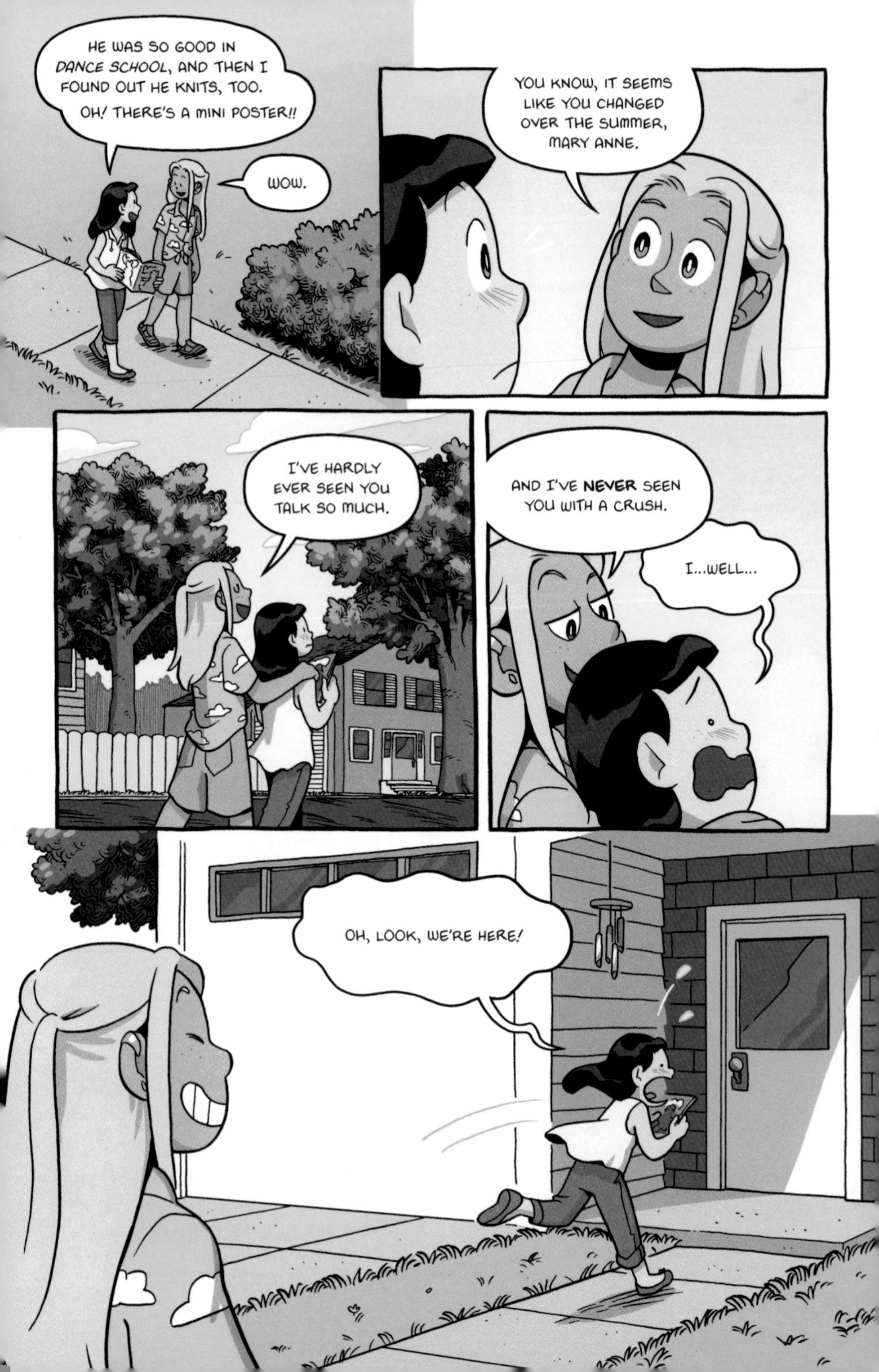
HE WAS SO GOOD IN *DANCE SCHOOL*, AND THEN I FOUND OUT HE KNITS, TOO.
OH! THERE'S A MINI POSTER!!
WOW.
YOU KNOW, IT SEEMS LIKE YOU CHANGED OVER THE SUMMER, MARY ANNE.
I'VE HARDLY EVER SEEN YOU TALK SO MUCH.
AND I'VE **NEVER** SEEN YOU WITH A CRUSH.
I...WELL...
OH, LOOK, WE'RE HERE!

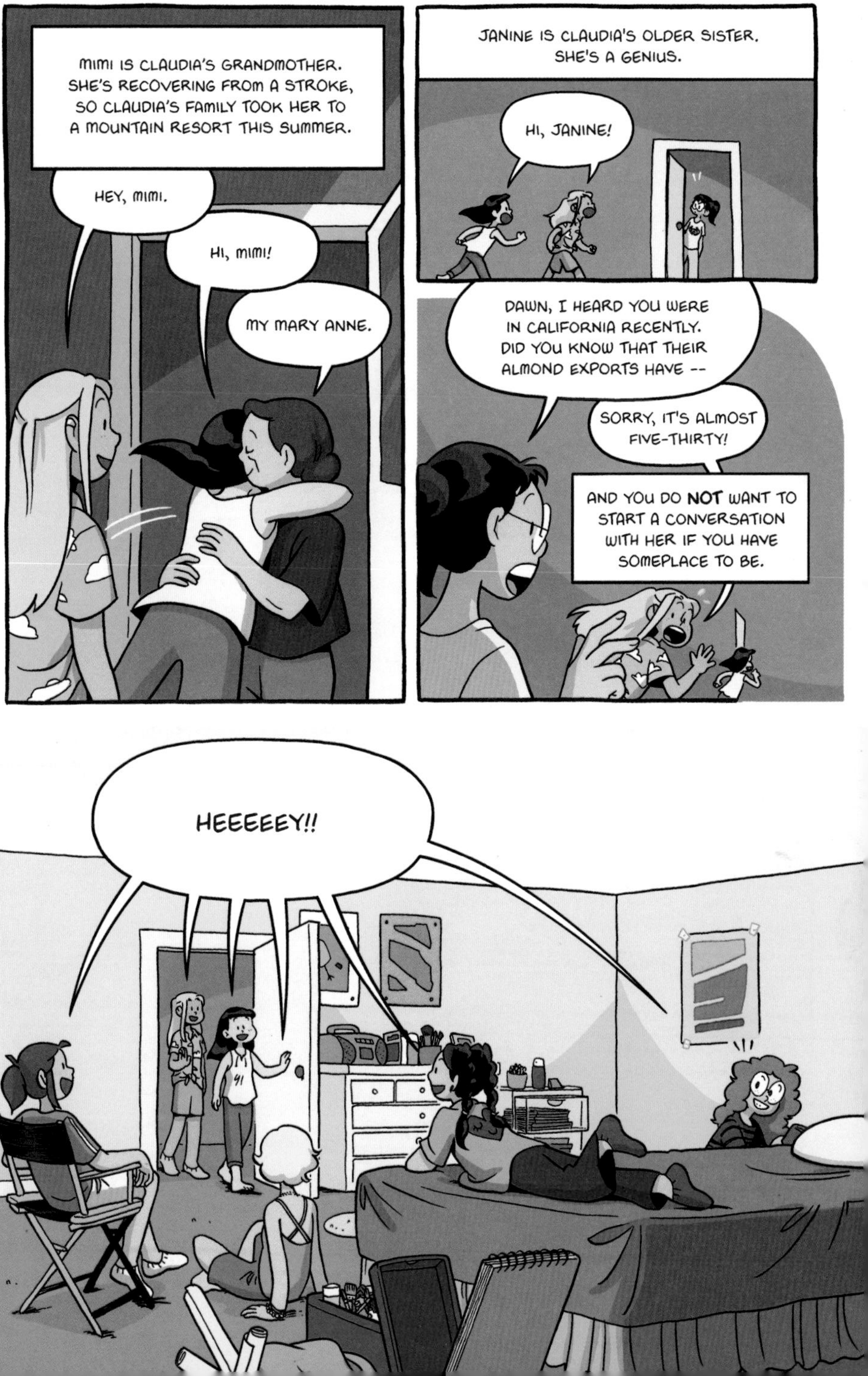
MIMI IS CLAUDIA'S GRANDMOTHER. SHE'S RECOVERING FROM A STROKE, SO CLAUDIA'S FAMILY TOOK HER TO A MOUNTAIN RESORT THIS SUMMER.
HEY, MIMI.
HI, MIMI!
MY MARY ANNE.
JANINE IS CLAUDIA'S OLDER SISTER. SHE'S A GENIUS.
HI, JANINE!
DAWN, I HEARD YOU WERE IN CALIFORNIA RECENTLY. DID YOU KNOW THAT THEIR ALMOND EXPORTS HAVE --
SORRY, IT'S ALMOST FIVE-THIRTY!
AND YOU DO **NOT** WANT TO START A CONVERSATION WITH HER IF YOU HAVE SOMEPLACE TO BE.
HEEEEEY!!

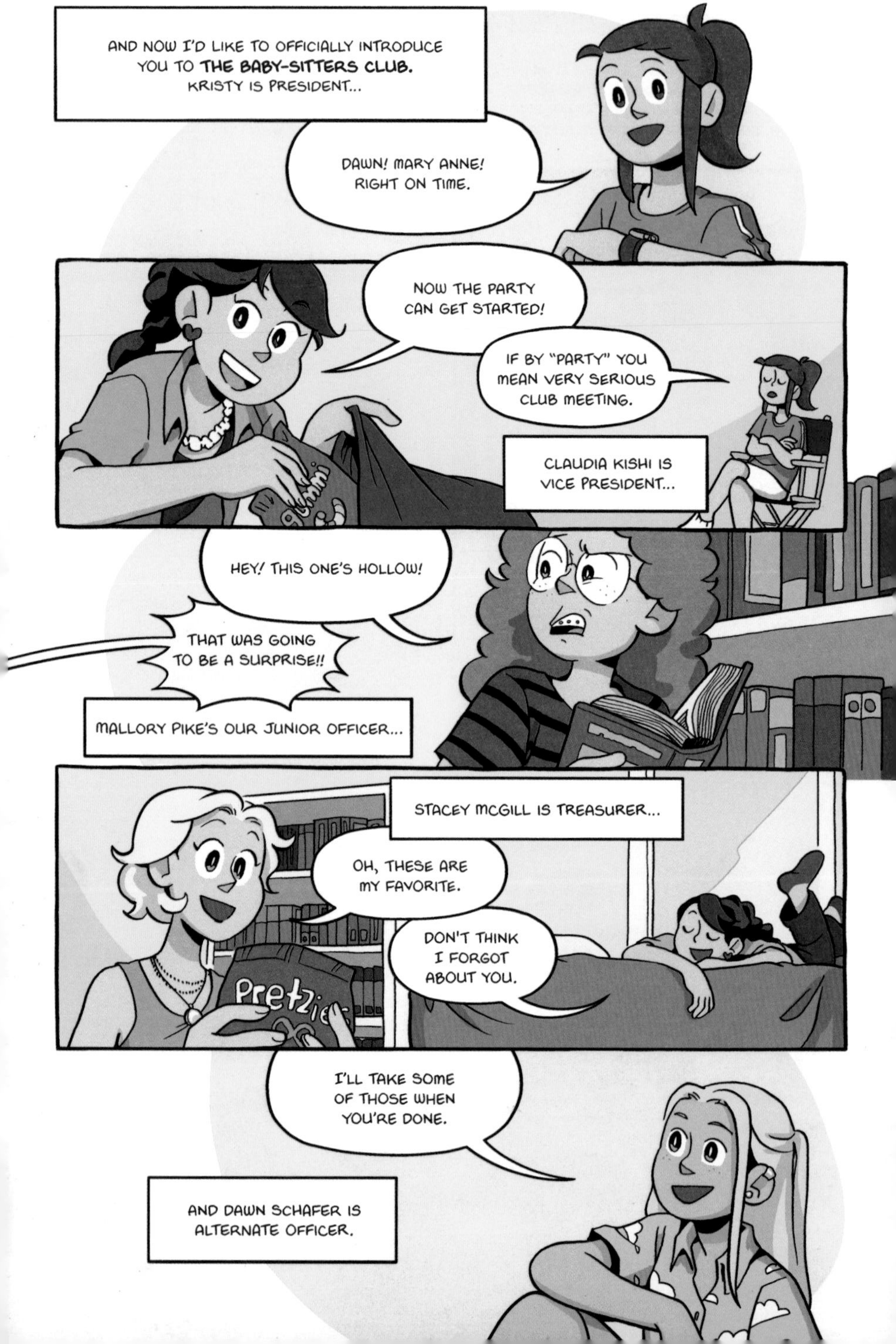
AND NOW I'D LIKE TO OFFICIALLY INTRODUCE YOU TO **THE BABY-SITTERS CLUB.** KRISTY IS PRESIDENT...
DAWN! MARY ANNE! RIGHT ON TIME.
NOW THE PARTY CAN GET STARTED!
IF BY "PARTY" YOU MEAN VERY SERIOUS CLUB MEETING.
CLAUDIA KISHI IS VICE PRESIDENT...
HEY! THIS ONE'S HOLLOW!
THAT WAS GOING TO BE A SURPRISE!!
MALLORY PIKE'S OUR JUNIOR OFFICER...
STACEY MCGILL IS TREASURER...
OH, THESE ARE MY FAVORITE.
DON'T THINK I FORGOT ABOUT YOU.
Pretzies
I'LL TAKE SOME OF THOSE WHEN YOU'RE DONE.
AND DAWN SCHAFER IS ALTERNATE OFFICER.

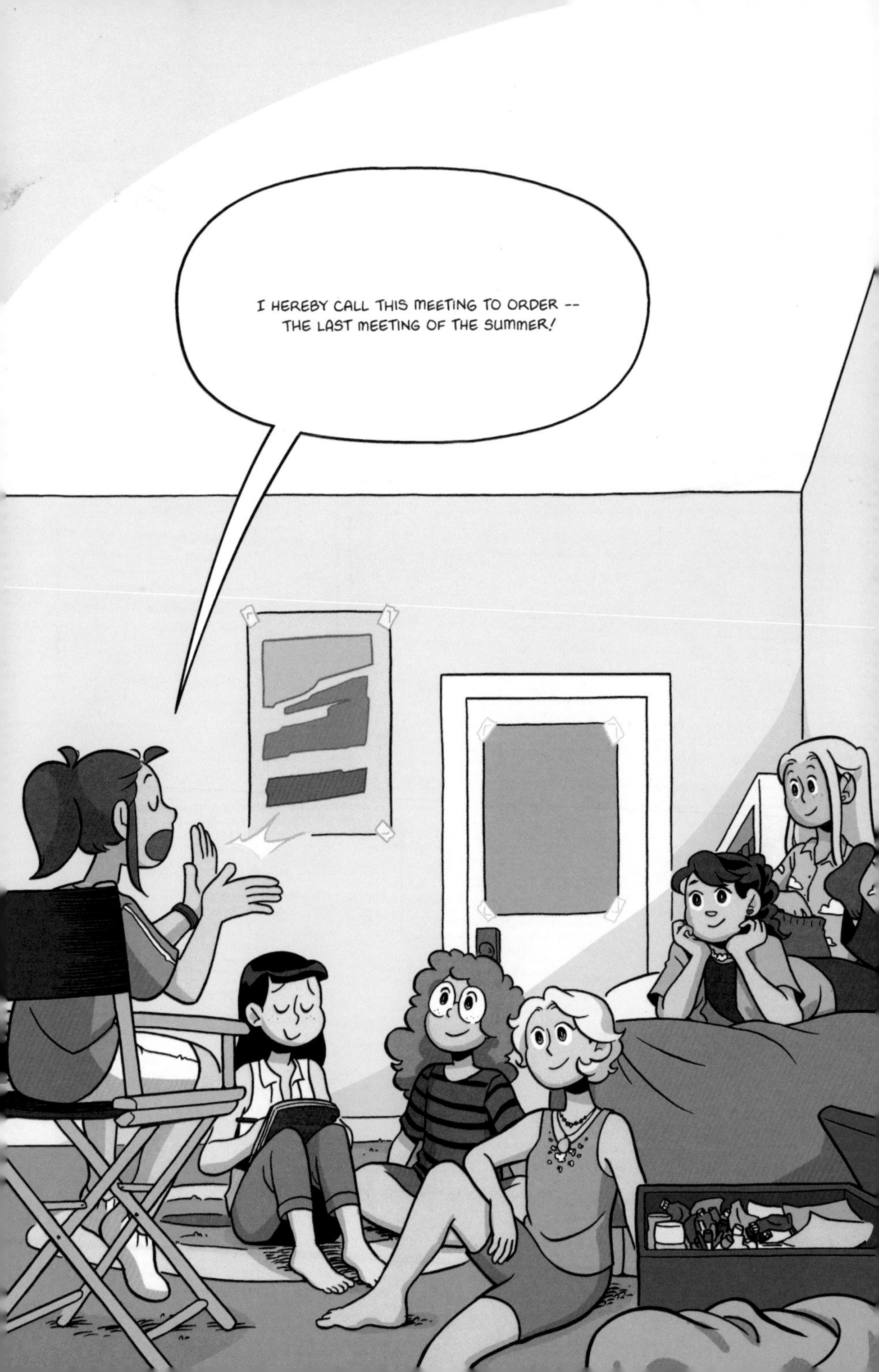
I HEREBY CALL THIS MEETING TO ORDER -- THE LAST MEETING OF THE SUMMER!

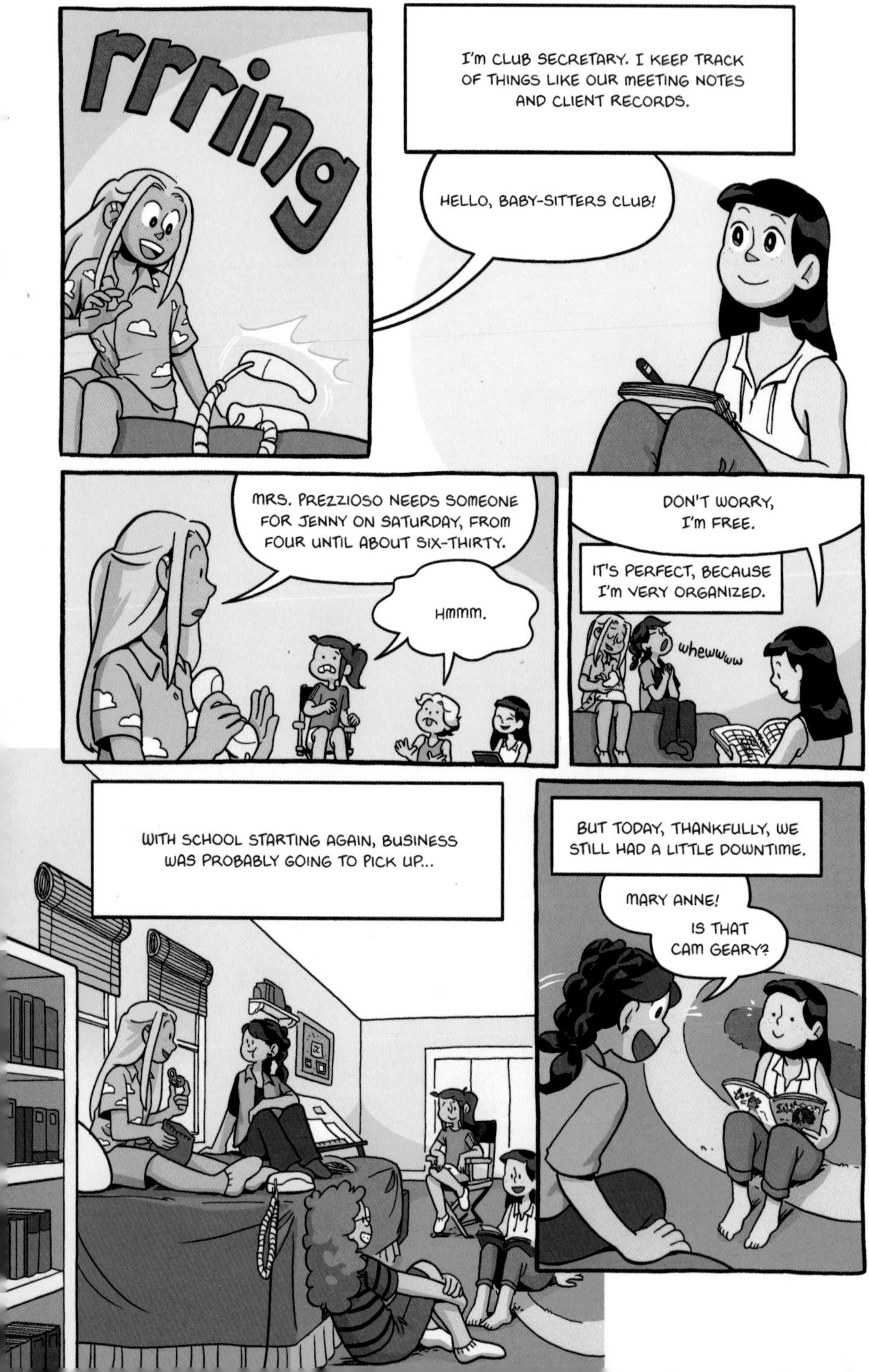
rrring
I'M CLUB SECRETARY. I KEEP TRACK OF THINGS LIKE OUR MEETING NOTES AND CLIENT RECORDS.
HELLO, BABY-SITTERS CLUB!
MRS. PREZZIOSO NEEDS SOMEONE FOR JENNY ON SATURDAY, FROM FOUR UNTIL ABOUT SIX-THIRTY.
HMMM.
DON'T WORRY, I'M FREE.
IT'S PERFECT, BECAUSE I'M VERY ORGANIZED.
whewwww
WITH SCHOOL STARTING AGAIN, BUSINESS WAS PROBABLY GOING TO PICK UP...
BUT TODAY, THANKFULLY, WE STILL HAD A LITTLE DOWNTIME.
MARY ANNE!
IS THAT CAM GEARY?

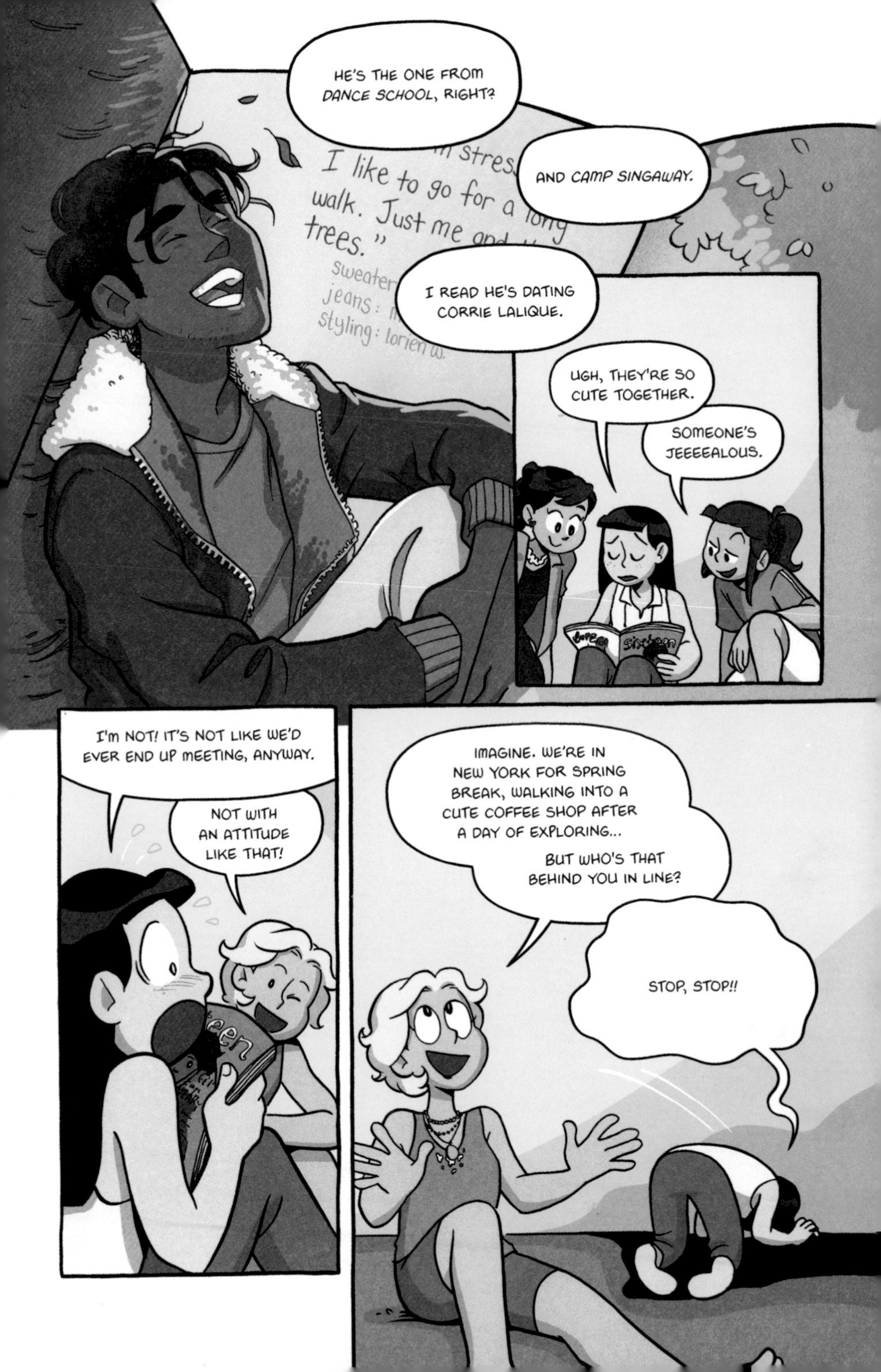
HE'S THE ONE FROM DANCE SCHOOL, RIGHT?
AND CAMP SINGAWAY.
I like to go for a long walk. Just me and ... trees."
sweater
jeans:
styling: lorien w.
I READ HE'S DATING CORRIE LALIQUE.
UGH, THEY'RE SO CUTE TOGETHER.
SOMEONE'S JEEEEALOUS.
sixteen
I'M NOT! IT'S NOT LIKE WE'D EVER END UP MEETING, ANYWAY.
NOT WITH AN ATTITUDE LIKE THAT!
IMAGINE. WE'RE IN NEW YORK FOR SPRING BREAK, WALKING INTO A CUTE COFFEE SHOP AFTER A DAY OF EXPLORING...
BUT WHO'S THAT BEHIND YOU IN LINE?
STOP, STOP!!

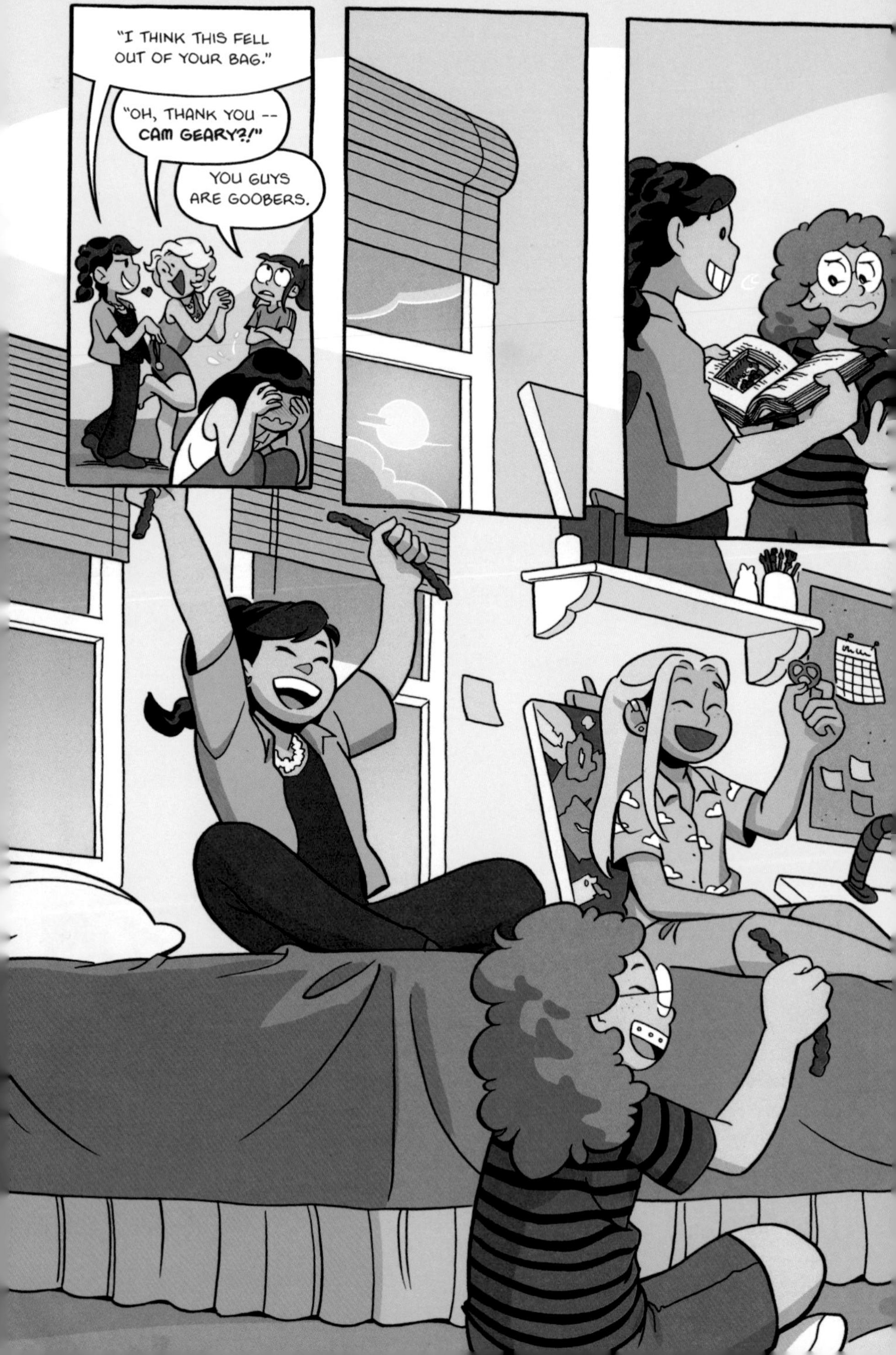
"I THINK THIS FELL OUT OF YOUR BAG."
"OH, THANK YOU -- CAM GEARY?!"
YOU GUYS ARE GOOBERS.

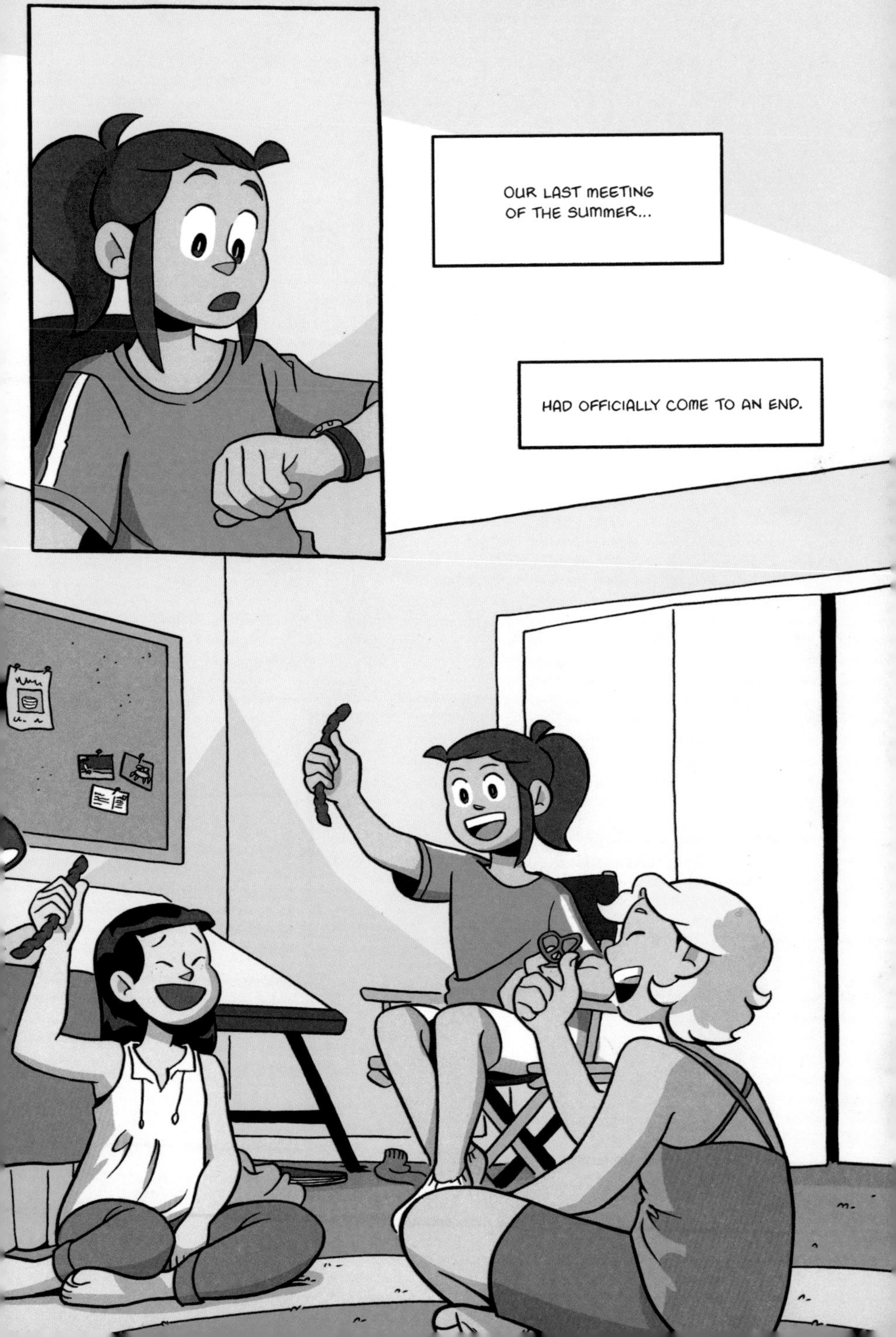
OUR LAST MEETING OF THE SUMMER...
HAD OFFICIALLY COME TO AN END.

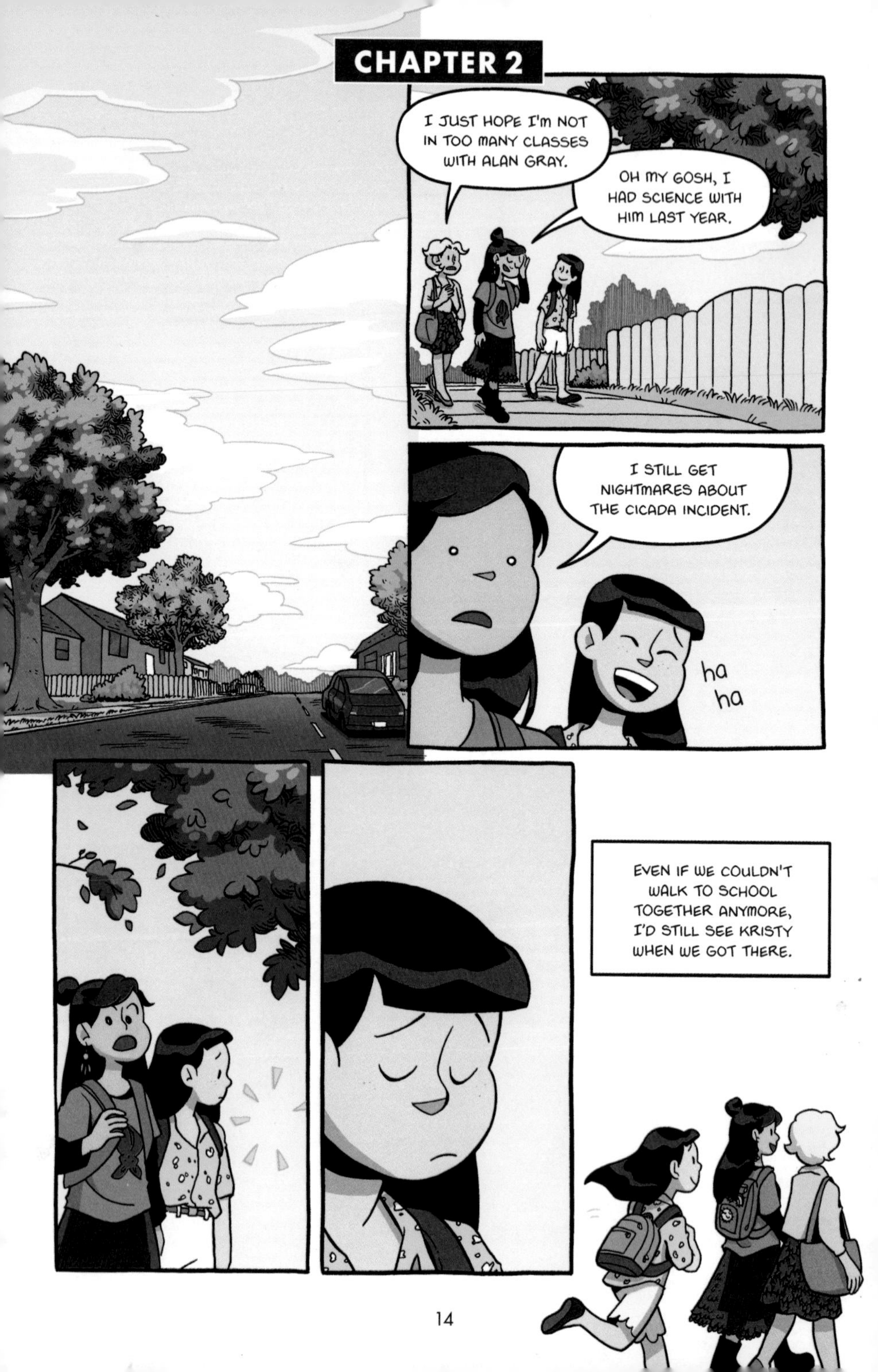
CHAPTER 2
I JUST HOPE I'm NOT IN TOO MANY CLASSES WITH ALAN GRAY.
OH MY GOSH, I HAD SCIENCE WITH HIM LAST YEAR.
I STILL GET NIGHTMARES ABOUT THE CICADA INCIDENT.
ha ha
EVEN IF WE COULDN'T WALK TO SCHOOL TOGETHER ANYMORE, I'D STILL SEE KRISTY WHEN WE GOT THERE.

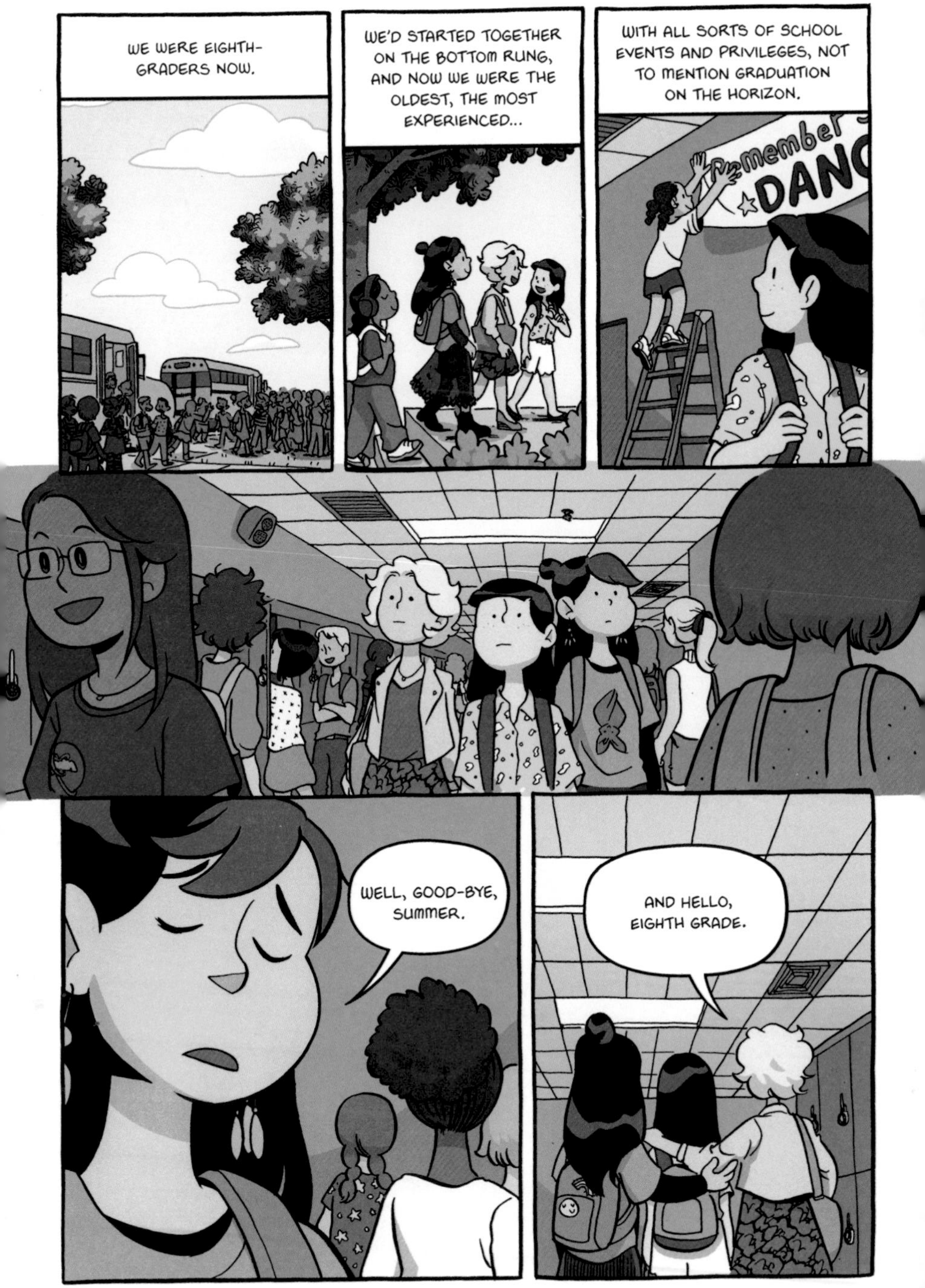
WE WERE EIGHTH-GRADERS NOW.
WE'D STARTED TOGETHER ON THE BOTTOM RUNG, AND NOW WE WERE THE OLDEST, THE MOST EXPERIENCED...
WITH ALL SORTS OF SCHOOL EVENTS AND PRIVILEGES, NOT TO MENTION GRADUATION ON THE HORIZON.
WELL, GOOD-BYE, SUMMER.
AND HELLO, EIGHTH GRADE.

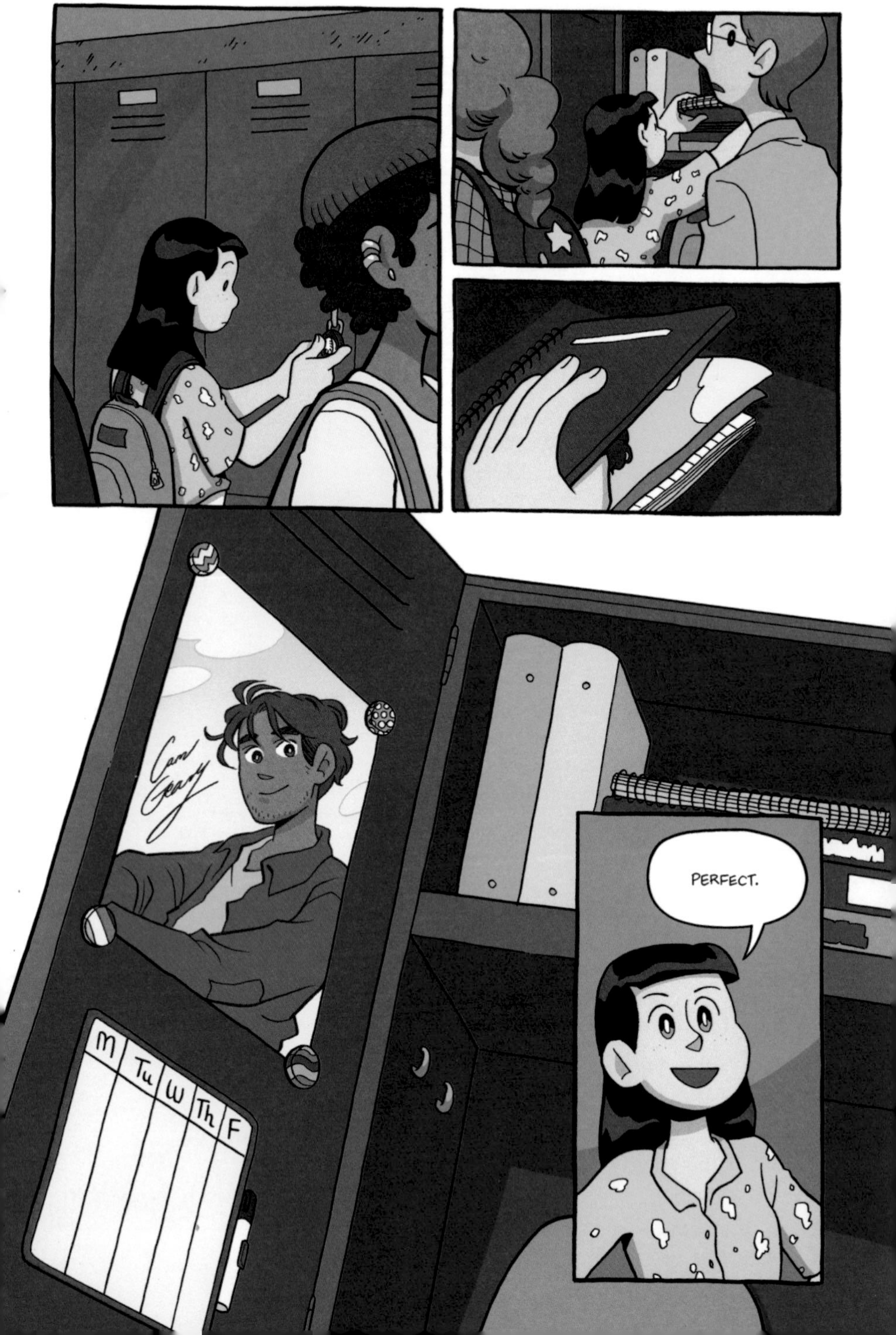
PERFECT.
Cam Gray
M
Tu
W
Th
F

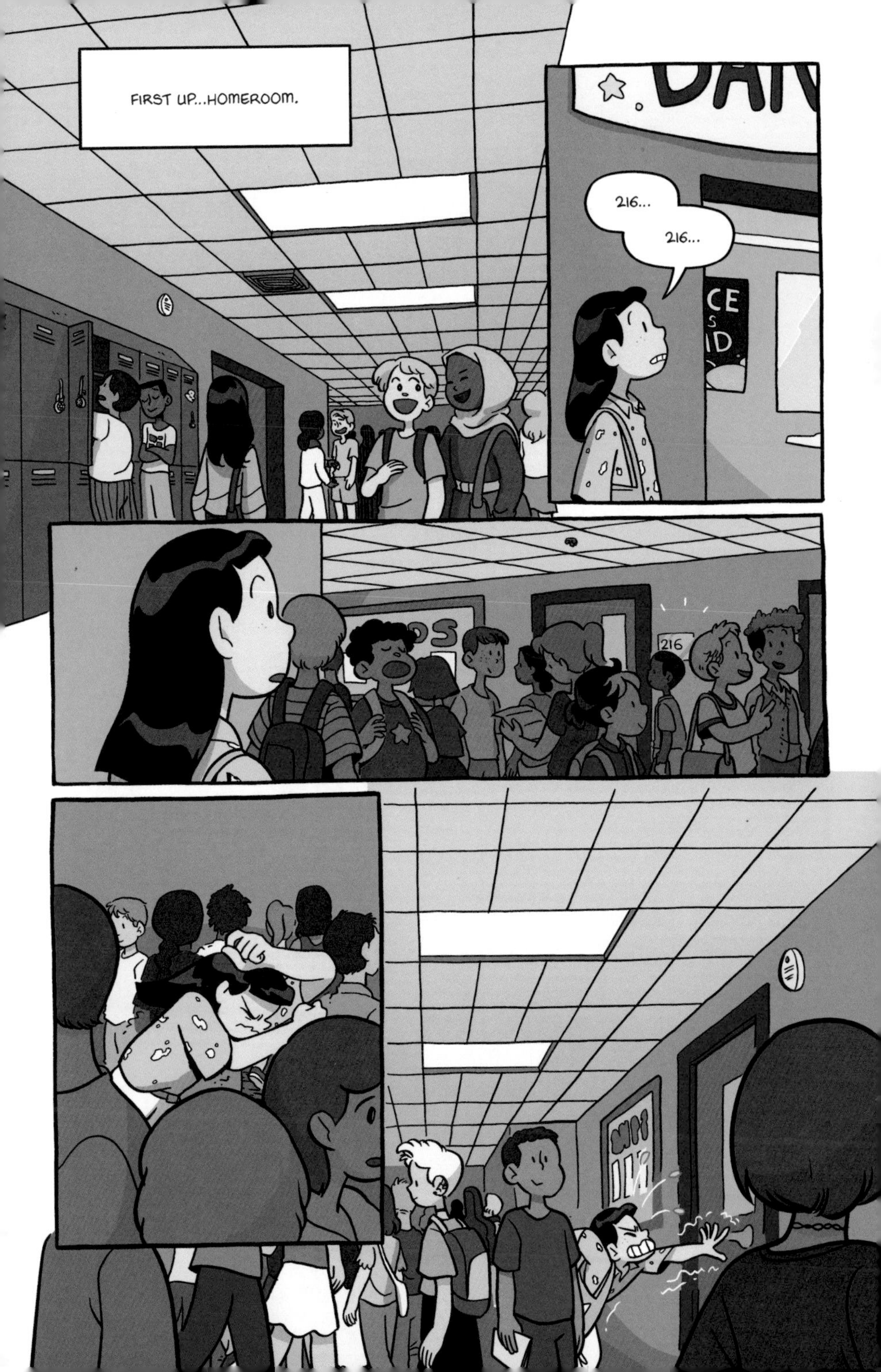
FIRST UP...HOMEROOM.
216...
216...
216

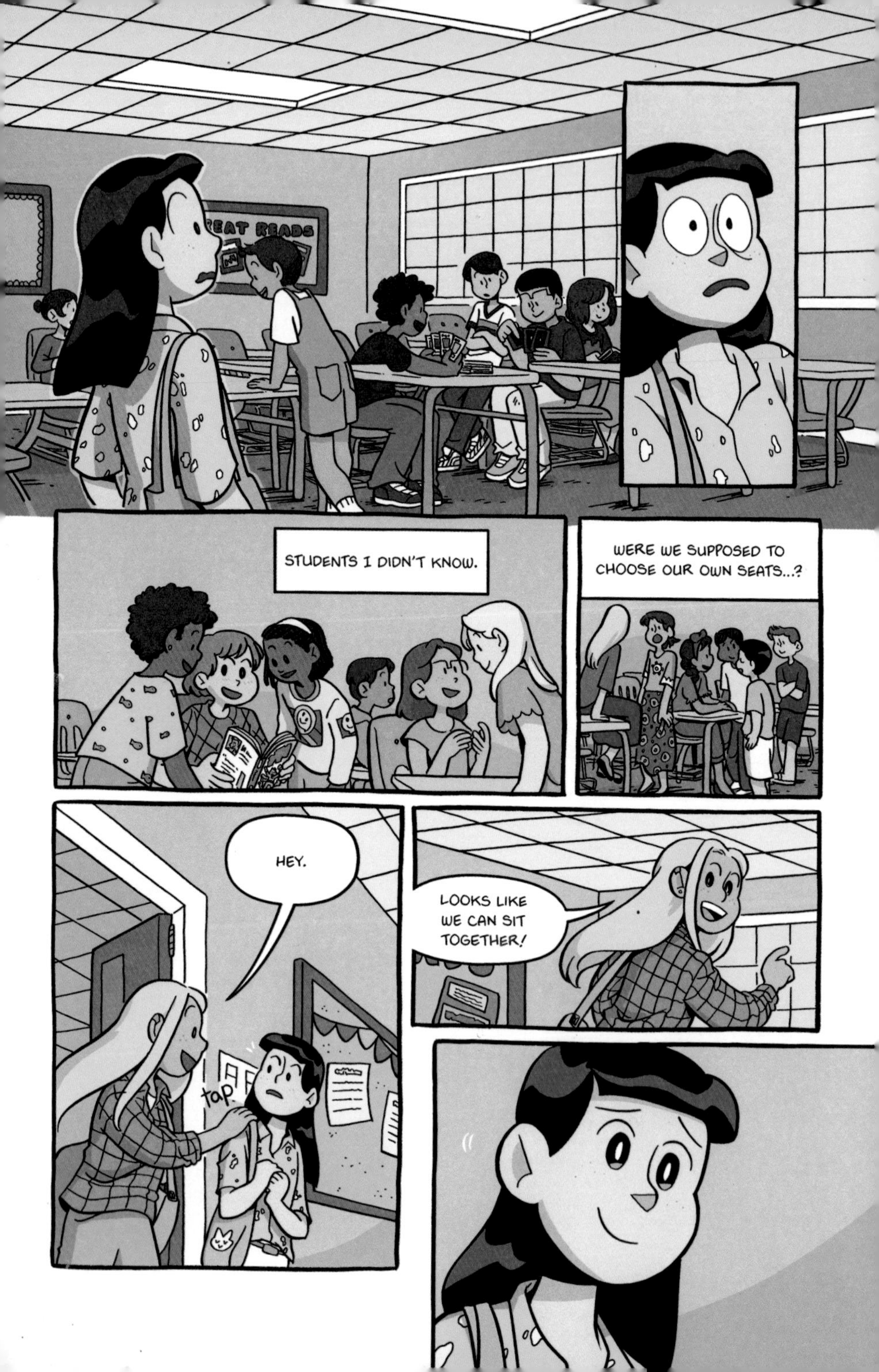
GREAT READS
STUDENTS I DIDN'T KNOW.
WERE WE SUPPOSED TO CHOOSE OUR OWN SEATS...?
HEY.
tap
LOOKS LIKE WE CAN SIT TOGETHER!

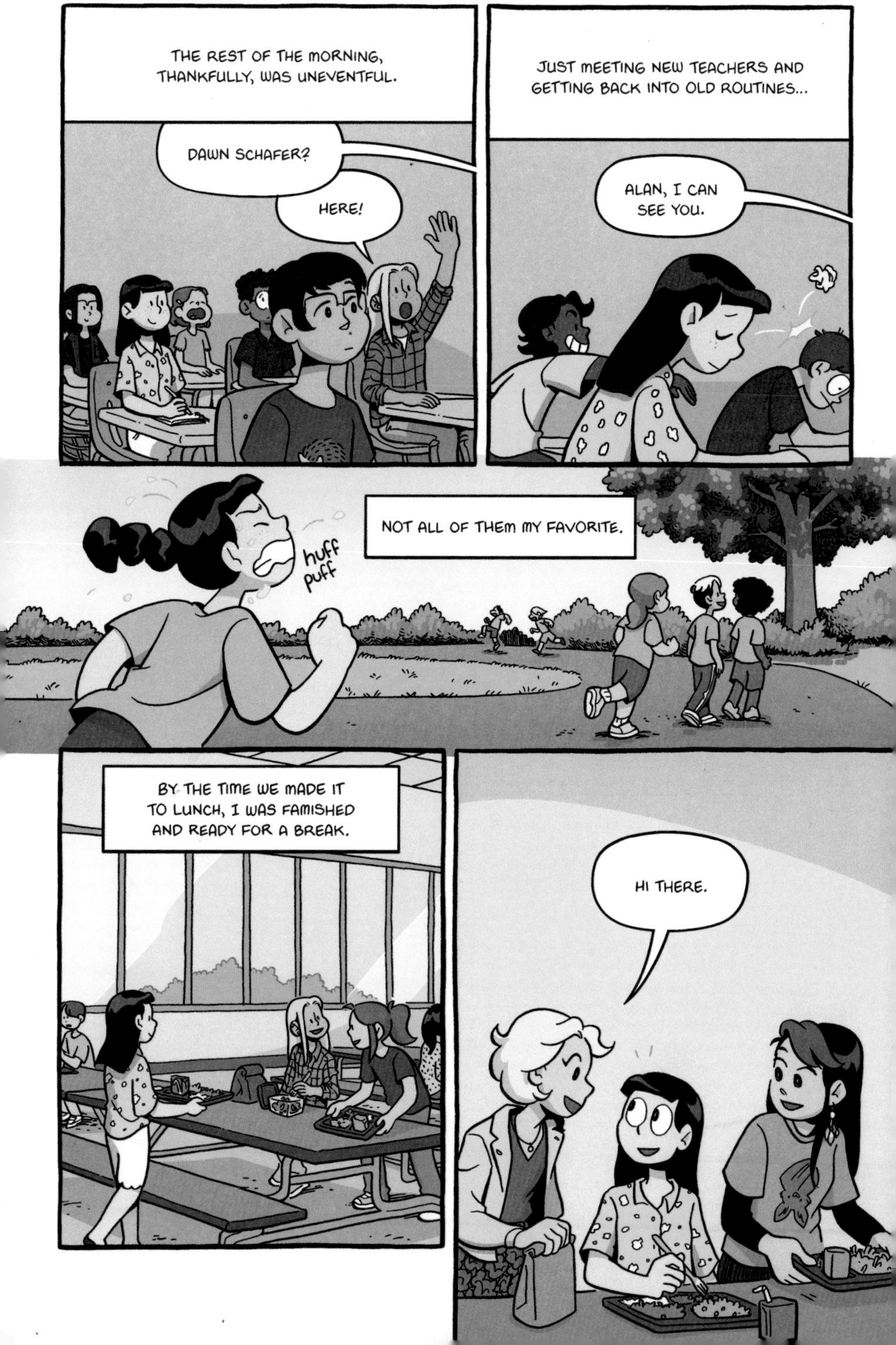
THE REST OF THE MORNING, THANKFULLY, WAS UNEVENTFUL.
DAWN SCHAFER?
HERE!
JUST MEETING NEW TEACHERS AND GETTING BACK INTO OLD ROUTINES...
ALAN, I CAN SEE YOU.
NOT ALL OF THEM MY FAVORITE.
huff puff
BY THE TIME WE MADE IT TO LUNCH, I WAS FAMISHED AND READY FOR A BREAK.
HI THERE.

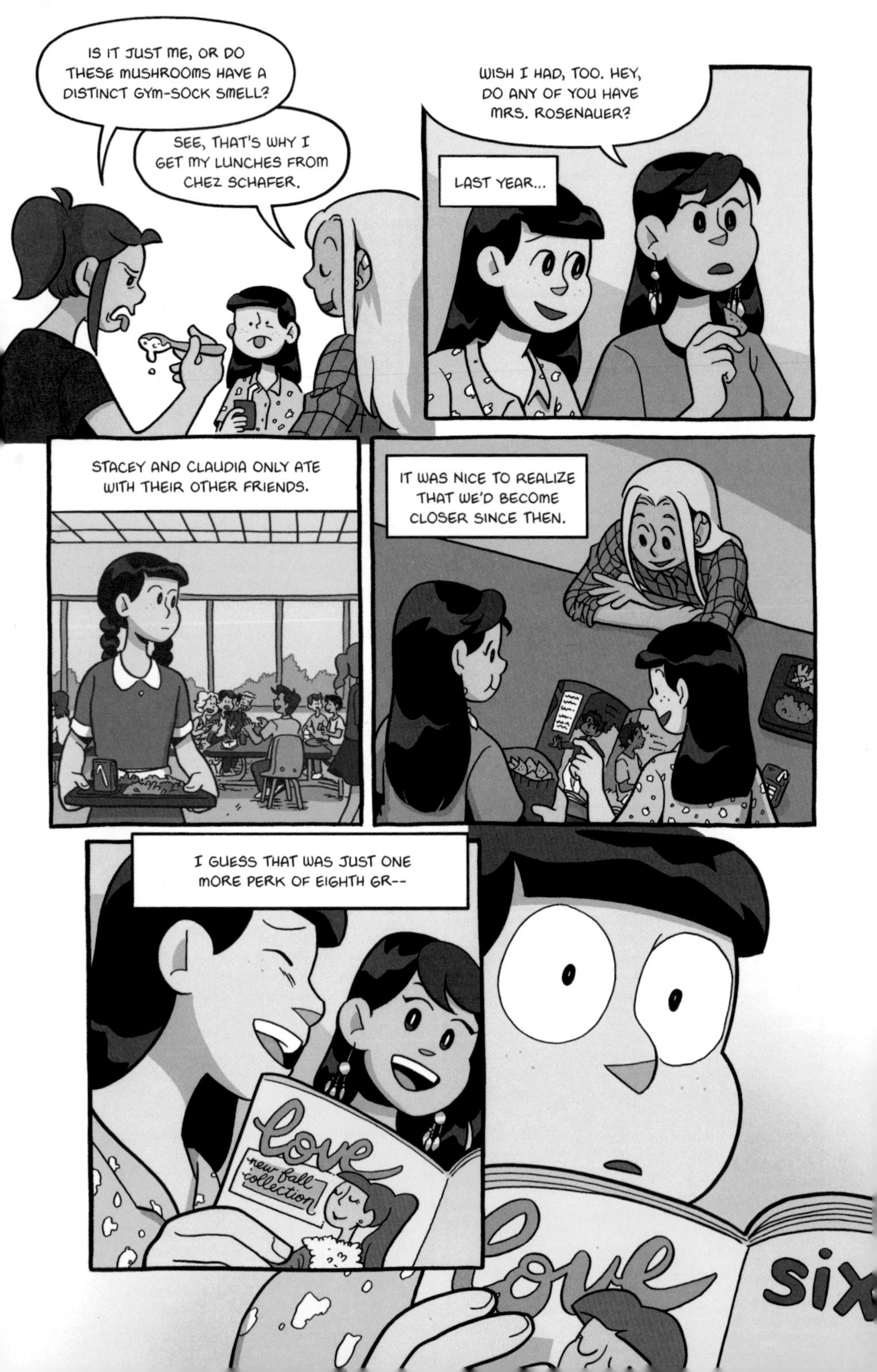
IS IT JUST ME, OR DO THESE MUSHROOMS HAVE A DISTINCT GYM-SOCK SMELL?
SEE, THAT'S WHY I GET MY LUNCHES FROM CHEZ SCHAFER.
WISH I HAD, TOO. HEY, DO ANY OF YOU HAVE MRS. ROSENAUER?
LAST YEAR...
STACEY AND CLAUDIA ONLY ATE WITH THEIR OTHER FRIENDS.
IT WAS NICE TO REALIZE THAT WE'D BECOME CLOSER SINCE THEN.
I GUESS THAT WAS JUST ONE MORE PERK OF EIGHTH GR--
love
new fall collection
love
six

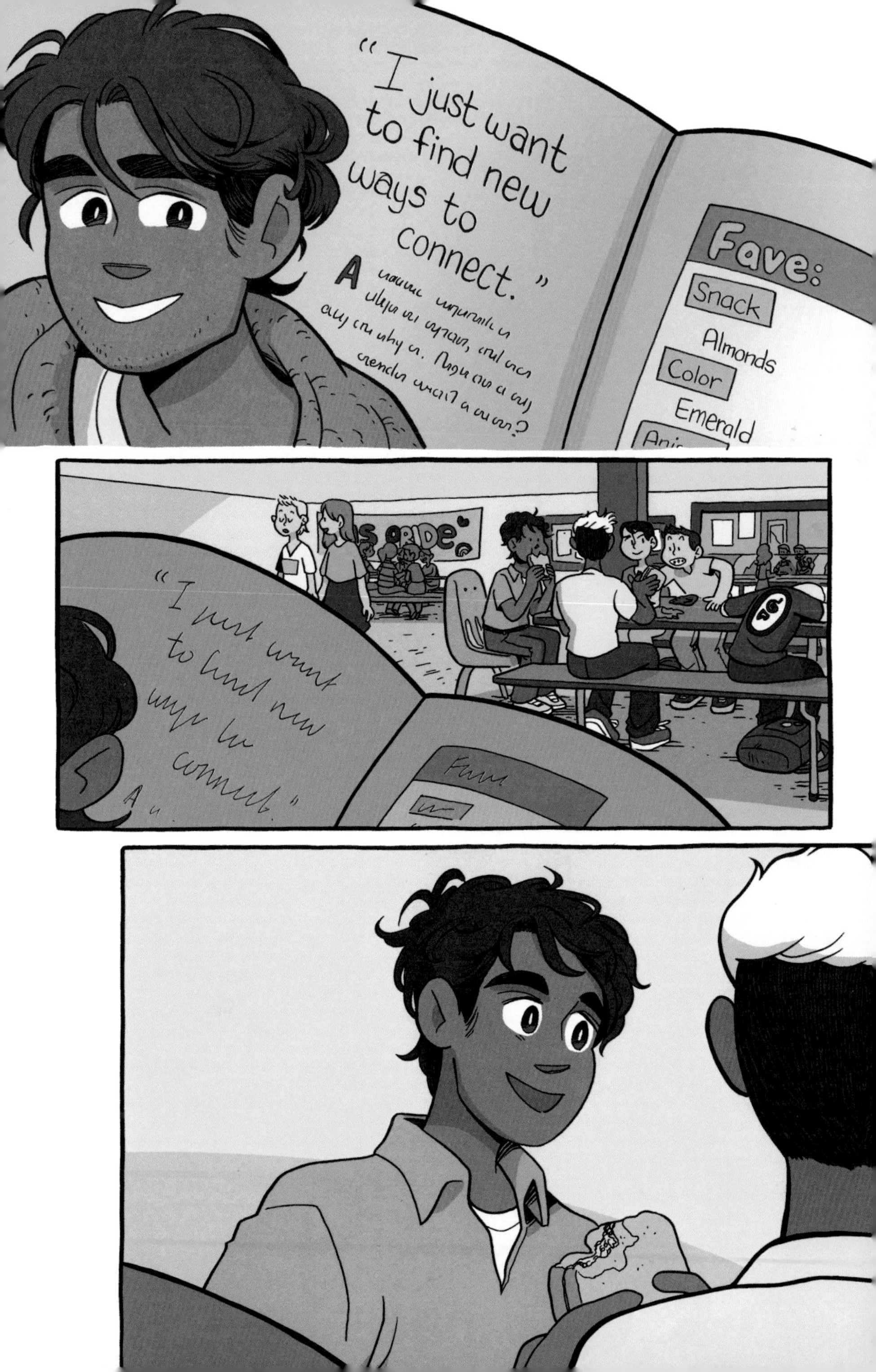
"I just want to find new ways to connect."
Fave:
Snack
Almonds
Color
Emerald

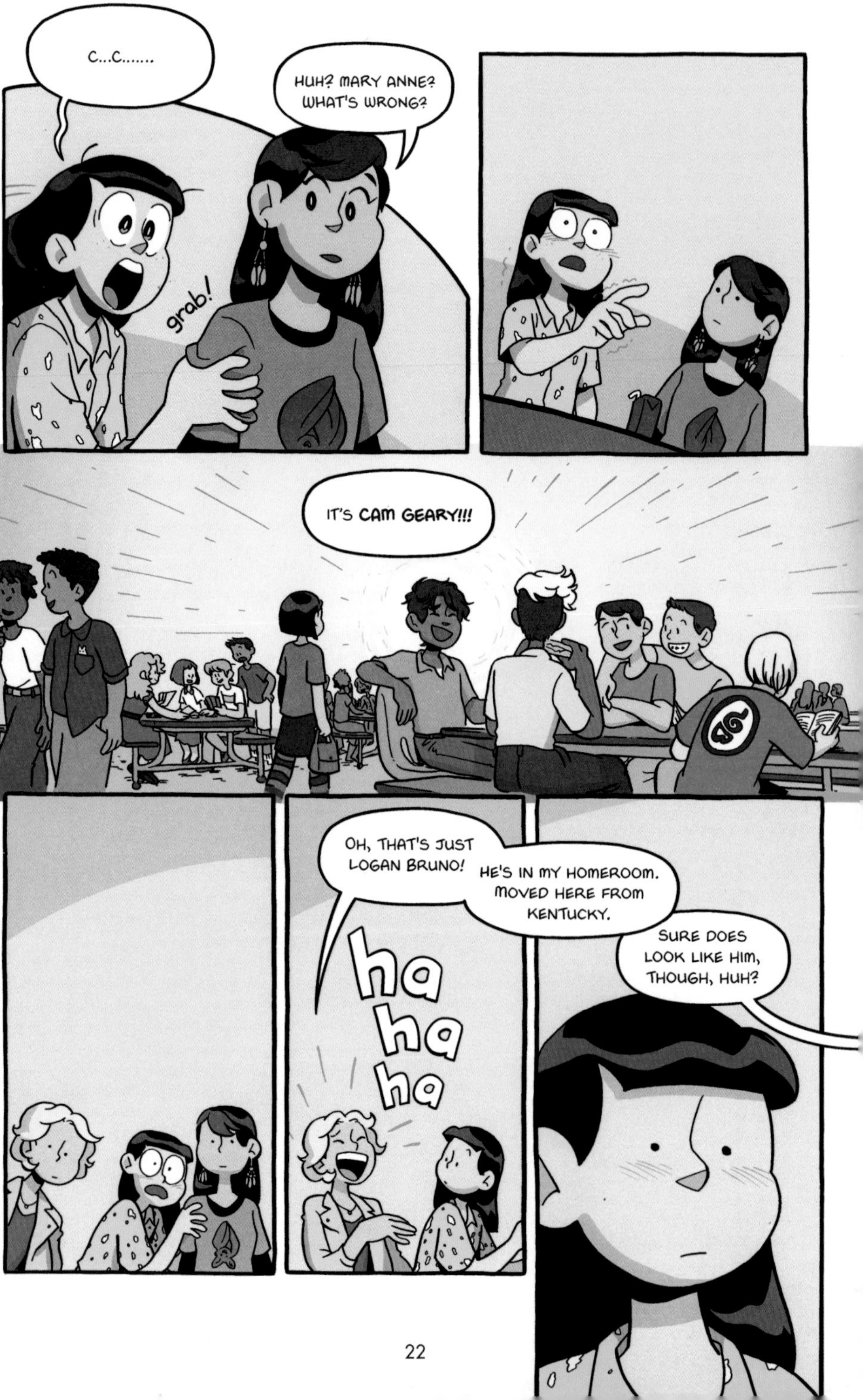
C...C.......
HUH? MARY ANNE? WHAT'S WRONG?
grab!
IT'S CAM GEARY!!!
OH, THAT'S JUST LOGAN BRUNO!
HE'S IN MY HOMEROOM. MOVED HERE FROM KENTUCKY.
ha ha ha
SURE DOES LOOK LIKE HIM, THOUGH, HUH?

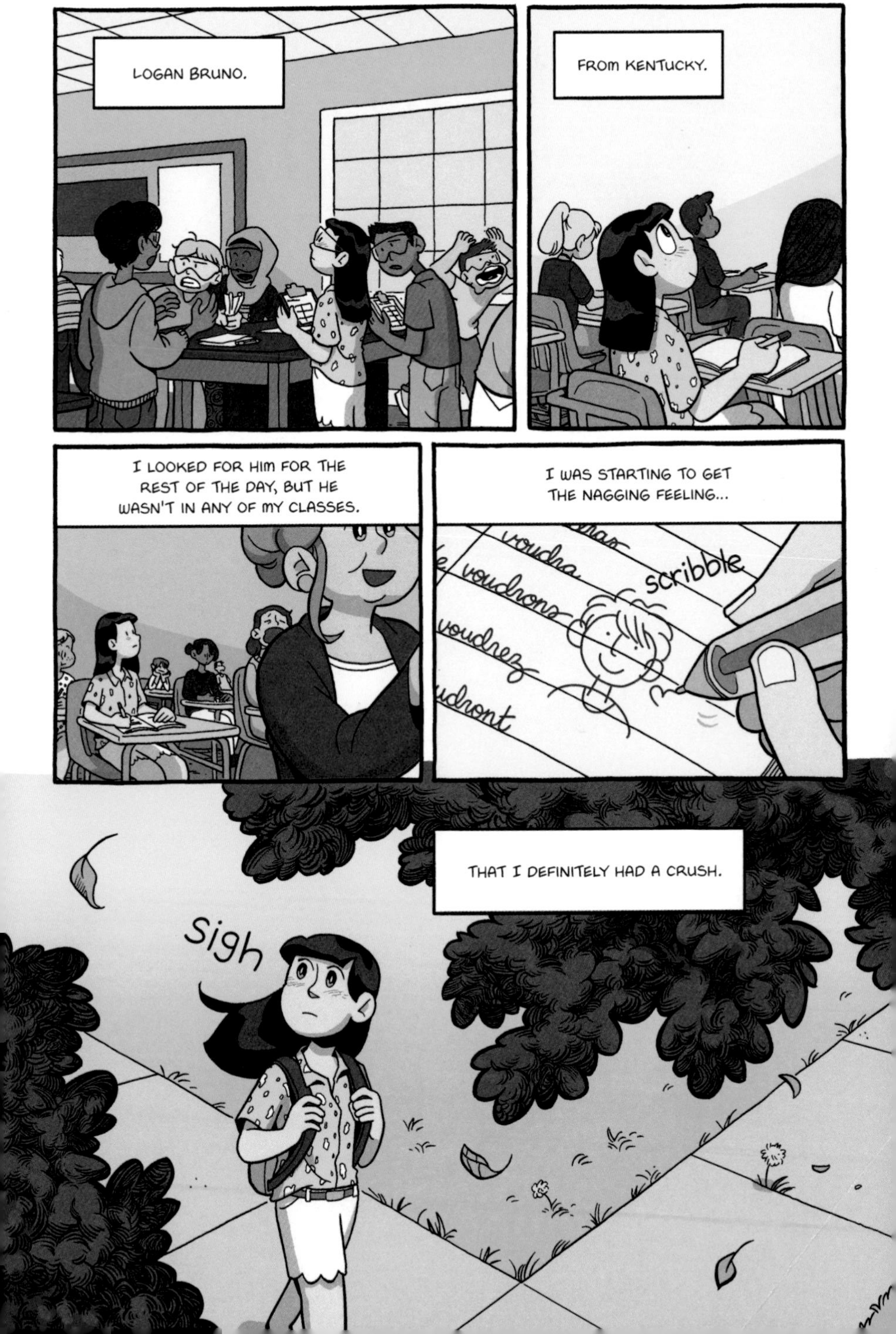
LOGAN BRUNO.
FROM KENTUCKY.
I LOOKED FOR HIM FOR THE REST OF THE DAY, BUT HE WASN'T IN ANY OF MY CLASSES.
I WAS STARTING TO GET THE NAGGING FEELING...
voudra
voudrons
voudrez
scribble
THAT I DEFINITELY HAD A CRUSH.
Sigh

CHAPTER 3

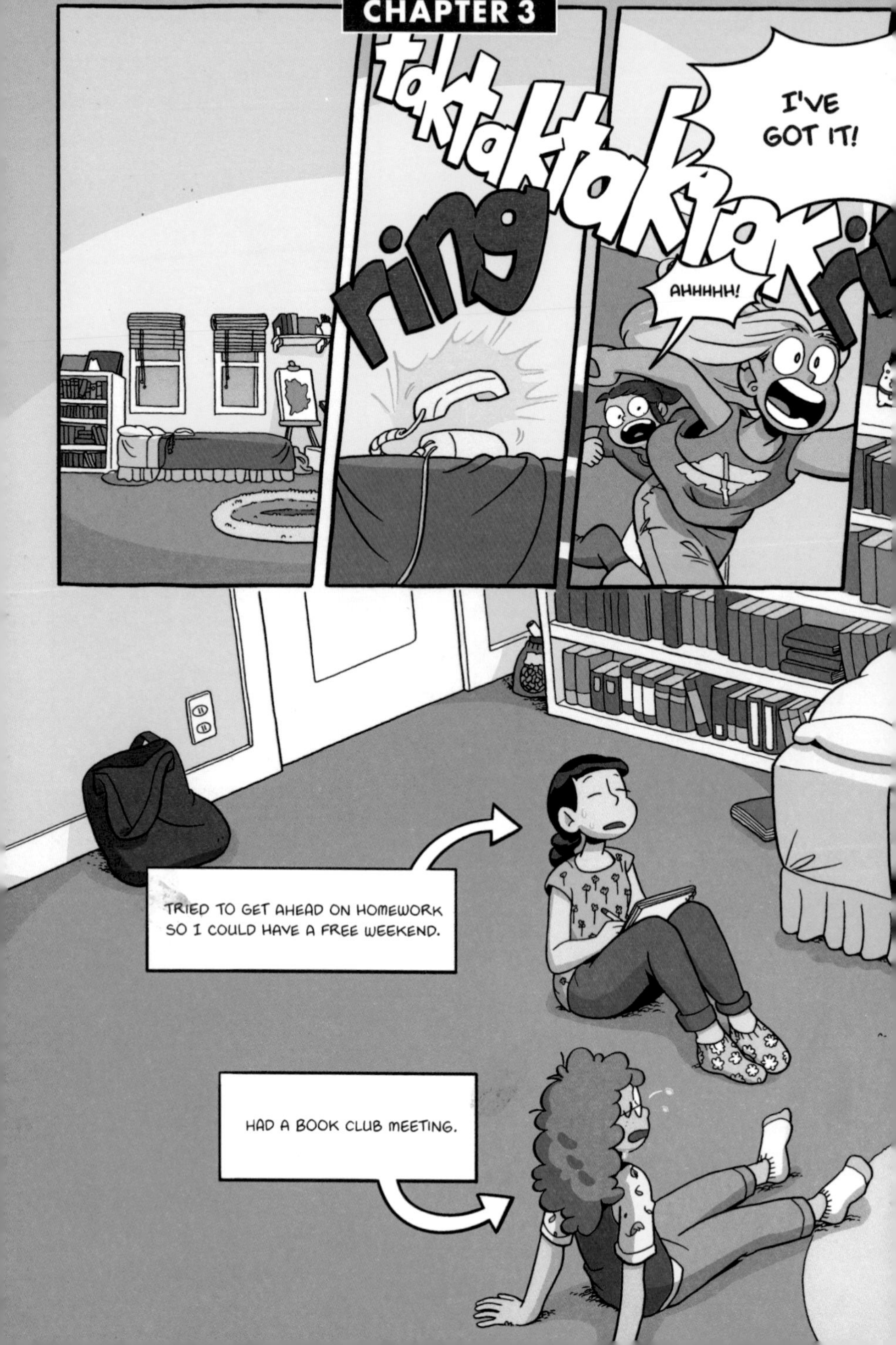
taktaktaktak
ring
I'VE GOT IT!
AHHHHH!
TRIED TO GET AHEAD ON HOMEWORK SO I COULD HAVE A FREE WEEKEND.
HAD A BOOK CLUB MEETING.

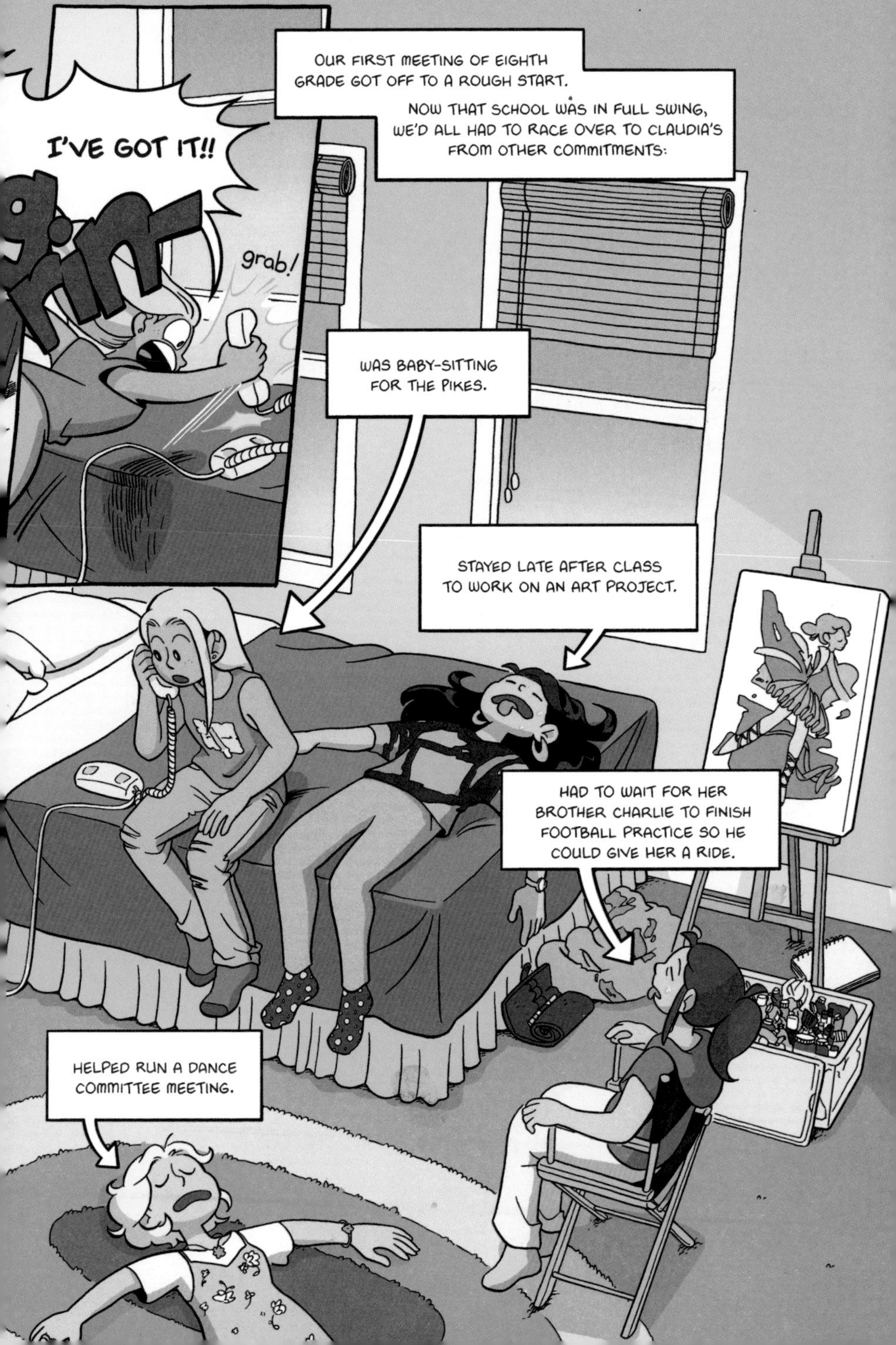
OUR FIRST MEETING OF EIGHTH GRADE GOT OFF TO A ROUGH START.
NOW THAT SCHOOL WAS IN FULL SWING, WE'D ALL HAD TO RACE OVER TO CLAUDIA'S FROM OTHER COMMITMENTS:
I'VE GOT IT!!
grab!
WAS BABY-SITTING FOR THE PIKES.
STAYED LATE AFTER CLASS TO WORK ON AN ART PROJECT.
HAD TO WAIT FOR HER BROTHER CHARLIE TO FINISH FOOTBALL PRACTICE SO HE COULD GIVE HER A RIDE.
HELPED RUN A DANCE COMMITTEE MEETING.

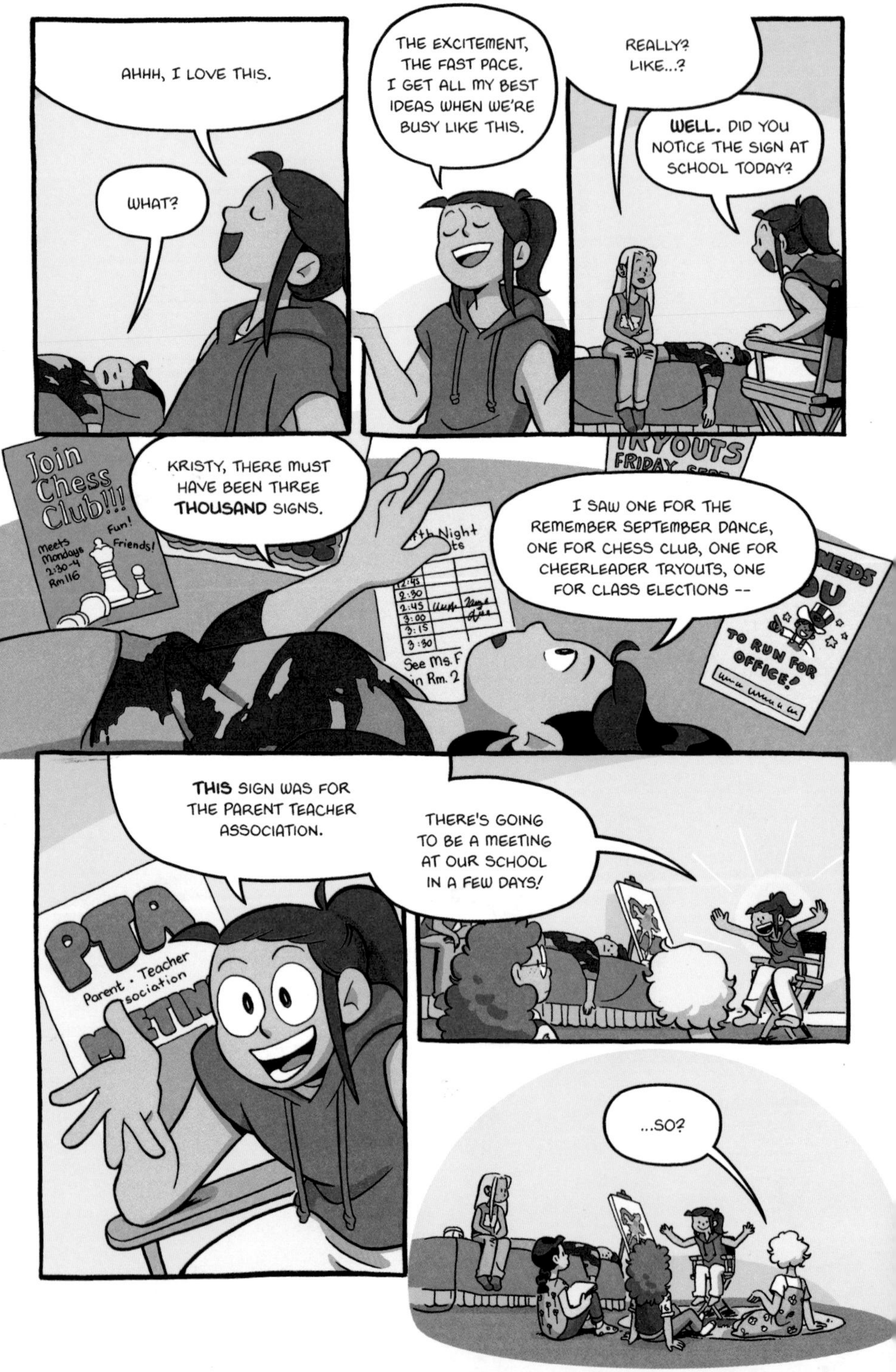
AHHH, I LOVE THIS.
WHAT?
THE EXCITEMENT, THE FAST PACE. I GET ALL MY BEST IDEAS WHEN WE'RE BUSY LIKE THIS.
REALLY? LIKE...?
WELL. DID YOU NOTICE THE SIGN AT SCHOOL TODAY?
Join Chess Club!!! Meets Mondays 2:30-4 Rm 116 Fun! Friends!
TRYOUTS FRIDAY
KRISTY, THERE MUST HAVE BEEN THREE **THOUSAND** SIGNS.
See Ms. F in Rm. 2
I SAW ONE FOR THE REMEMBER SEPTEMBER DANCE, ONE FOR CHESS CLUB, ONE FOR CHEERLEADER TRYOUTS, ONE FOR CLASS ELECTIONS --
TO RUN FOR OFFICE!
THIS SIGN WAS FOR THE PARENT TEACHER ASSOCIATION.
THERE'S GOING TO BE A MEETING AT OUR SCHOOL IN A FEW DAYS!
PTA Parent · Teacher Association
...SO?

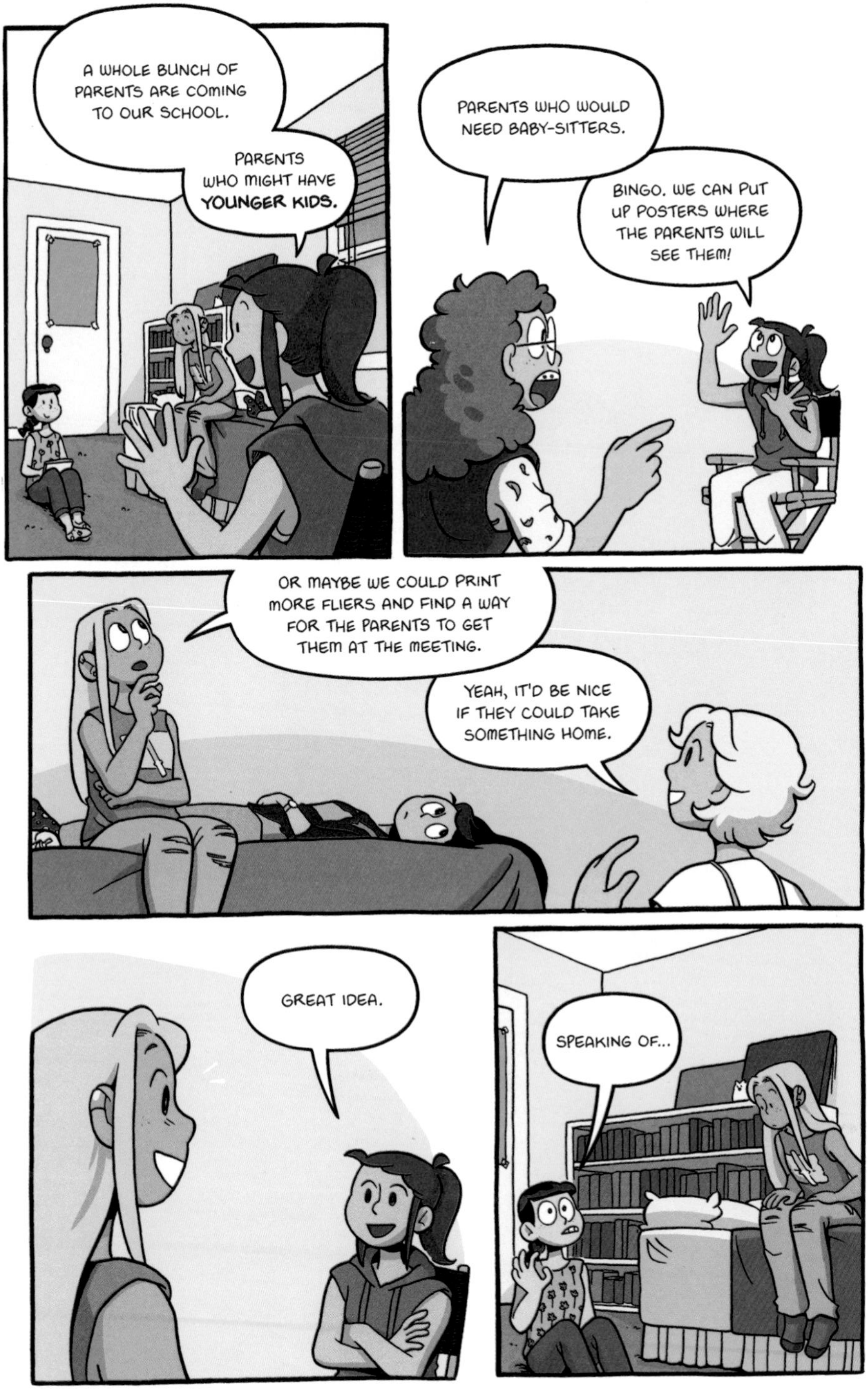
A WHOLE BUNCH OF PARENTS ARE COMING TO OUR SCHOOL.
PARENTS WHO MIGHT HAVE **YOUNGER KIDS.**
PARENTS WHO WOULD NEED BABY-SITTERS.
BINGO. WE CAN PUT UP POSTERS WHERE THE PARENTS WILL SEE THEM!
OR MAYBE WE COULD PRINT MORE FLIERS AND FIND A WAY FOR THE PARENTS TO GET THEM AT THE MEETING.
YEAH, IT'D BE NICE IF THEY COULD TAKE SOMETHING HOME.
GREAT IDEA.
SPEAKING OF...

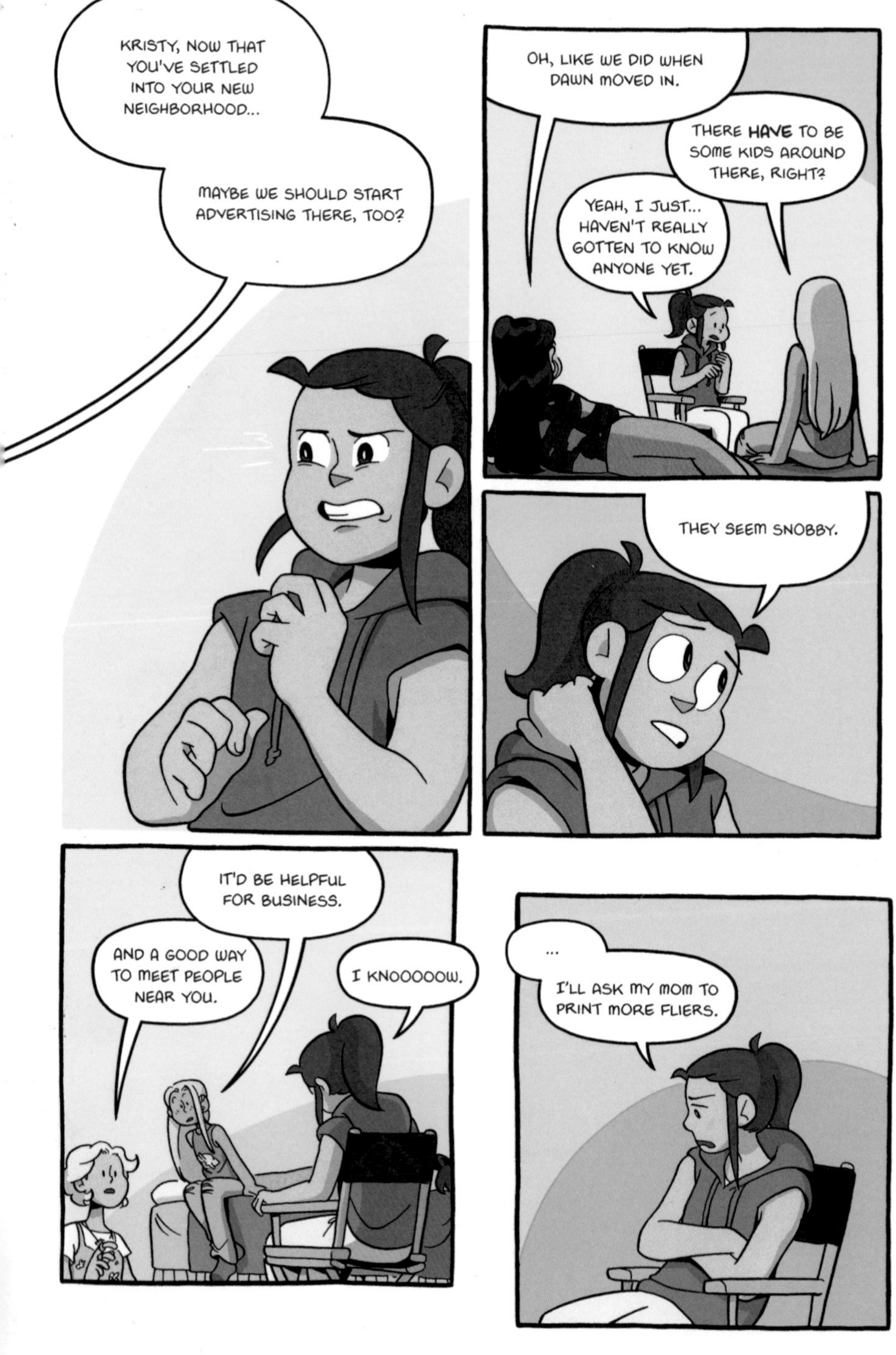
KRISTY, NOW THAT YOU'VE SETTLED INTO YOUR NEW NEIGHBORHOOD...
MAYBE WE SHOULD START ADVERTISING THERE, TOO?
OH, LIKE WE DID WHEN DAWN MOVED IN.
THERE **HAVE** TO BE SOME KIDS AROUND THERE, RIGHT?
YEAH, I JUST... HAVEN'T REALLY GOTTEN TO KNOW ANYONE YET.
THEY SEEM SNOBBY.
IT'D BE HELPFUL FOR BUSINESS.
AND A GOOD WAY TO MEET PEOPLE NEAR YOU.
I KNOOOOOW.
...
I'LL ASK MY MOM TO PRINT MORE FLIERS.

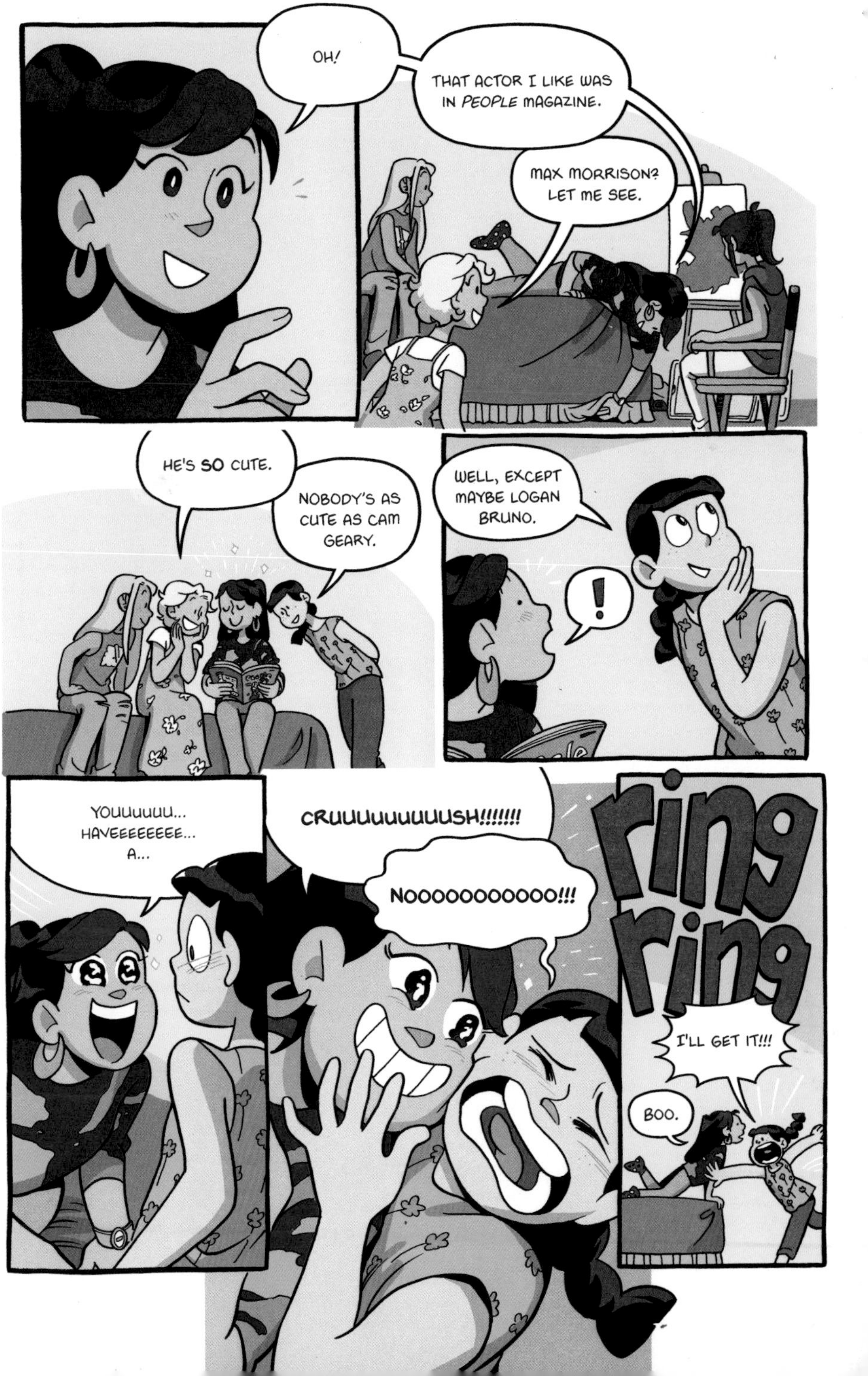
OH!
THAT ACTOR I LIKE WAS IN *PEOPLE* MAGAZINE.
MAX MORRISON? LET ME SEE.
HE'S **SO** CUTE.
NOBODY'S AS CUTE AS CAM GEARY.
WELL, EXCEPT MAYBE LOGAN BRUNO.
!
YOUUUUUU... HAVEEEEEEEE... A...
CRUUUUUUUUUSH!!!!!!!
NOOOOOOOOOOO!!!
ring ring
I'LL GET IT!!!
BOO.

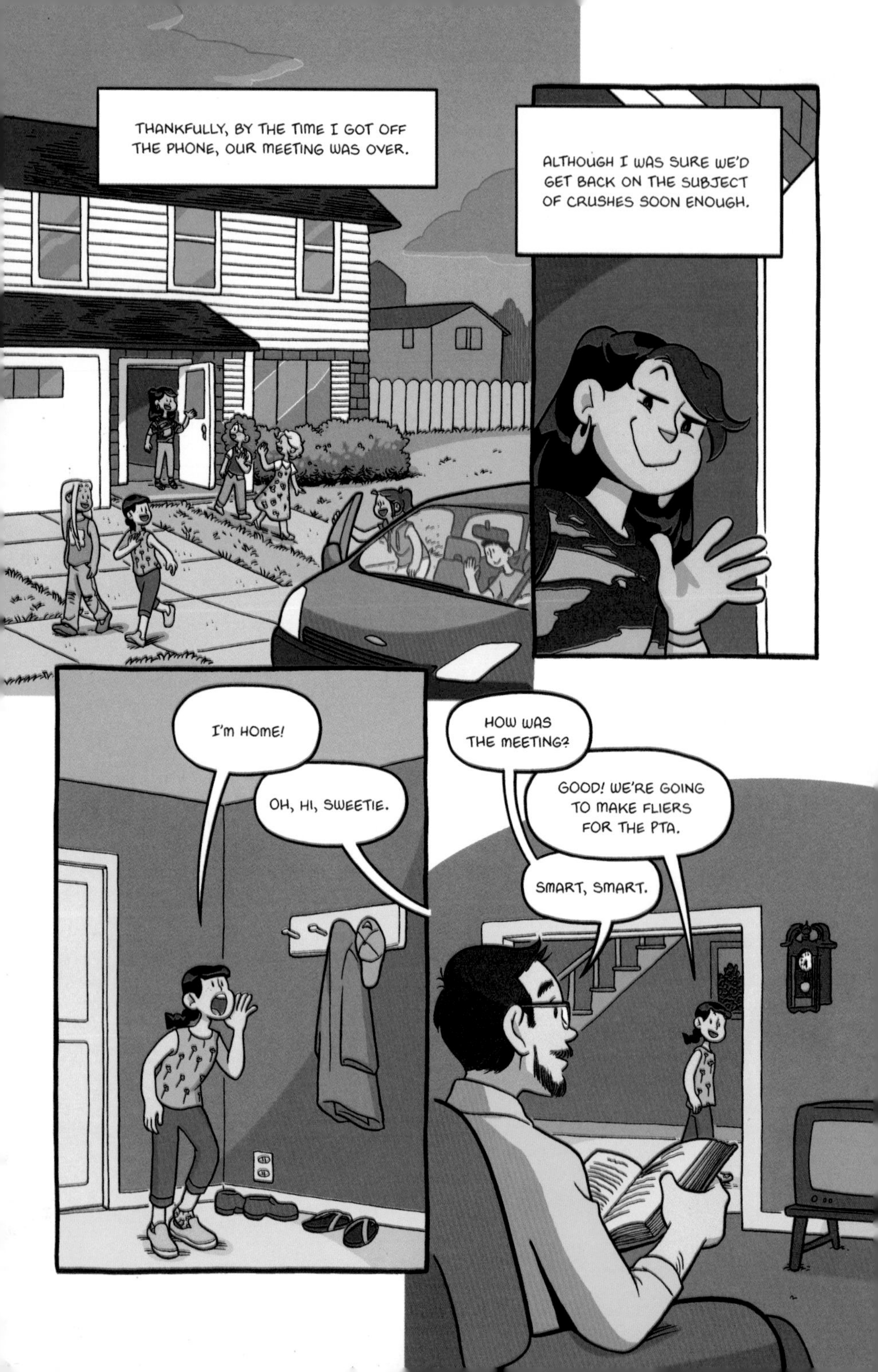

THANKFULLY, BY THE TIME I GOT OFF THE PHONE, OUR MEETING WAS OVER.
ALTHOUGH I WAS SURE WE'D GET BACK ON THE SUBJECT OF CRUSHES SOON ENOUGH.
I'M HOME!
OH, HI, SWEETIE.
HOW WAS THE MEETING?
GOOD! WE'RE GOING TO MAKE FLIERS FOR THE PTA.
SMART, SMART.

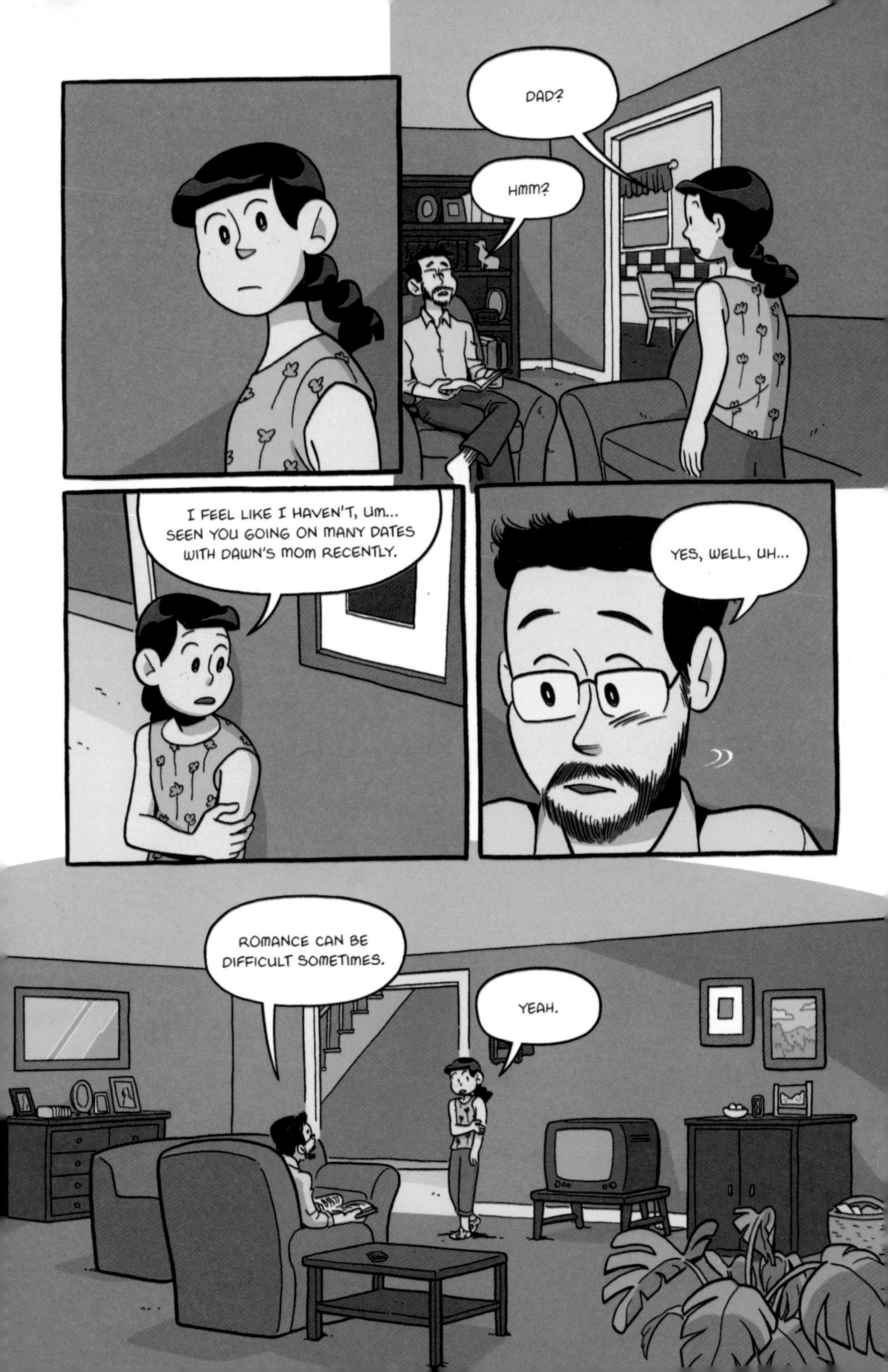
DAD?
HMM?
I FEEL LIKE I HAVEN'T, UM... SEEN YOU GOING ON MANY DATES WITH DAWN'S MOM RECENTLY.
YES, WELL, UH...
ROMANCE CAN BE DIFFICULT SOMETIMES.
YEAH.

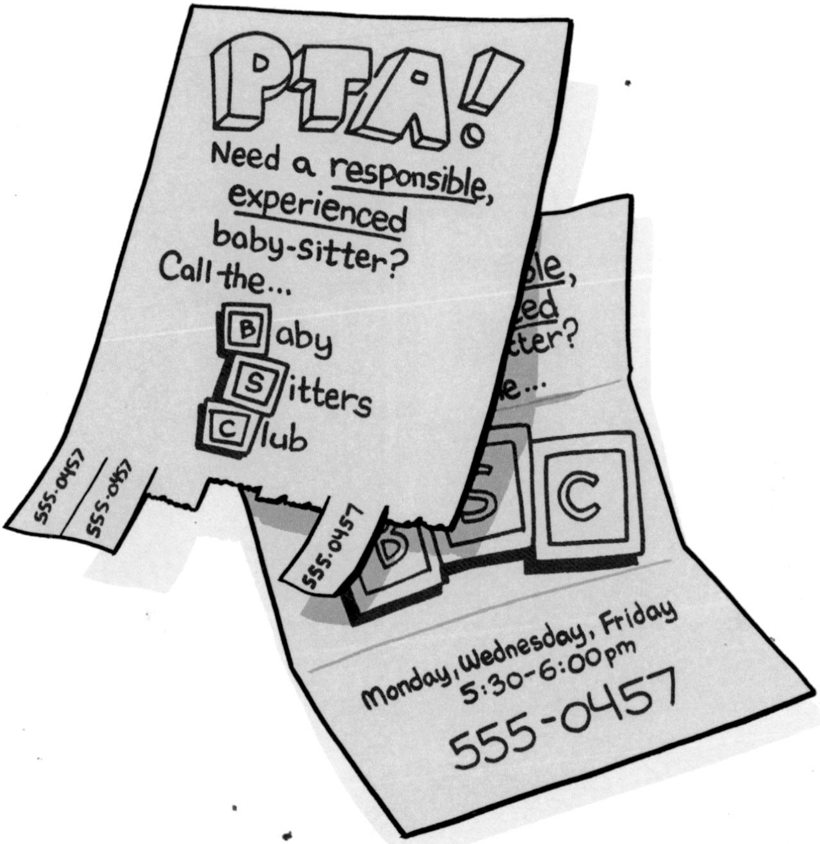
PTA!
Need a responsible, experienced baby-sitter?
Call the...
Baby Sitters Club
555-0457
555-0457
555-0457
BSC
Monday, Wednesday, Friday
5:30-6:00 pm
555-0457

CHAPTER 4

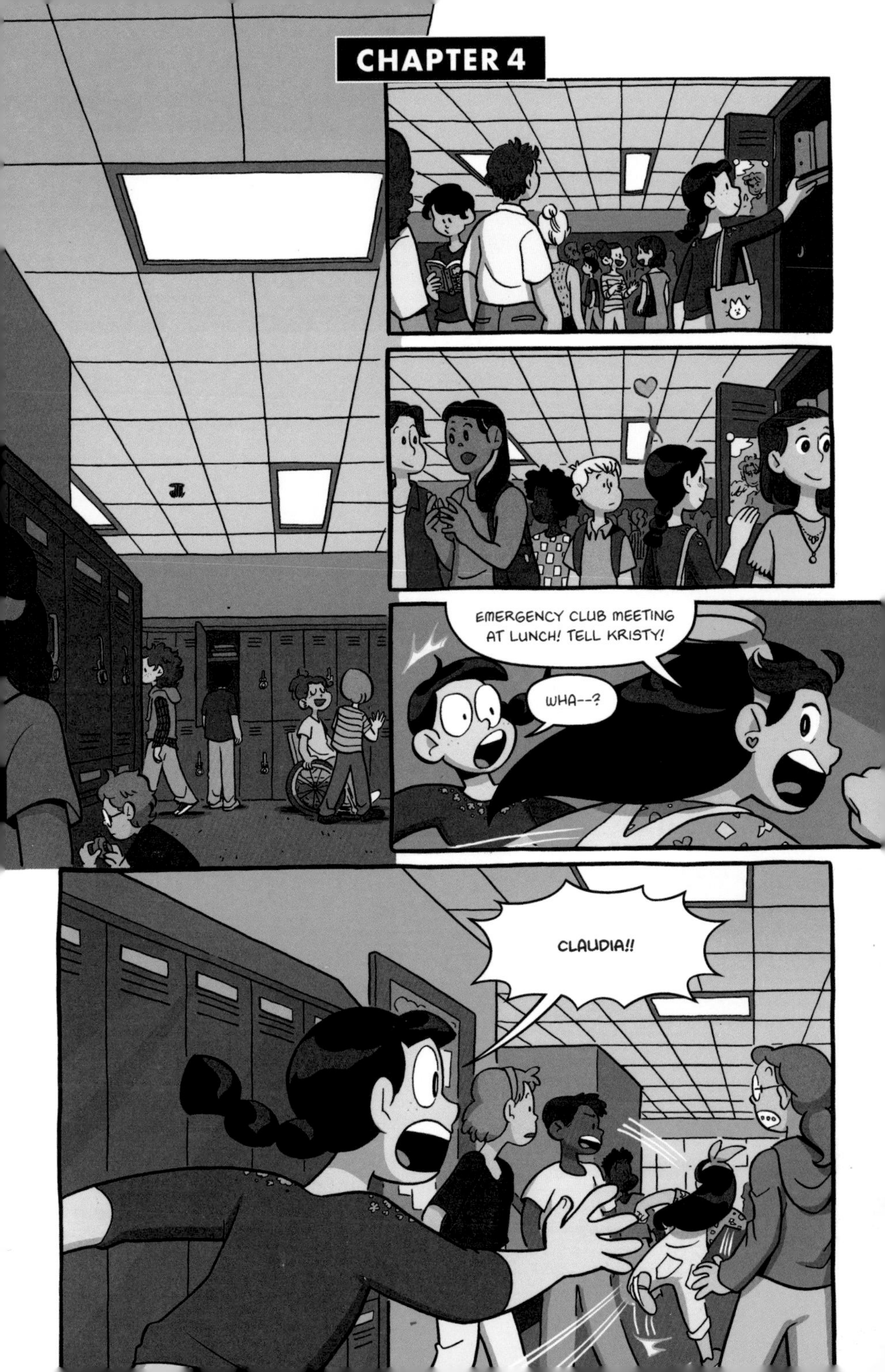
EMERGENCY CLUB MEETING AT LUNCH! TELL KRISTY!
WHA--?
CLAUDIA!!

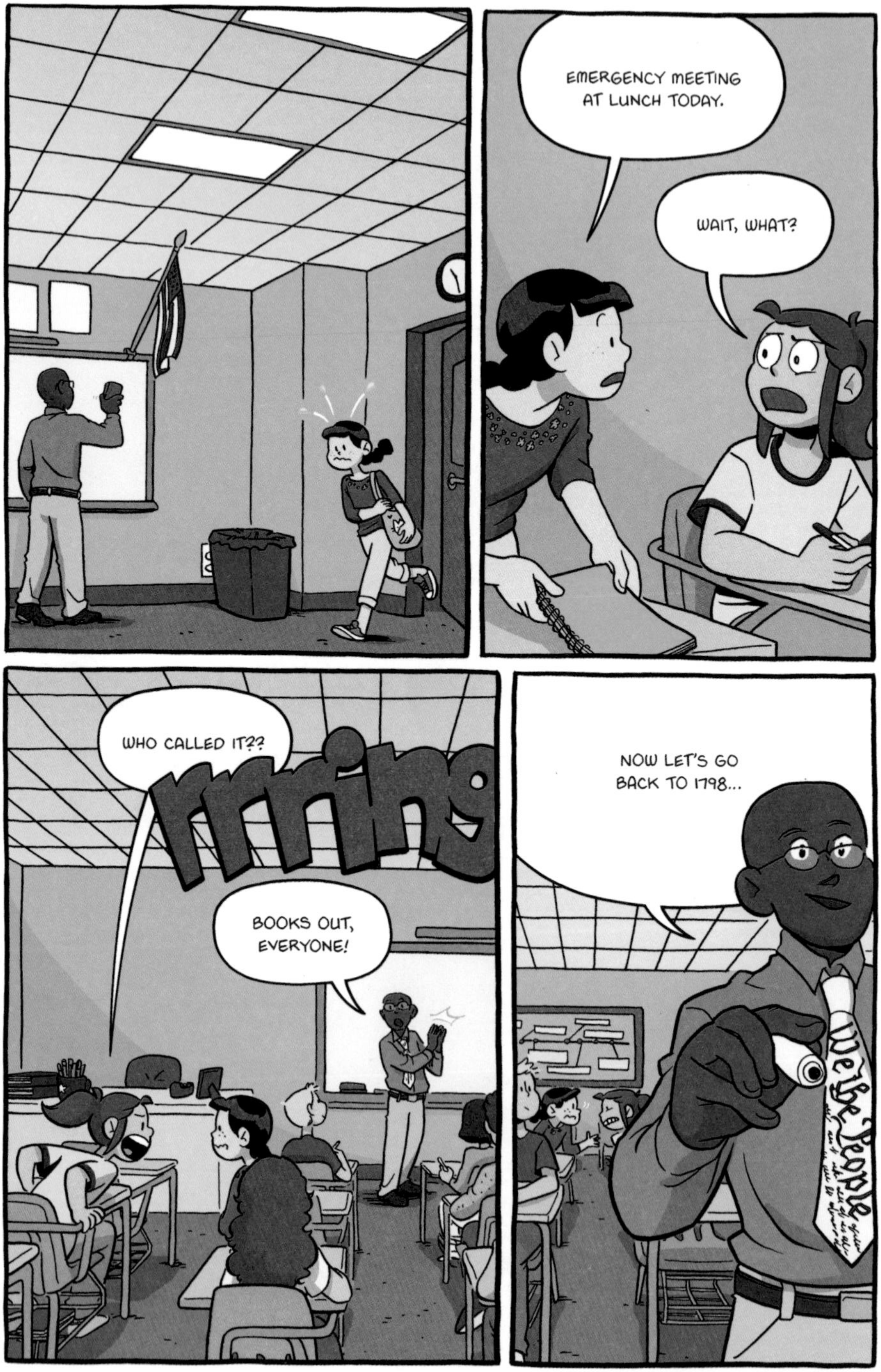
EMERGENCY MEETING AT LUNCH TODAY.
WAIT, WHAT?
WHO CALLED IT??
rrring
BOOKS OUT, EVERYONE!
NOW LET'S GO BACK TO 1798...
We the People

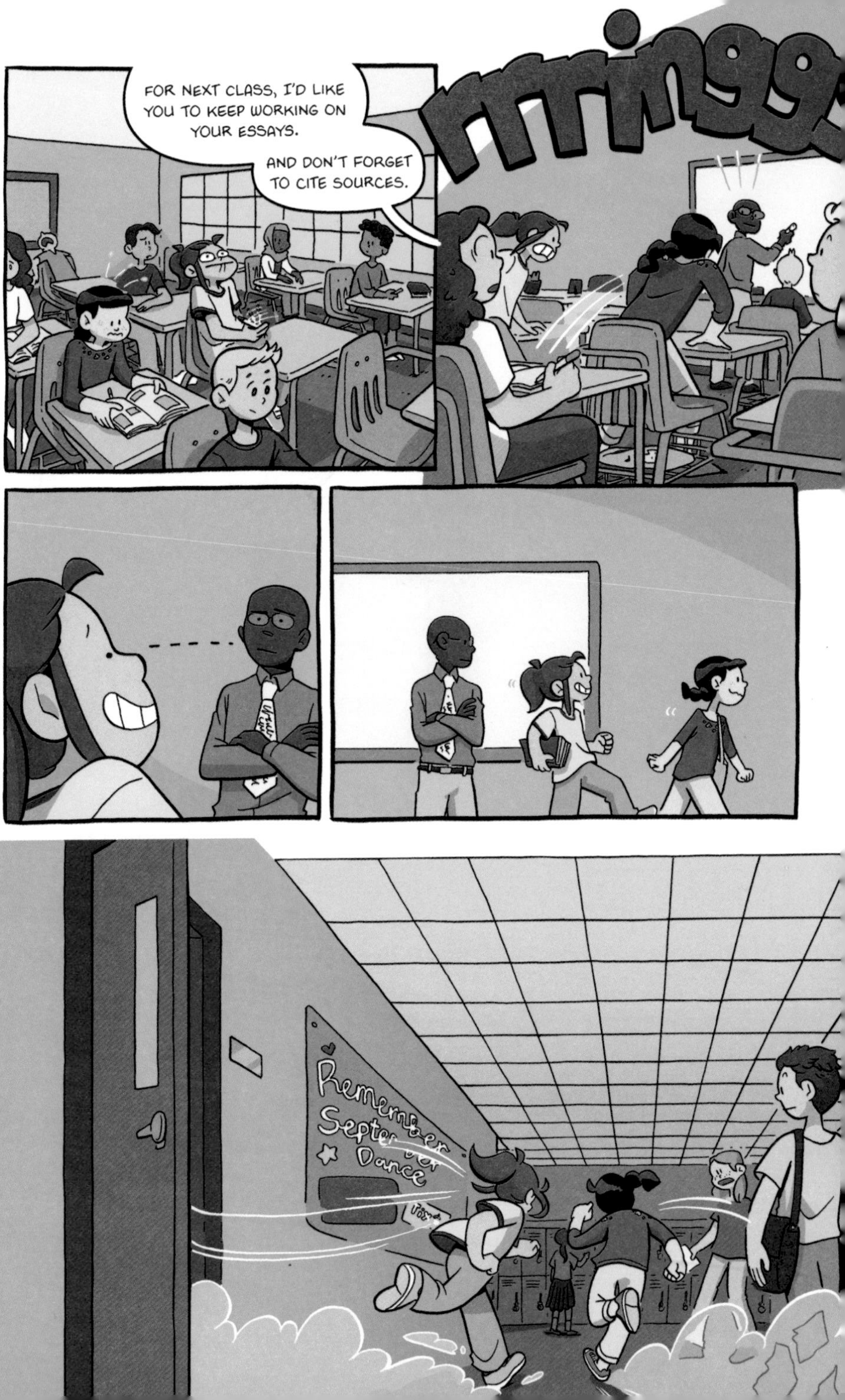
FOR NEXT CLASS, I'D LIKE YOU TO KEEP WORKING ON YOUR ESSAYS.
AND DON'T FORGET TO CITE SOURCES.
rrrringgg
Remember September Dance

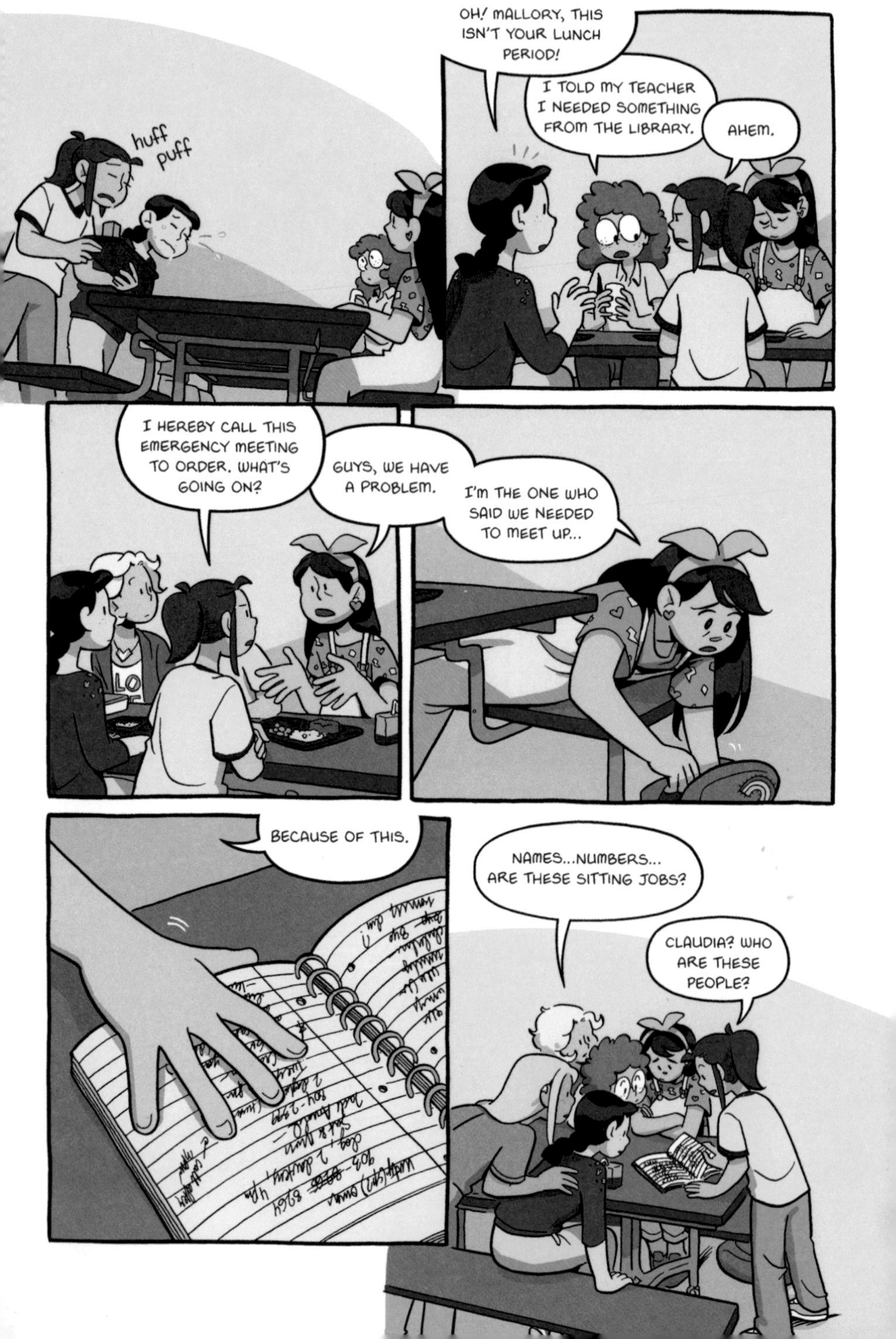
huff
puff
OH! MALLORY, THIS ISN'T YOUR LUNCH PERIOD!
I TOLD MY TEACHER I NEEDED SOMETHING FROM THE LIBRARY.
AHEM.
I HEREBY CALL THIS EMERGENCY MEETING TO ORDER. WHAT'S GOING ON?
GUYS, WE HAVE A PROBLEM.
I'M THE ONE WHO SAID WE NEEDED TO MEET UP...
BECAUSE OF THIS.
NAMES...NUMBERS... ARE THESE SITTING JOBS?
CLAUDIA? WHO ARE THESE PEOPLE?

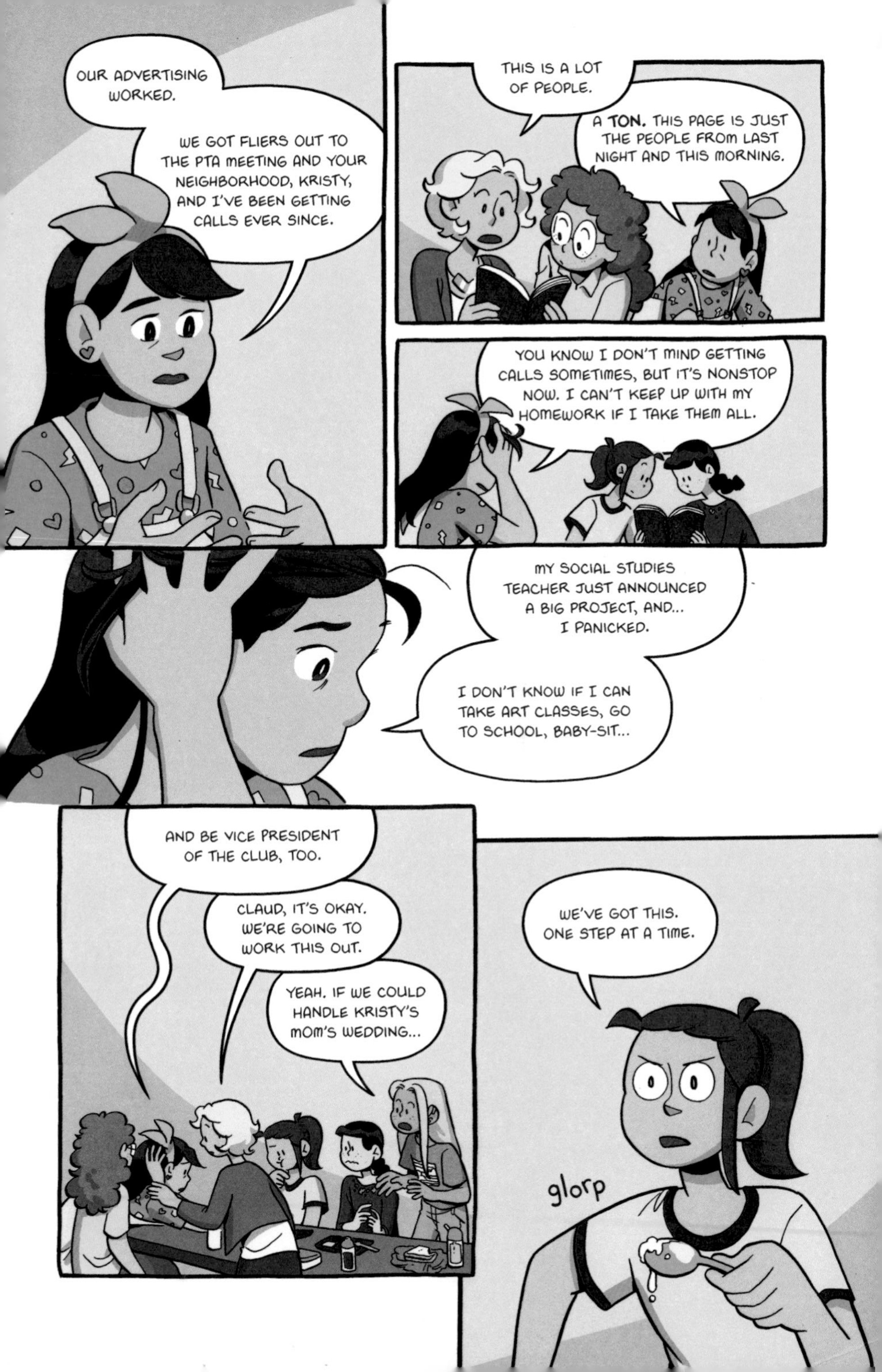
OUR ADVERTISING WORKED.
WE GOT FLIERS OUT TO THE PTA MEETING AND YOUR NEIGHBORHOOD, KRISTY, AND I'VE BEEN GETTING CALLS EVER SINCE.
THIS IS A LOT OF PEOPLE.
A **TON.** THIS PAGE IS JUST THE PEOPLE FROM LAST NIGHT AND THIS MORNING.
YOU KNOW I DON'T MIND GETTING CALLS SOMETIMES, BUT IT'S NONSTOP NOW. I CAN'T KEEP UP WITH MY HOMEWORK IF I TAKE THEM ALL.
MY SOCIAL STUDIES TEACHER JUST ANNOUNCED A BIG PROJECT, AND... I PANICKED.
I DON'T KNOW IF I CAN TAKE ART CLASSES, GO TO SCHOOL, BABY-SIT...
AND BE VICE PRESIDENT OF THE CLUB, TOO.
CLAUD, IT'S OKAY. WE'RE GOING TO WORK THIS OUT.
YEAH. IF WE COULD HANDLE KRISTY'S MOM'S WEDDING...
WE'VE GOT THIS. ONE STEP AT A TIME.
glorp

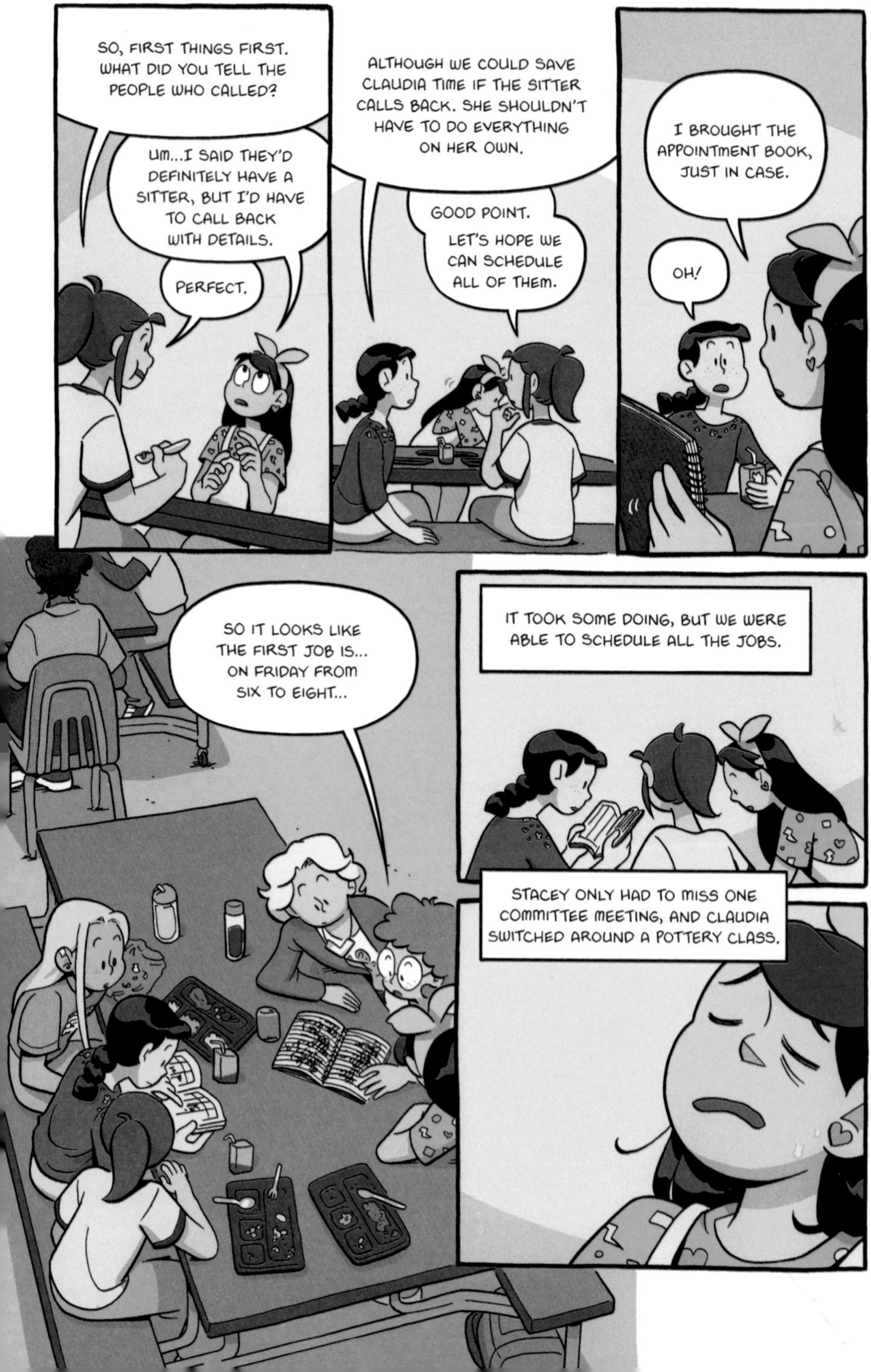
SO, FIRST THINGS FIRST. WHAT DID YOU TELL THE PEOPLE WHO CALLED?
UM...I SAID THEY'D DEFINITELY HAVE A SITTER, BUT I'D HAVE TO CALL BACK WITH DETAILS.
PERFECT.
ALTHOUGH WE COULD SAVE CLAUDIA TIME IF THE SITTER CALLS BACK. SHE SHOULDN'T HAVE TO DO EVERYTHING ON HER OWN.
GOOD POINT.
LET'S HOPE WE CAN SCHEDULE ALL OF THEM.
I BROUGHT THE APPOINTMENT BOOK, JUST IN CASE.
OH!
SO IT LOOKS LIKE THE FIRST JOB IS... ON FRIDAY FROM SIX TO EIGHT...
IT TOOK SOME DOING, BUT WE WERE ABLE TO SCHEDULE ALL THE JOBS.
STACEY ONLY HAD TO MISS ONE COMMITTEE MEETING, AND CLAUDIA SWITCHED AROUND A POTTERY CLASS.

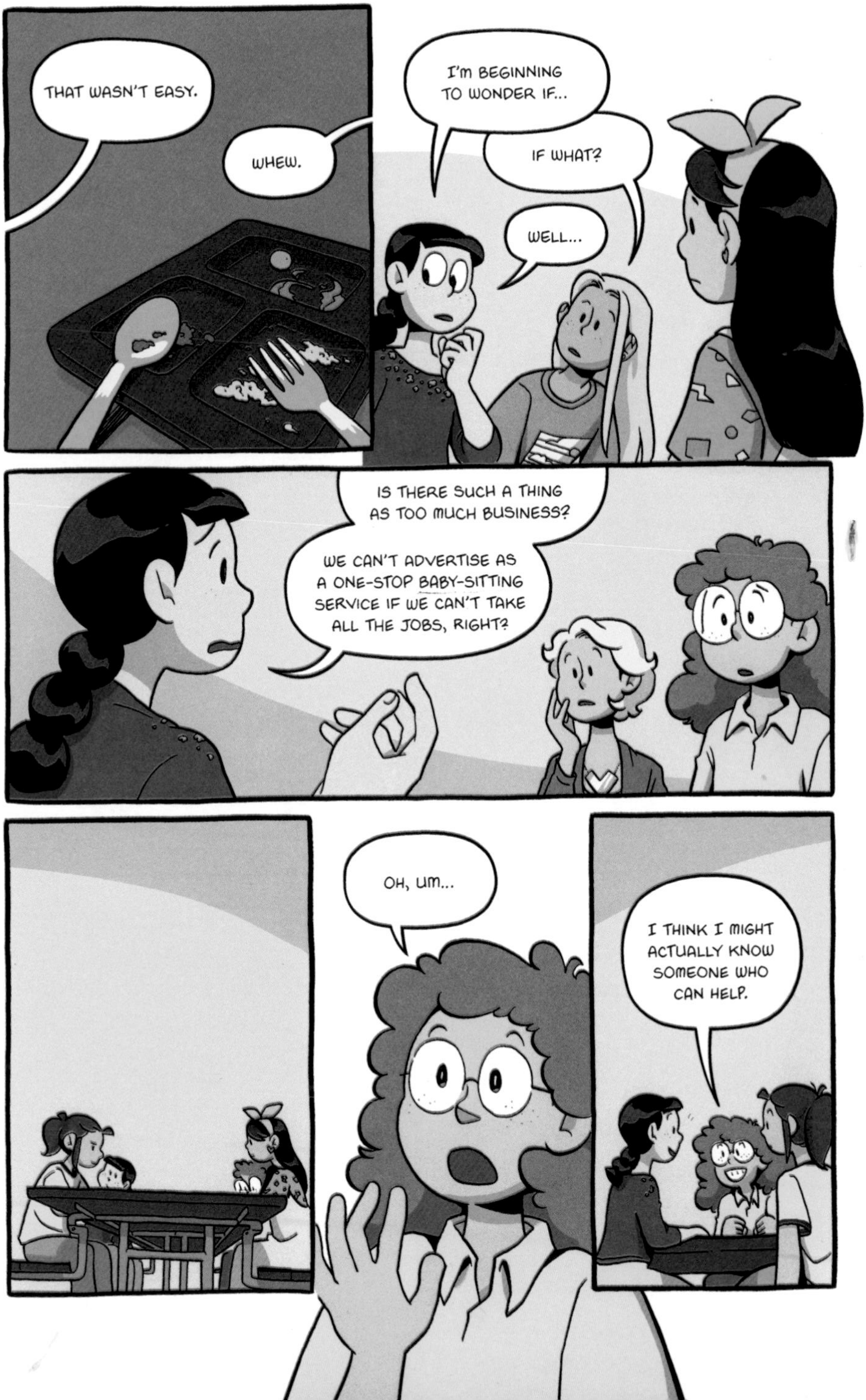
THAT WASN'T EASY.
WHEW.
I'M BEGINNING TO WONDER IF...
IF WHAT?
WELL...
IS THERE SUCH A THING AS TOO MUCH BUSINESS?
WE CAN'T ADVERTISE AS A ONE-STOP BABY-SITTING SERVICE IF WE CAN'T TAKE ALL THE JOBS, RIGHT?
OH, UM...
I THINK I MIGHT ACTUALLY KNOW SOMEONE WHO CAN HELP.

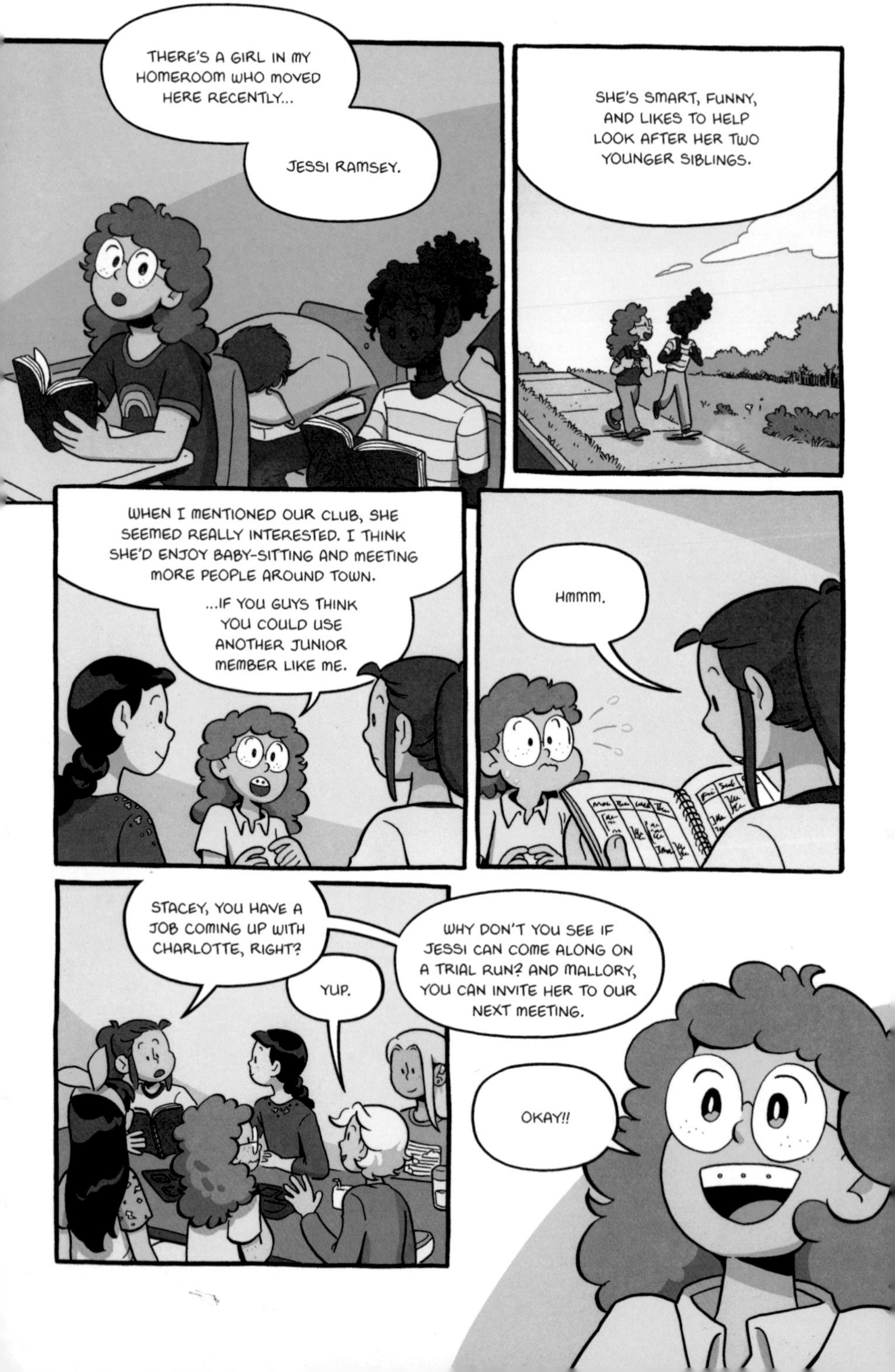
THERE'S A GIRL IN MY HOMEROOM WHO MOVED HERE RECENTLY...
JESSI RAMSEY.
SHE'S SMART, FUNNY, AND LIKES TO HELP LOOK AFTER HER TWO YOUNGER SIBLINGS.
WHEN I MENTIONED OUR CLUB, SHE SEEMED REALLY INTERESTED. I THINK SHE'D ENJOY BABY-SITTING AND MEETING MORE PEOPLE AROUND TOWN.
...IF YOU GUYS THINK YOU COULD USE ANOTHER JUNIOR MEMBER LIKE ME.
HMMM.
STACEY, YOU HAVE A JOB COMING UP WITH CHARLOTTE, RIGHT?
YUP.
WHY DON'T YOU SEE IF JESSI CAN COME ALONG ON A TRIAL RUN? AND MALLORY, YOU CAN INVITE HER TO OUR NEXT MEETING.
OKAY!!

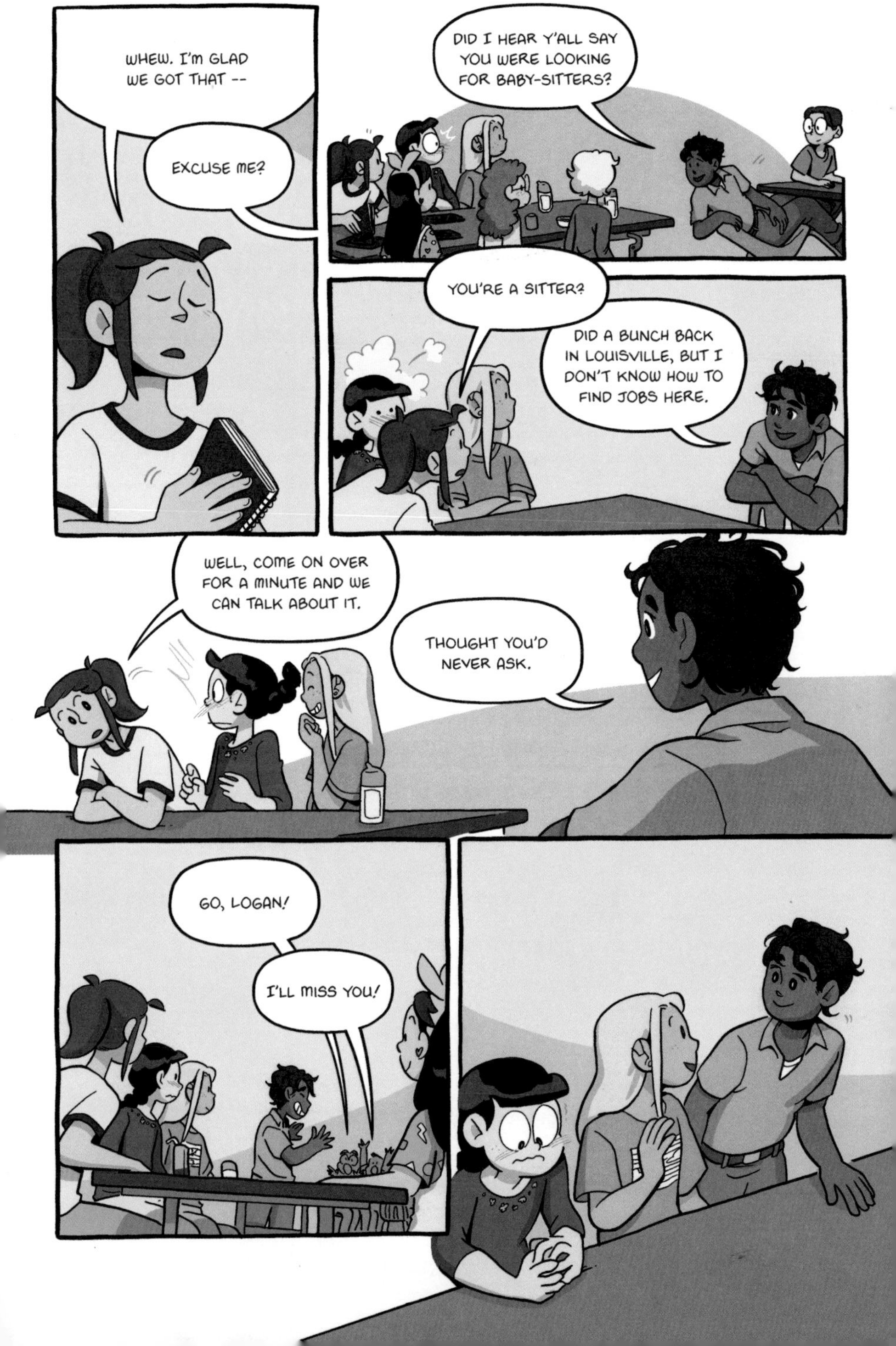
WHEW. I'M GLAD WE GOT THAT --
EXCUSE ME?
DID I HEAR Y'ALL SAY YOU WERE LOOKING FOR BABY-SITTERS?
YOU'RE A SITTER?
DID A BUNCH BACK IN LOUISVILLE, BUT I DON'T KNOW HOW TO FIND JOBS HERE.
WELL, COME ON OVER FOR A MINUTE AND WE CAN TALK ABOUT IT.
THOUGHT YOU'D NEVER ASK.
GO, LOGAN!
I'LL MISS YOU!

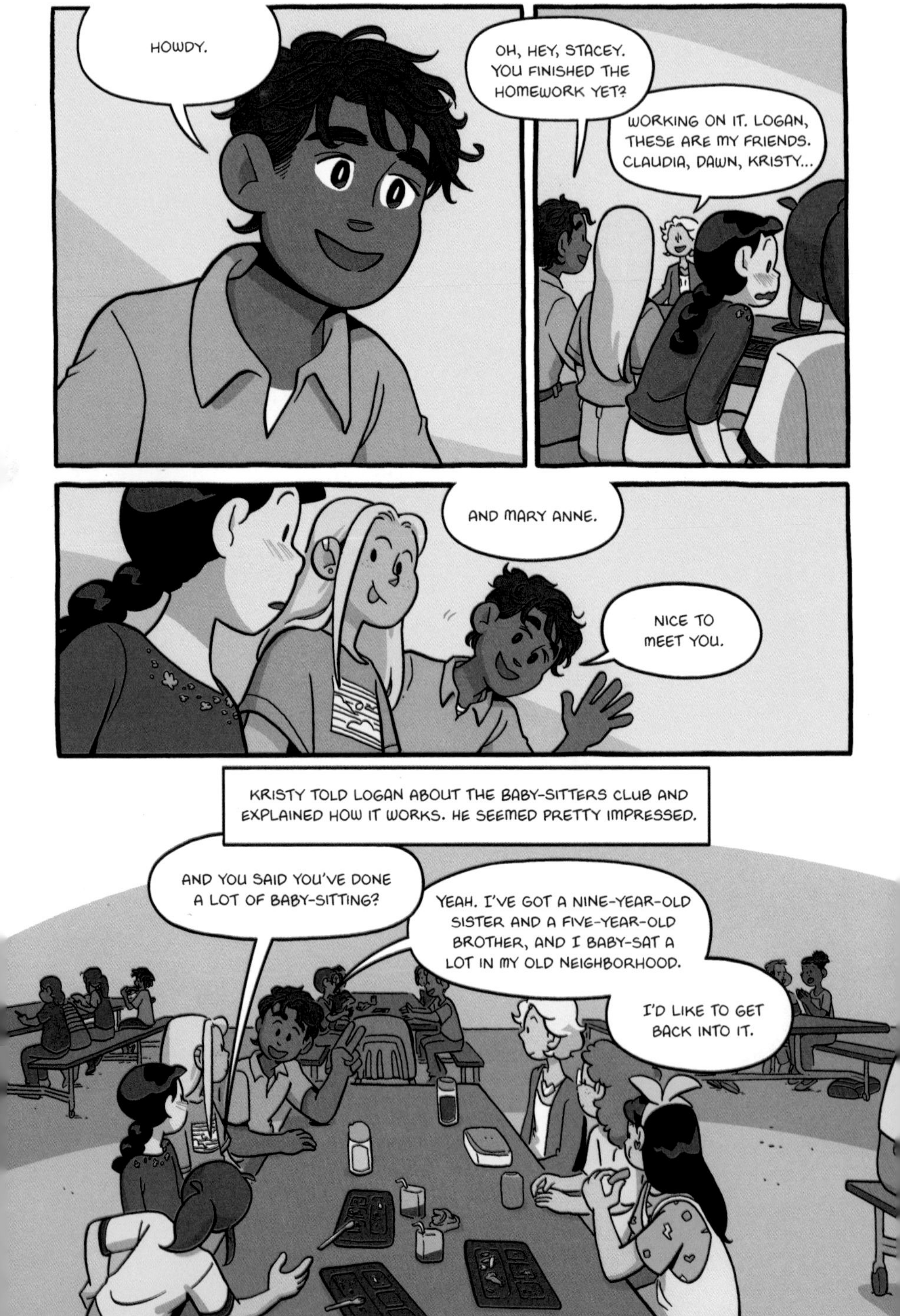
HOWDY.
OH, HEY, STACEY. YOU FINISHED THE HOMEWORK YET?
WORKING ON IT. LOGAN, THESE ARE MY FRIENDS. CLAUDIA, DAWN, KRISTY...
AND MARY ANNE.
NICE TO MEET YOU.
KRISTY TOLD LOGAN ABOUT THE BABY-SITTERS CLUB AND EXPLAINED HOW IT WORKS. HE SEEMED PRETTY IMPRESSED.
AND YOU SAID YOU'VE DONE A LOT OF BABY-SITTING?
YEAH. I'VE GOT A NINE-YEAR-OLD SISTER AND A FIVE-YEAR-OLD BROTHER, AND I BABY-SAT A LOT IN MY OLD NEIGHBORHOOD.
I'D LIKE TO GET BACK INTO IT.

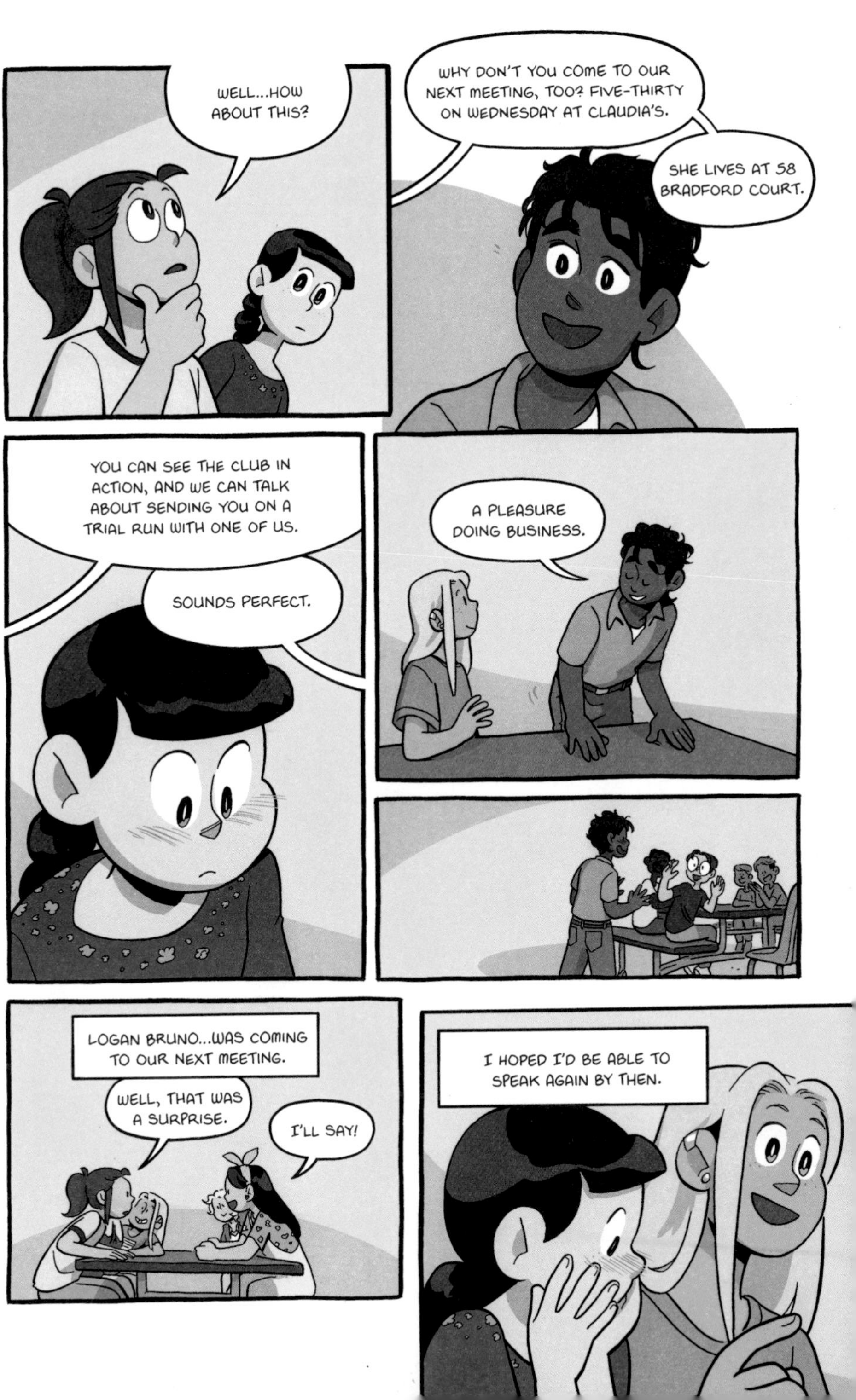
WELL...HOW ABOUT THIS?
WHY DON'T YOU COME TO OUR NEXT MEETING, TOO? FIVE-THIRTY ON WEDNESDAY AT CLAUDIA'S.
SHE LIVES AT 58 BRADFORD COURT.
YOU CAN SEE THE CLUB IN ACTION, AND WE CAN TALK ABOUT SENDING YOU ON A TRIAL RUN WITH ONE OF US.
SOUNDS PERFECT.
A PLEASURE DOING BUSINESS.
LOGAN BRUNO...WAS COMING TO OUR NEXT MEETING.
WELL, THAT WAS A SURPRISE.
I'LL SAY!
I HOPED I'D BE ABLE TO SPEAK AGAIN BY THEN.

CHAPTER 5

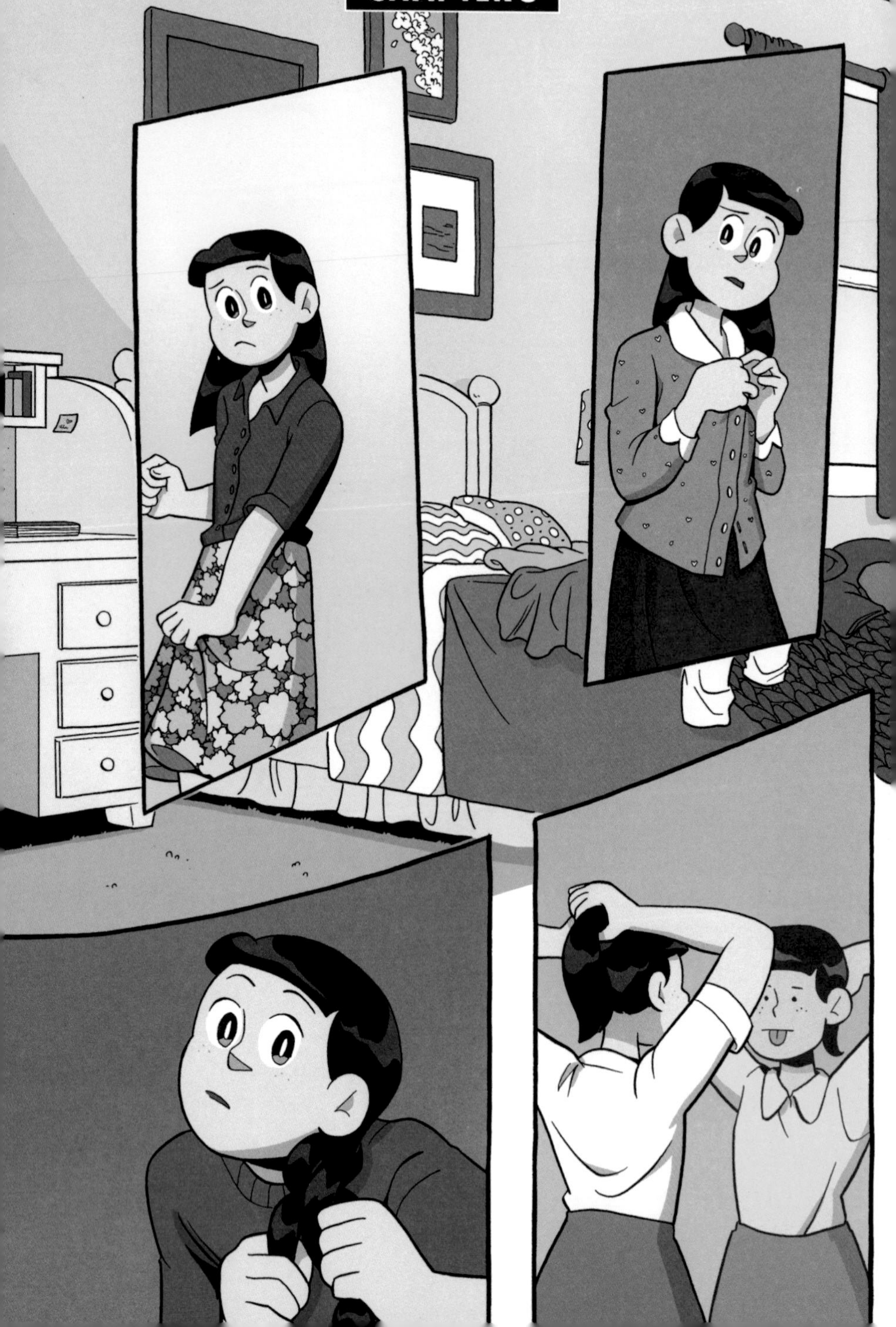

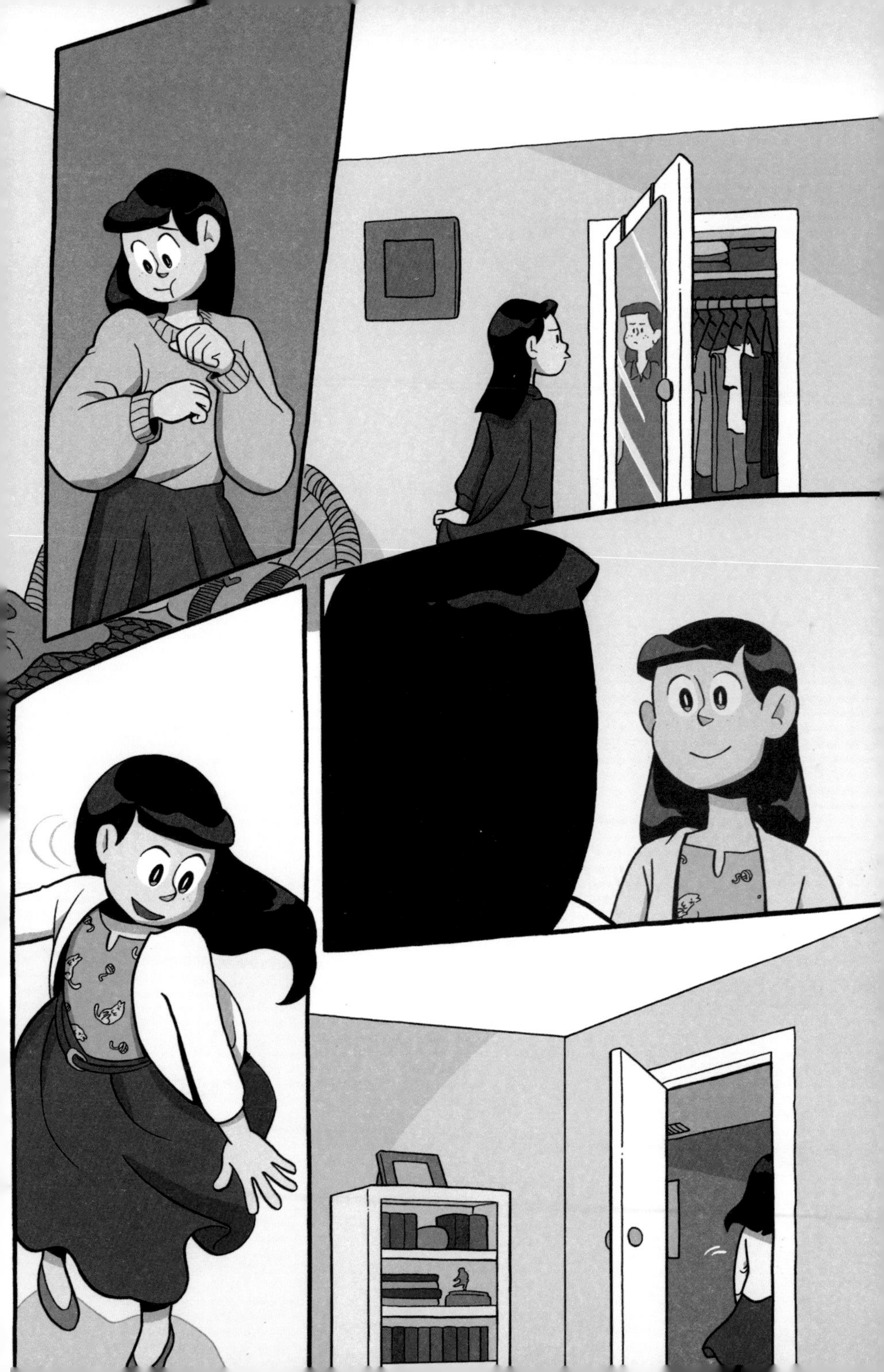

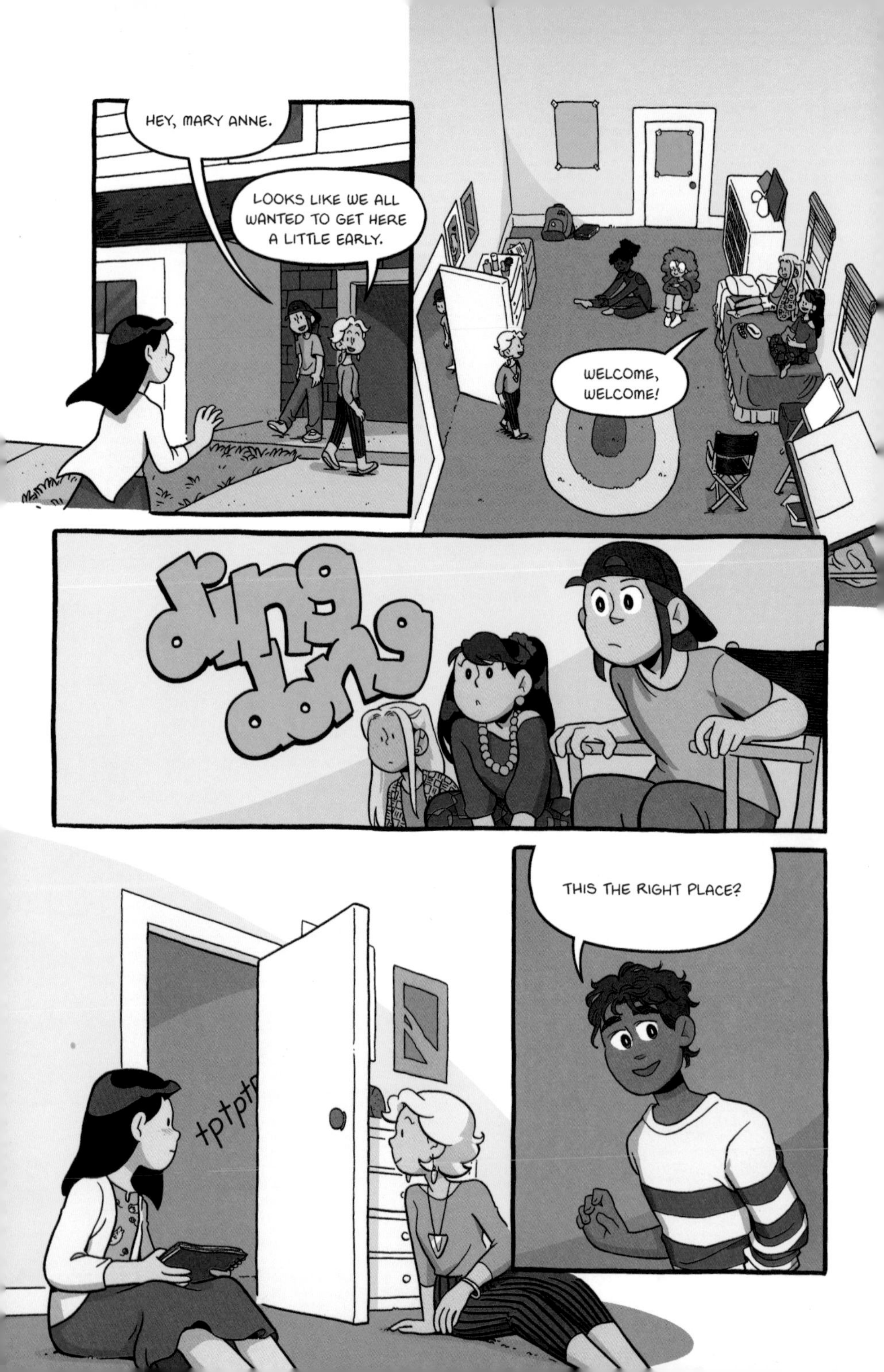

HEY, MARY ANNE.
LOOKS LIKE WE ALL WANTED TO GET HERE A LITTLE EARLY.
WELCOME, WELCOME!
ding dong
THIS THE RIGHT PLACE?
tptpt

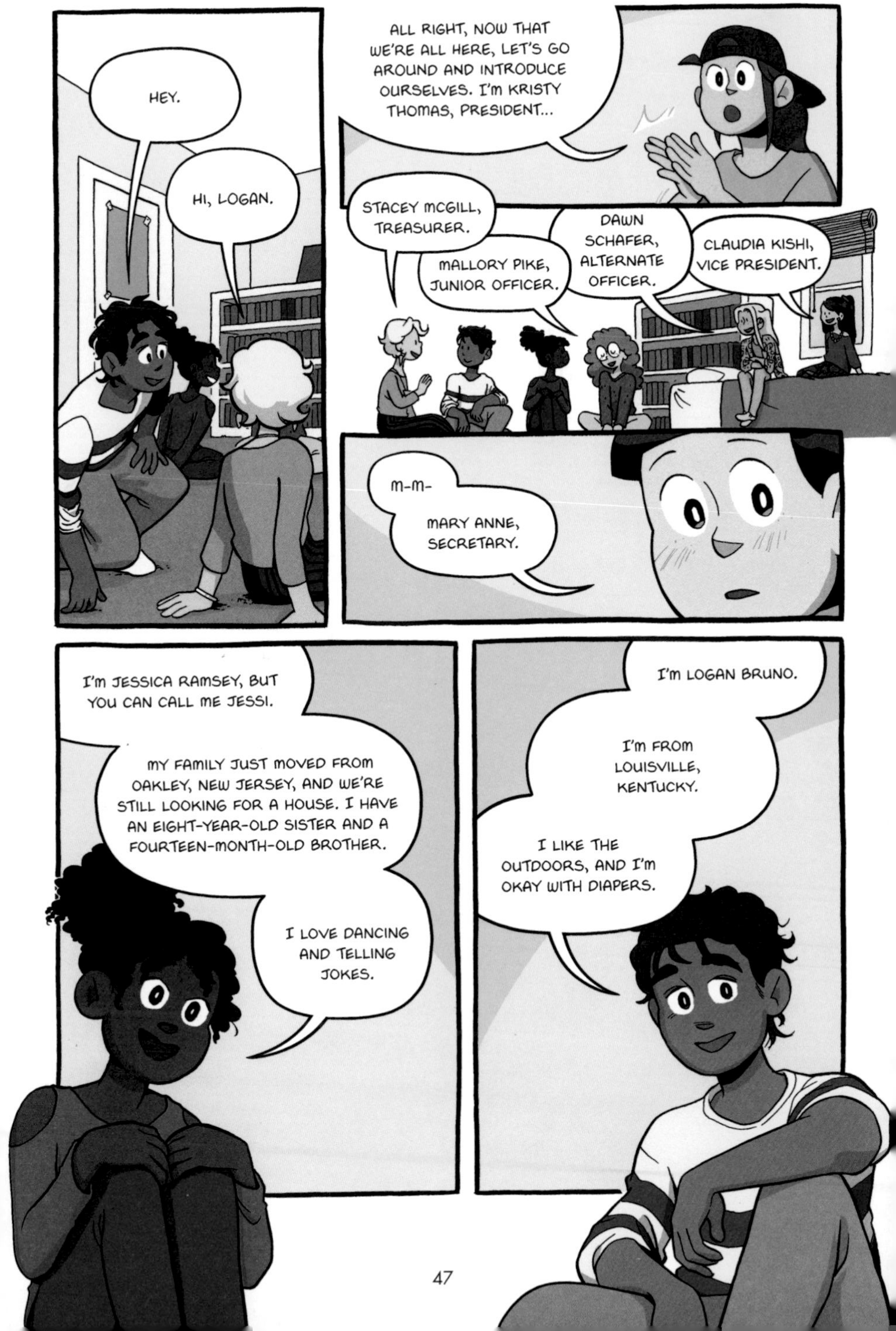
HEY.
HI, LOGAN.
ALL RIGHT, NOW THAT WE'RE ALL HERE, LET'S GO AROUND AND INTRODUCE OURSELVES. I'M KRISTY THOMAS, PRESIDENT...
STACEY MCGILL, TREASURER.
MALLORY PIKE, JUNIOR OFFICER.
DAWN SCHAFER, ALTERNATE OFFICER.
CLAUDIA KISHI, VICE PRESIDENT.
M-M-
MARY ANNE, SECRETARY.
I'M JESSICA RAMSEY, BUT YOU CAN CALL ME JESSI.
MY FAMILY JUST MOVED FROM OAKLEY, NEW JERSEY, AND WE'RE STILL LOOKING FOR A HOUSE. I HAVE AN EIGHT-YEAR-OLD SISTER AND A FOURTEEN-MONTH-OLD BROTHER.
I LOVE DANCING AND TELLING JOKES.
I'M LOGAN BRUNO.
I'M FROM LOUISVILLE, KENTUCKY.
I LIKE THE OUTDOORS, AND I'M OKAY WITH DIAPERS.

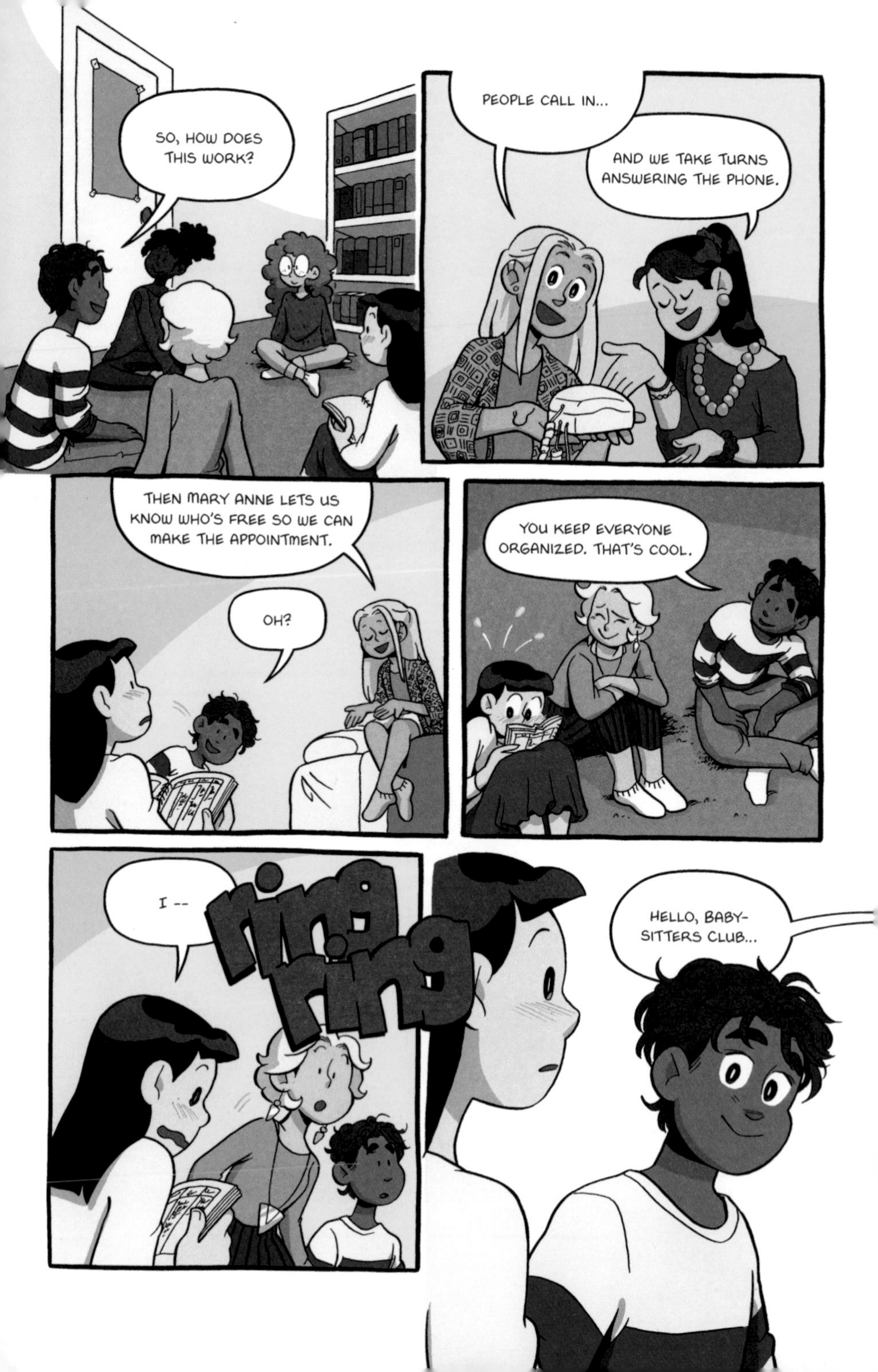
SO, HOW DOES THIS WORK?
PEOPLE CALL IN...
AND WE TAKE TURNS ANSWERING THE PHONE.
THEN MARY ANNE LETS US KNOW WHO'S FREE SO WE CAN MAKE THE APPOINTMENT.
OH?
YOU KEEP EVERYONE ORGANIZED. THAT'S COOL.
I --
ring ring
HELLO, BABY-SITTERS CLUB...

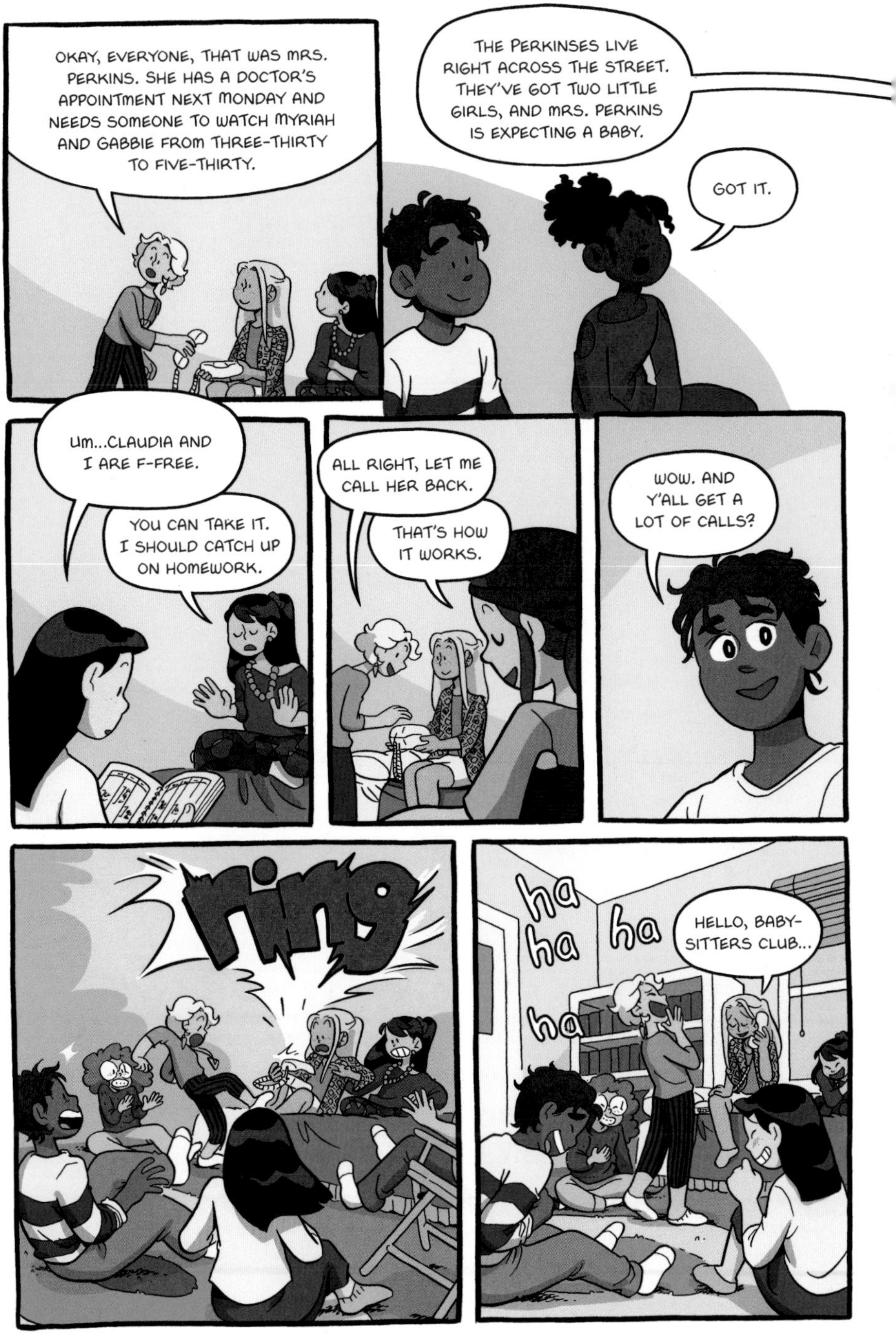
OKAY, EVERYONE, THAT WAS MRS. PERKINS. SHE HAS A DOCTOR'S APPOINTMENT NEXT MONDAY AND NEEDS SOMEONE TO WATCH MYRIAH AND GABBIE FROM THREE-THIRTY TO FIVE-THIRTY.
THE PERKINSES LIVE RIGHT ACROSS THE STREET. THEY'VE GOT TWO LITTLE GIRLS, AND MRS. PERKINS IS EXPECTING A BABY.
GOT IT.
UM...CLAUDIA AND I ARE F-FREE.
YOU CAN TAKE IT. I SHOULD CATCH UP ON HOMEWORK.
ALL RIGHT, LET ME CALL HER BACK.
THAT'S HOW IT WORKS.
WOW. AND Y'ALL GET A LOT OF CALLS?
RING
HA HA HA HA
HELLO, BABY-SITTERS CLUB...

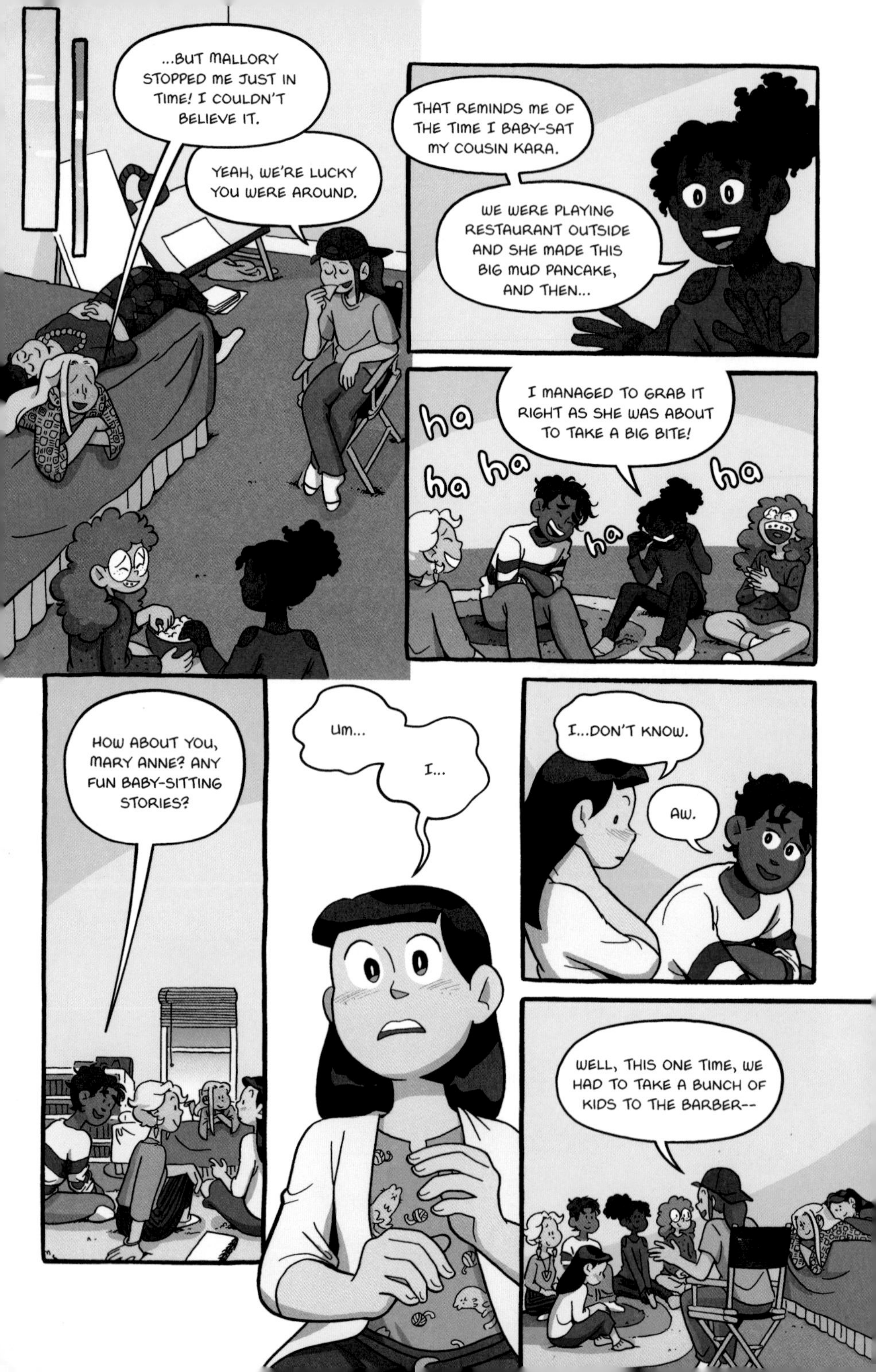
...BUT MALLORY STOPPED ME JUST IN TIME! I COULDN'T BELIEVE IT.
YEAH, WE'RE LUCKY YOU WERE AROUND.
THAT REMINDS ME OF THE TIME I BABY-SAT MY COUSIN KARA.
WE WERE PLAYING RESTAURANT OUTSIDE AND SHE MADE THIS BIG MUD PANCAKE, AND THEN...
ha
ha ha
I MANAGED TO GRAB IT RIGHT AS SHE WAS ABOUT TO TAKE A BIG BITE!
ha
ha
HOW ABOUT YOU, MARY ANNE? ANY FUN BABY-SITTING STORIES?
UM...
I...
I...DON'T KNOW.
AW.
WELL, THIS ONE TIME, WE HAD TO TAKE A BUNCH OF KIDS TO THE BARBER--

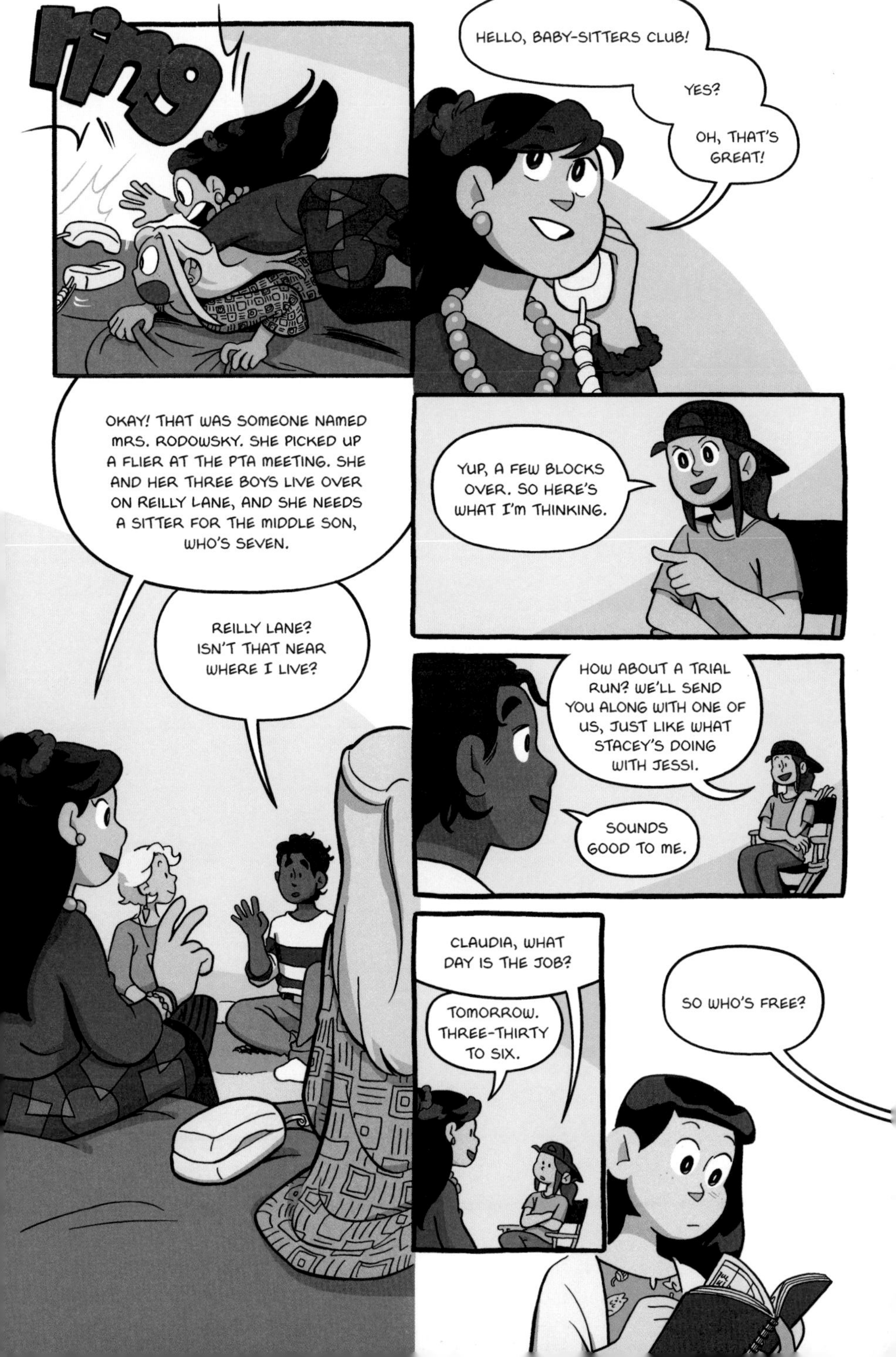
ring
HELLO, BABY-SITTERS CLUB!
YES?
OH, THAT'S GREAT!
OKAY! THAT WAS SOMEONE NAMED MRS. RODOWSKY. SHE PICKED UP A FLIER AT THE PTA MEETING. SHE AND HER THREE BOYS LIVE OVER ON REILLY LANE, AND SHE NEEDS A SITTER FOR THE MIDDLE SON, WHO'S SEVEN.
REILLY LANE? ISN'T THAT NEAR WHERE I LIVE?
YUP, A FEW BLOCKS OVER. SO HERE'S WHAT I'M THINKING.
HOW ABOUT A TRIAL RUN? WE'LL SEND YOU ALONG WITH ONE OF US, JUST LIKE WHAT STACEY'S DOING WITH JESSI.
SOUNDS GOOD TO ME.
CLAUDIA, WHAT DAY IS THE JOB?
TOMORROW. THREE-THIRTY TO SIX.
SO WHO'S FREE?

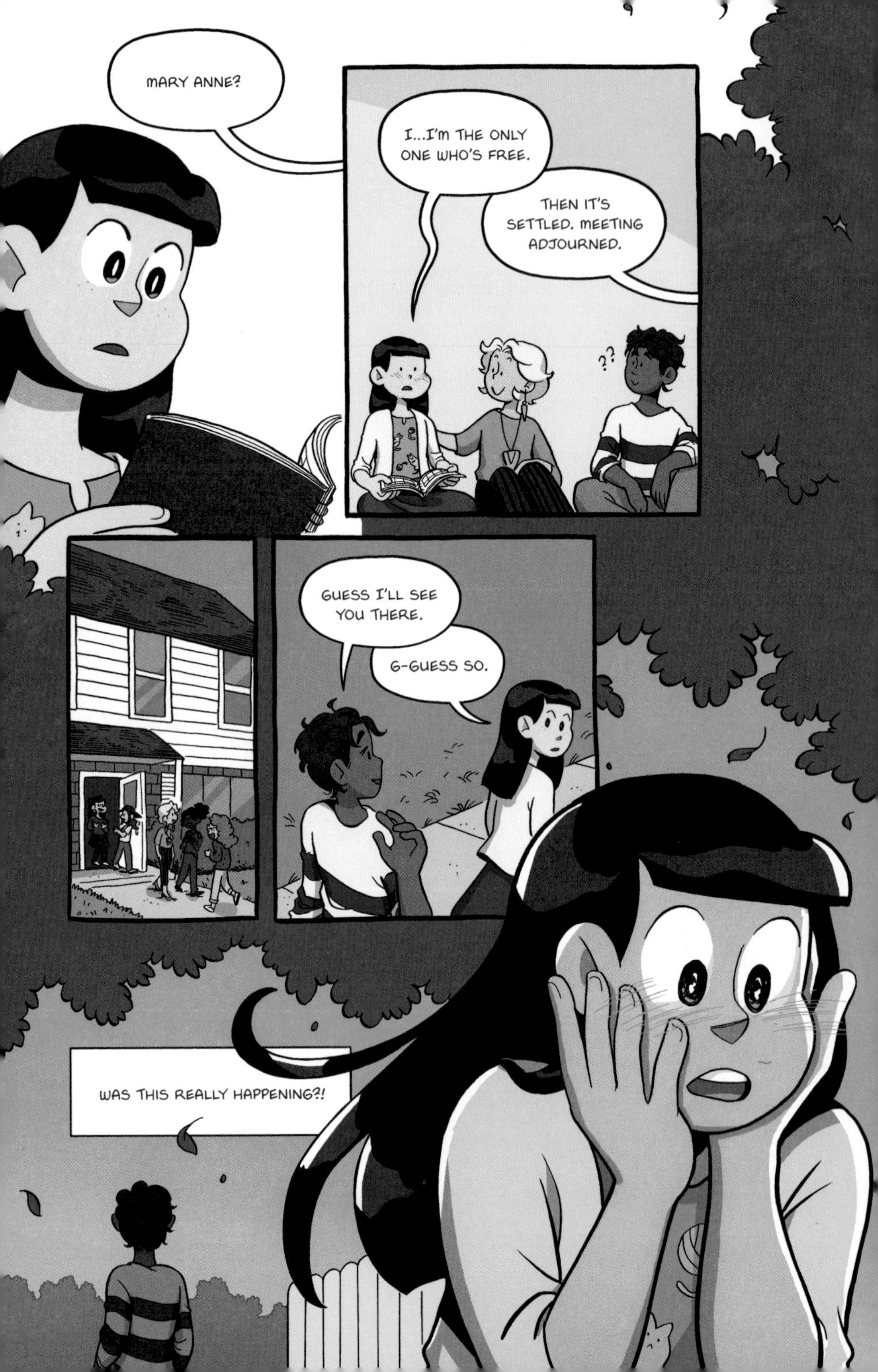
MARY ANNE?
I...I'M THE ONLY ONE WHO'S FREE.
THEN IT'S SETTLED. MEETING ADJOURNED.
??
GUESS I'LL SEE YOU THERE.
G-GUESS SO.
WAS THIS REALLY HAPPENING?!

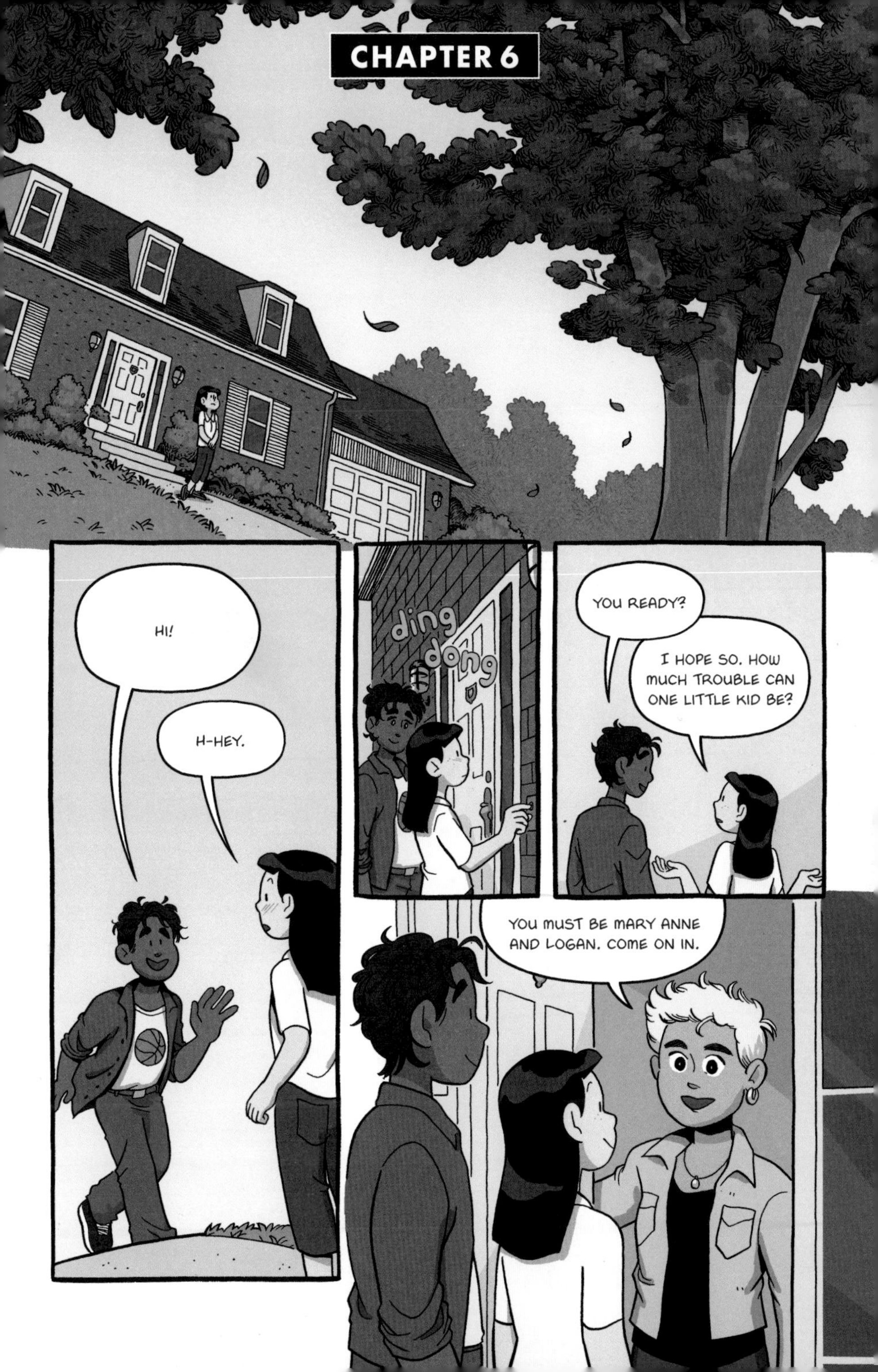
CHAPTER 6
HI!
H-HEY.
ding dong
YOU READY?
I HOPE SO. HOW MUCH TROUBLE CAN ONE LITTLE KID BE?
YOU MUST BE MARY ANNE AND LOGAN. COME ON IN.

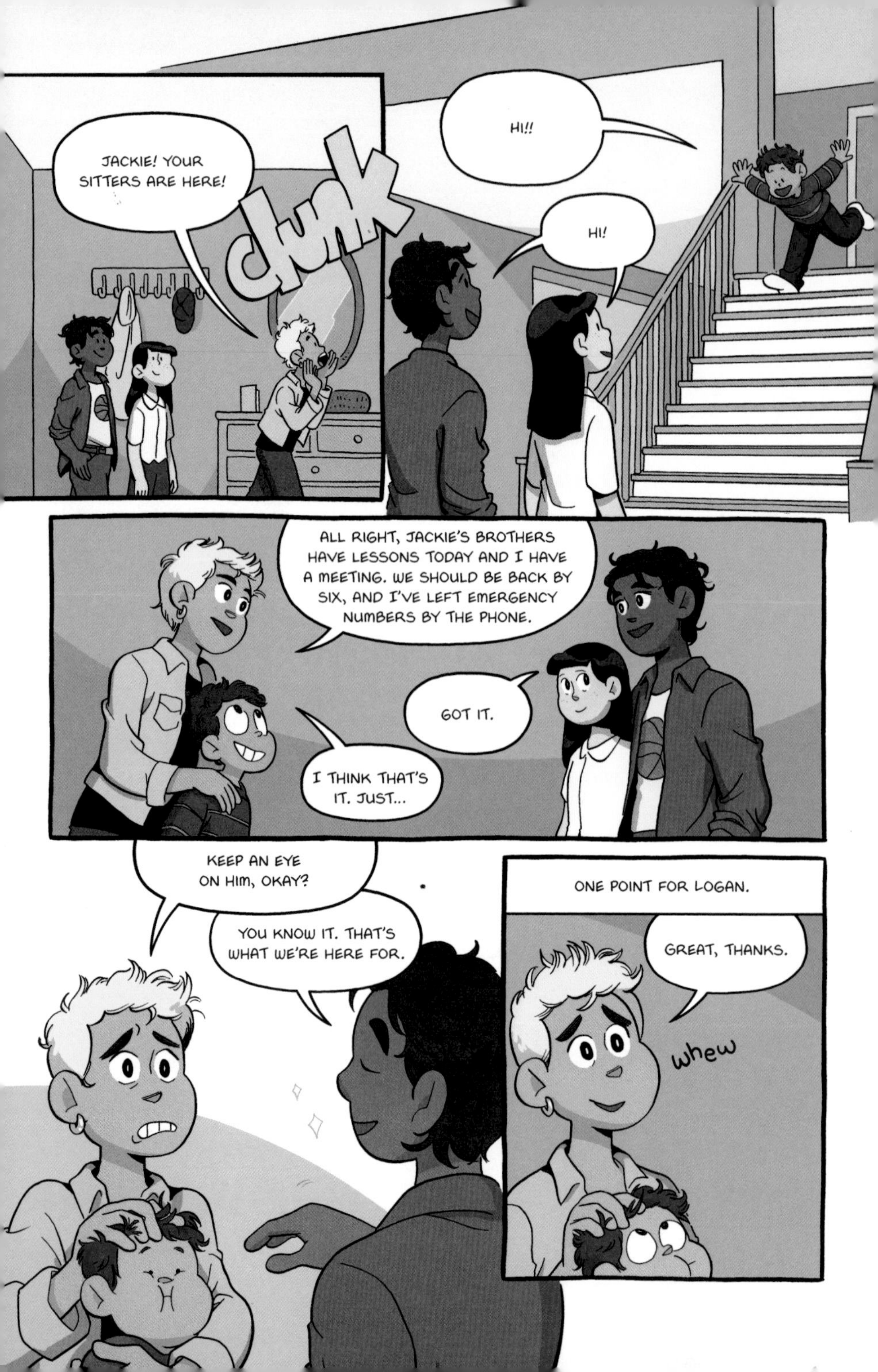
JACKIE! YOUR SITTERS ARE HERE!
clunk
HI!!
HI!
ALL RIGHT, JACKIE'S BROTHERS HAVE LESSONS TODAY AND I HAVE A MEETING. WE SHOULD BE BACK BY SIX, AND I'VE LEFT EMERGENCY NUMBERS BY THE PHONE.
GOT IT.
I THINK THAT'S IT. JUST...
KEEP AN EYE ON HIM, OKAY?
YOU KNOW IT. THAT'S WHAT WE'RE HERE FOR.
ONE POINT FOR LOGAN.
GREAT, THANKS.
whew

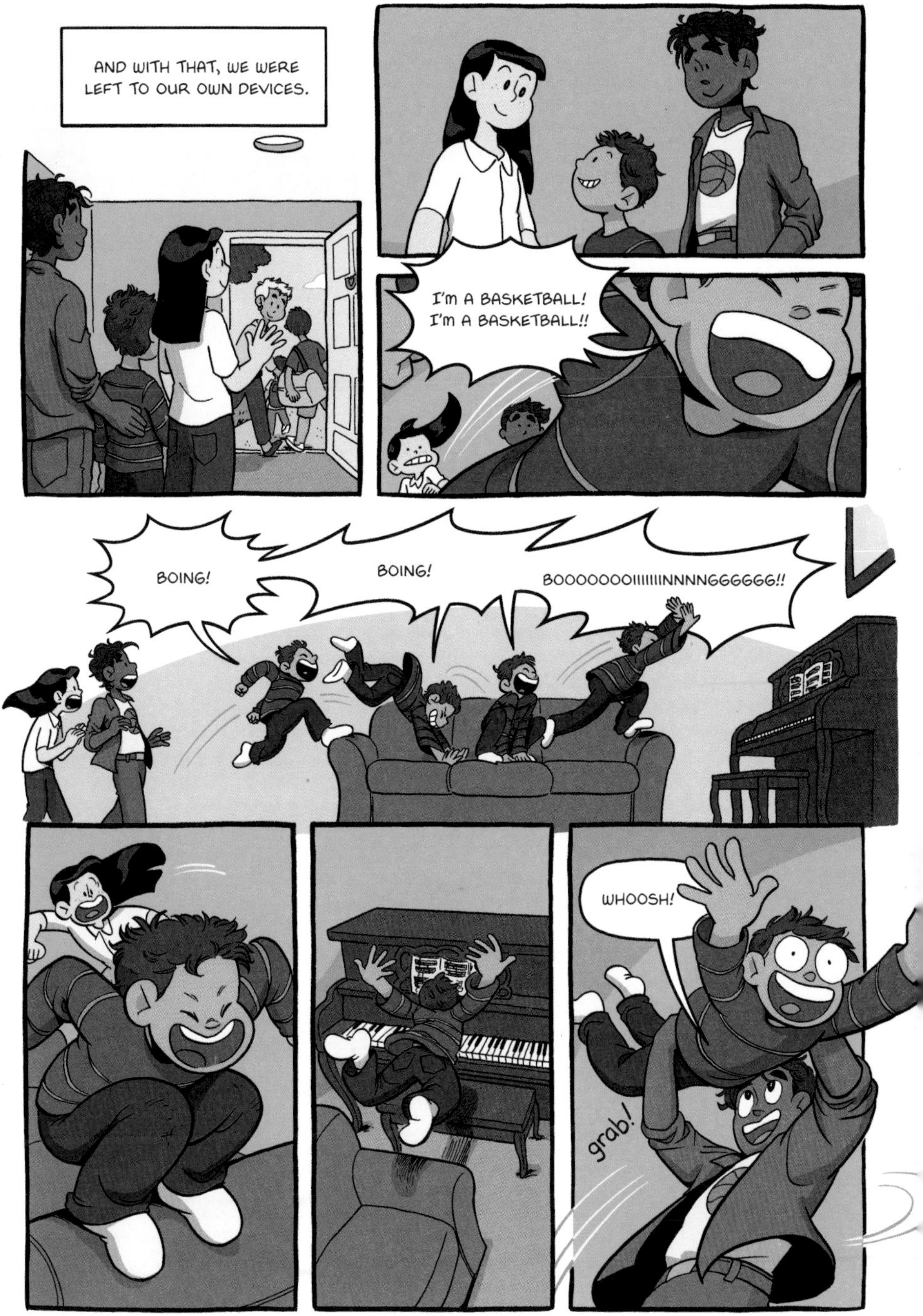
AND WITH THAT, WE WERE LEFT TO OUR OWN DEVICES.
I'M A BASKETBALL! I'M A BASKETBALL!!
BOING!
BOING!
BOOOOOOOIIIIIIINNNNGGGGGG!!
WHOOSH!
grab!

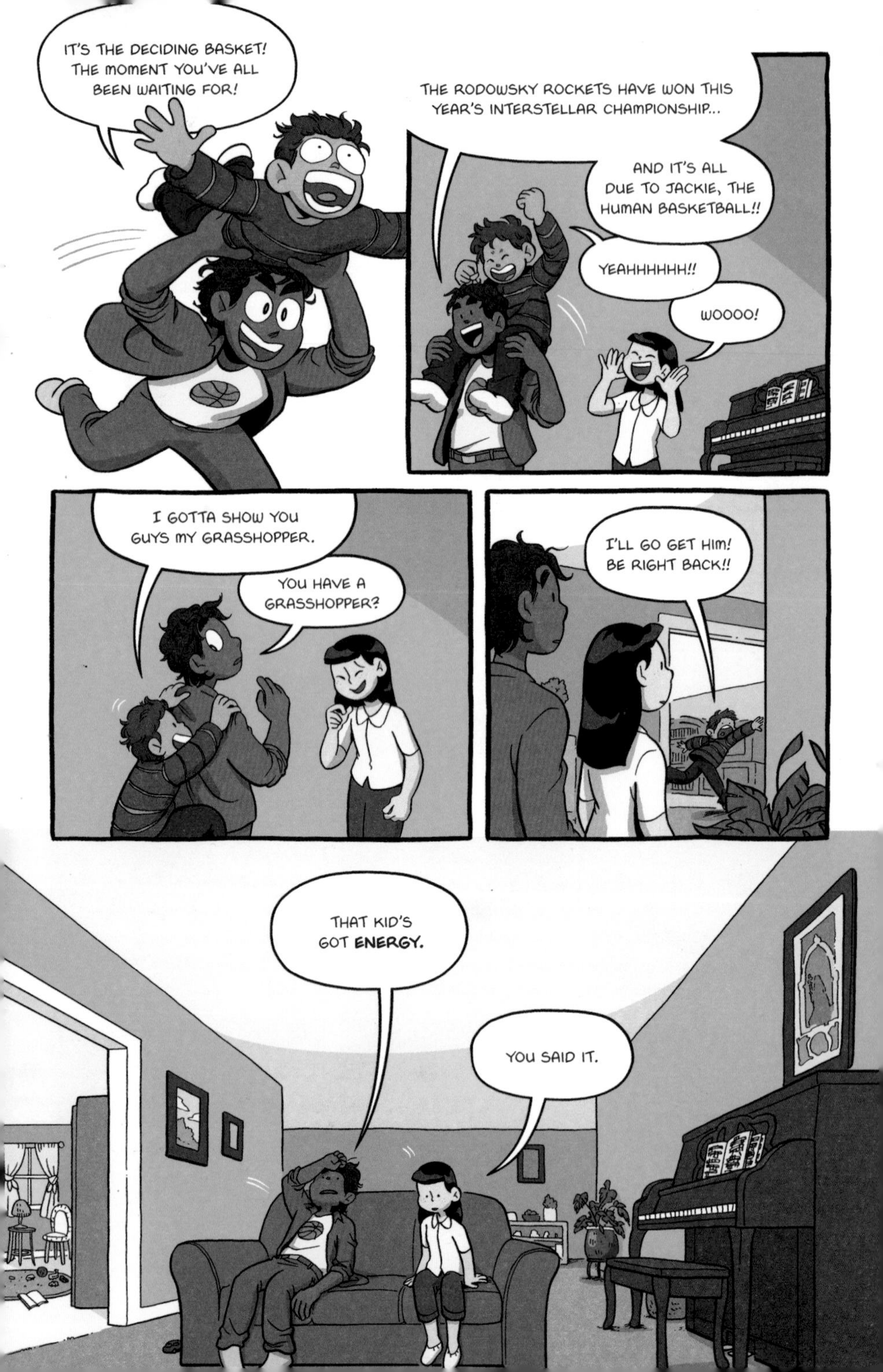
IT'S THE DECIDING BASKET! THE MOMENT YOU'VE ALL BEEN WAITING FOR!
THE RODOWSKY ROCKETS HAVE WON THIS YEAR'S INTERSTELLAR CHAMPIONSHIP...
AND IT'S ALL DUE TO JACKIE, THE HUMAN BASKETBALL!!
YEAHHHHHHH!!
WOOOO!
I GOTTA SHOW YOU GUYS MY GRASSHOPPER.
YOU HAVE A GRASSHOPPER?
I'LL GO GET HIM! BE RIGHT BACK!!
THAT KID'S GOT **ENERGY.**
YOU SAID IT.

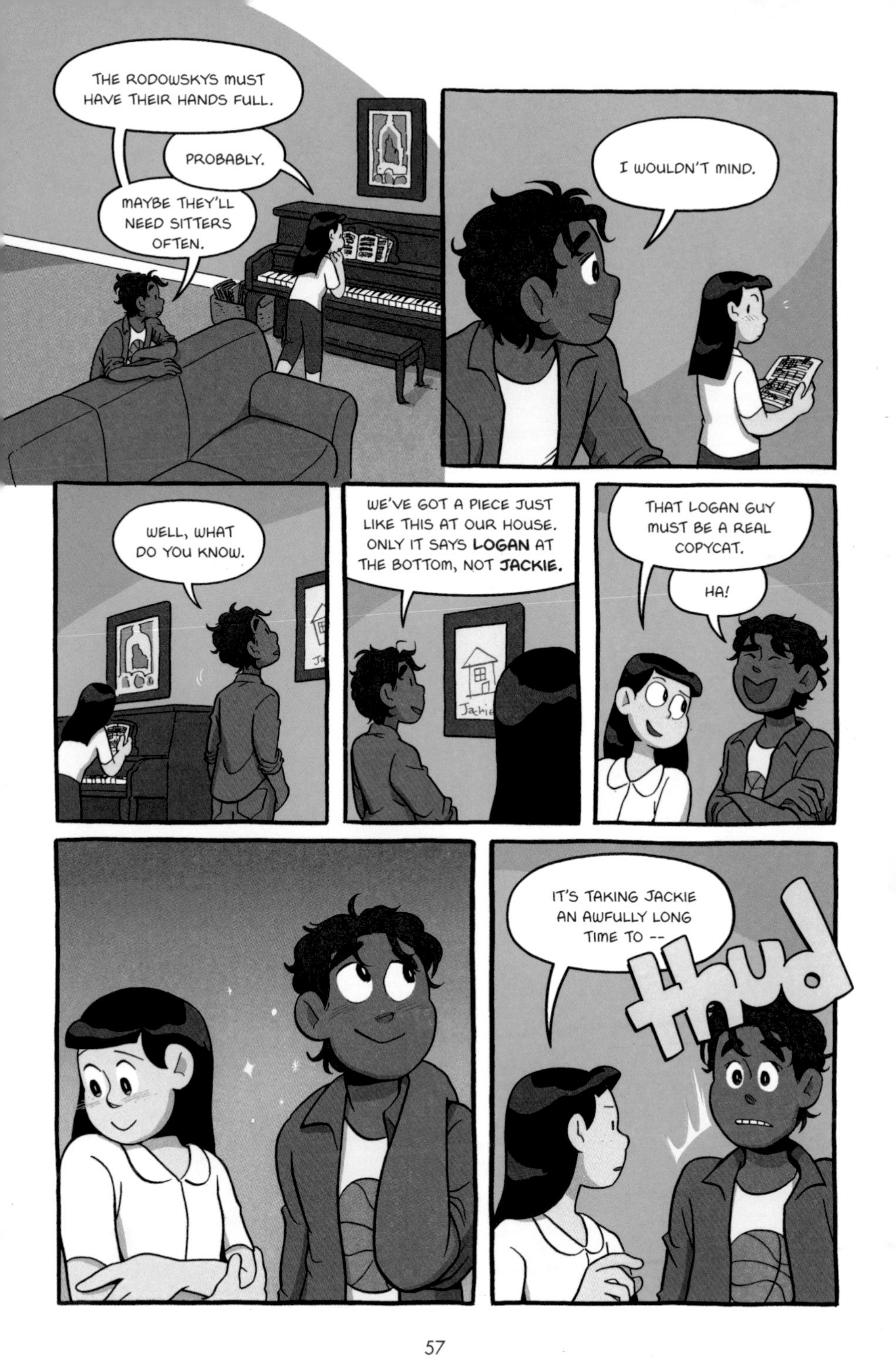
THE RODOWSKYS MUST HAVE THEIR HANDS FULL.
PROBABLY.
MAYBE THEY'LL NEED SITTERS OFTEN.
I WOULDN'T MIND.
WELL, WHAT DO YOU KNOW.
Jackie
WE'VE GOT A PIECE JUST LIKE THIS AT OUR HOUSE. ONLY IT SAYS **LOGAN** AT THE BOTTOM, NOT **JACKIE.**
THAT LOGAN GUY MUST BE A REAL COPYCAT.
HA!
IT'S TAKING JACKIE AN AWFULLY LONG TIME TO --
thud

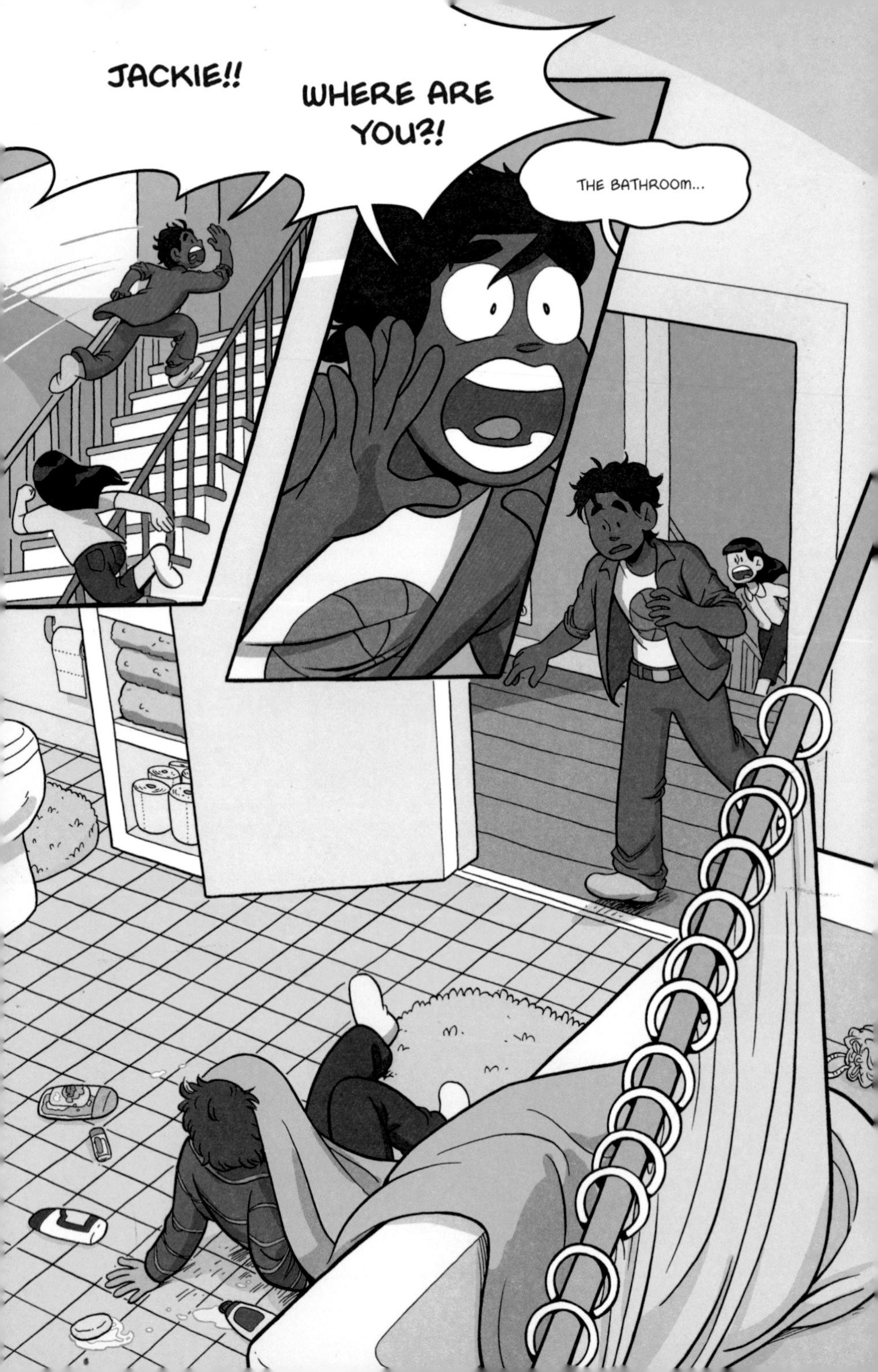
JACKIE!!
WHERE ARE YOU?!
THE BATHROOM...

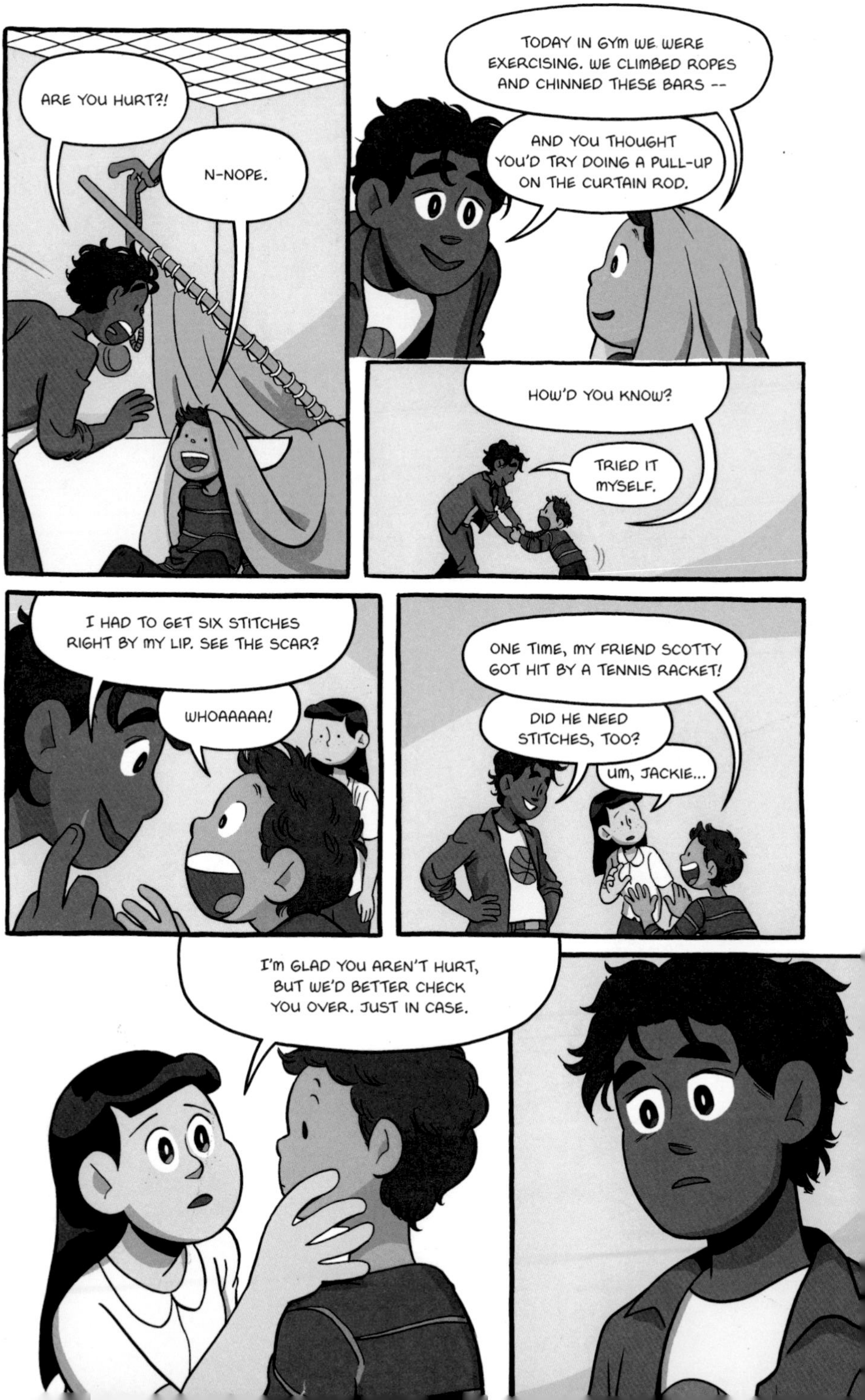
ARE YOU HURT?!
N-NOPE.
TODAY IN GYM WE WERE EXERCISING. WE CLIMBED ROPES AND CHINNED THESE BARS --
AND YOU THOUGHT YOU'D TRY DOING A PULL-UP ON THE CURTAIN ROD.
HOW'D YOU KNOW?
TRIED IT MYSELF.
I HAD TO GET SIX STITCHES RIGHT BY MY LIP. SEE THE SCAR?
WHOAAAAA!
ONE TIME, MY FRIEND SCOTTY GOT HIT BY A TENNIS RACKET!
DID HE NEED STITCHES, TOO?
UM, JACKIE...
I'M GLAD YOU AREN'T HURT, BUT WE'D BETTER CHECK YOU OVER. JUST IN CASE.

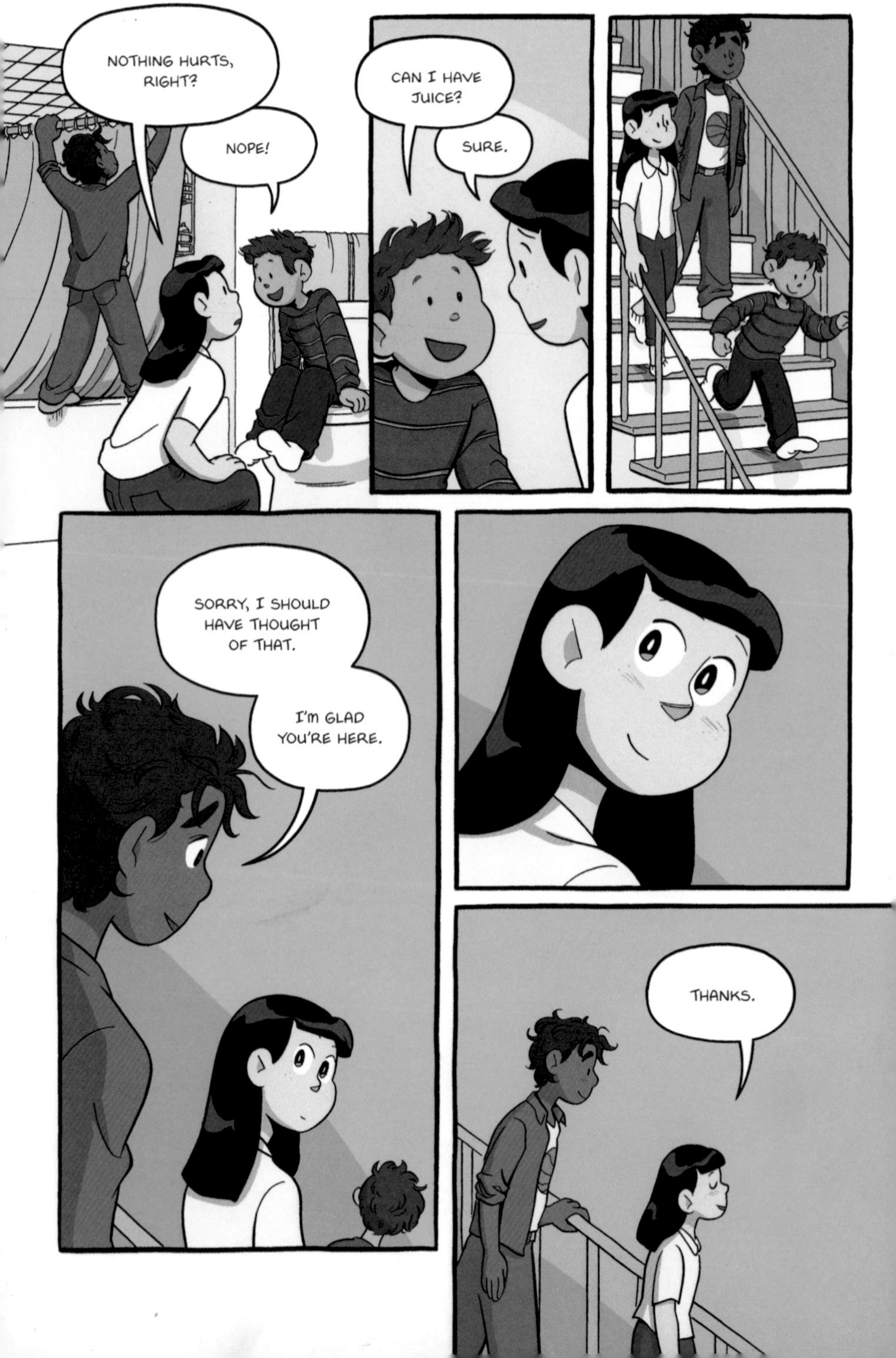
NOTHING HURTS, RIGHT?
NOPE!
CAN I HAVE JUICE?
SURE.
SORRY, I SHOULD HAVE THOUGHT OF THAT.
I'M GLAD YOU'RE HERE.
THANKS.

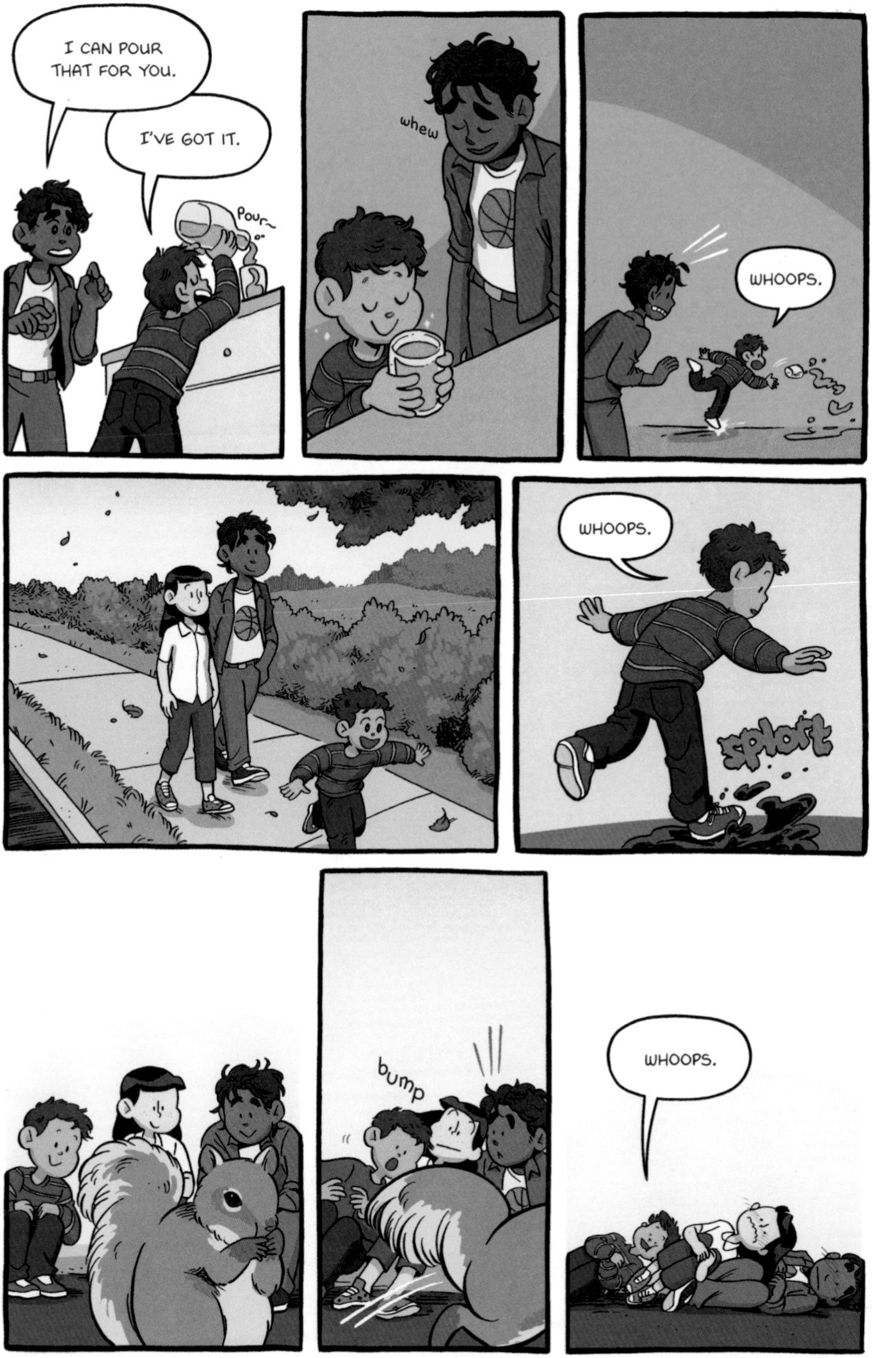
I CAN POUR THAT FOR YOU.
I'VE GOT IT.
Pour~
whew
WHOOPS.
WHOOPS.
splort
bump
WHOOPS.

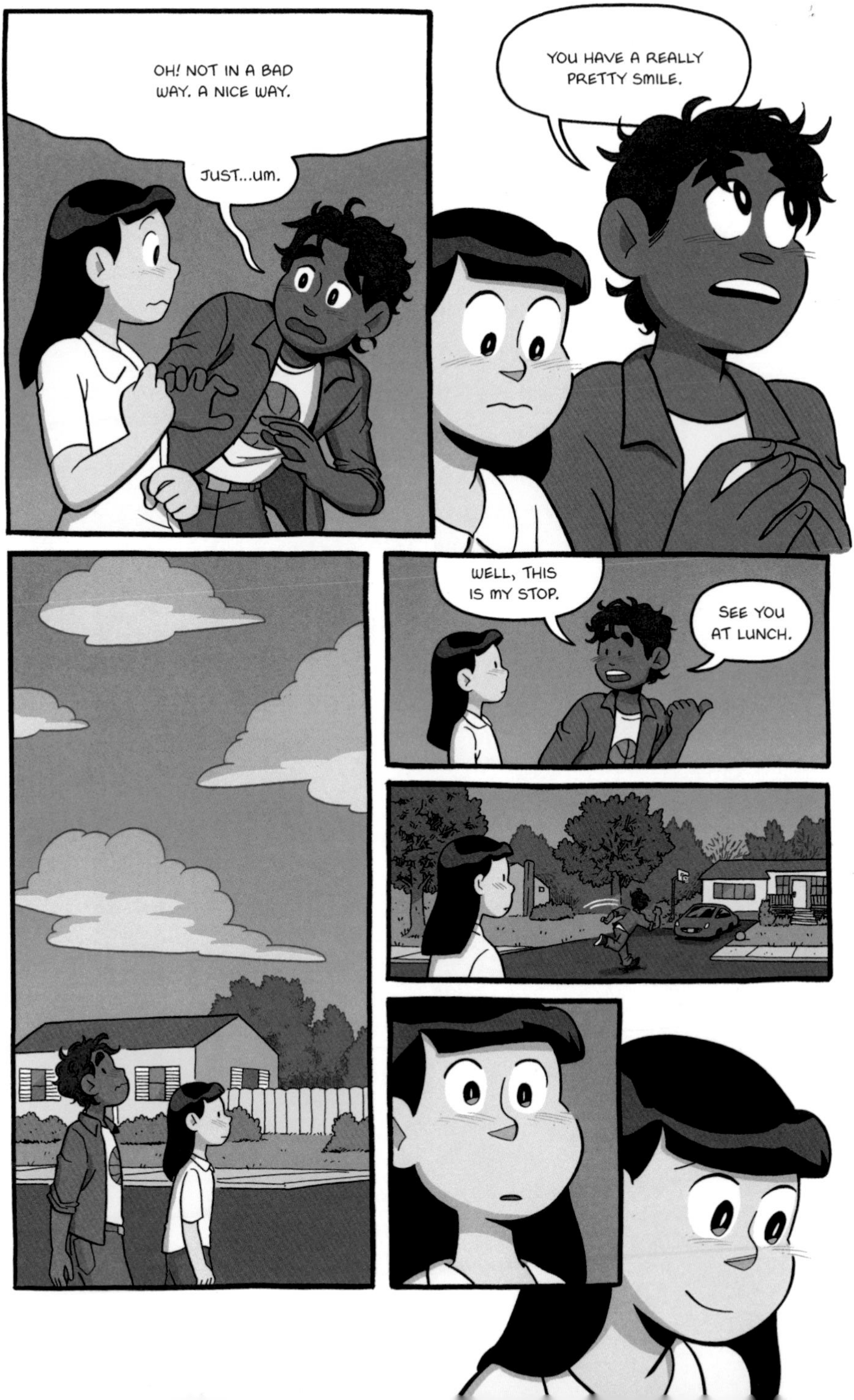
OH! NOT IN A BAD WAY. A NICE WAY.
JUST...um.
YOU HAVE A REALLY PRETTY SMILE.
WELL, THIS IS MY STOP.
SEE YOU AT LUNCH.

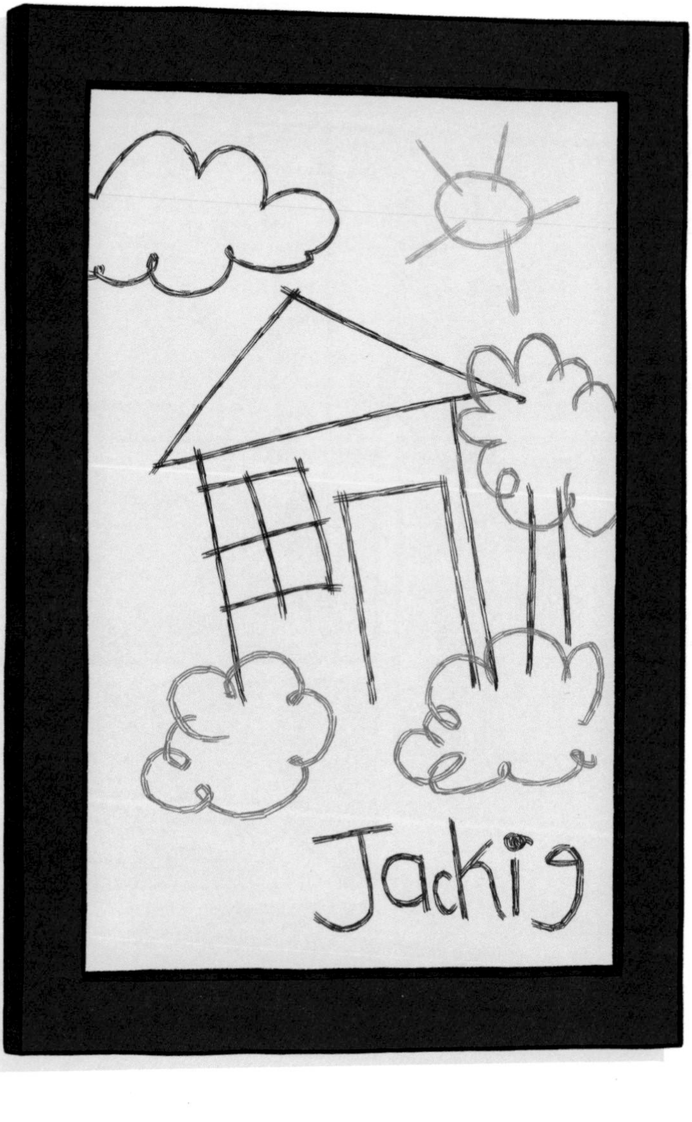
Jackie

CHAPTER 7

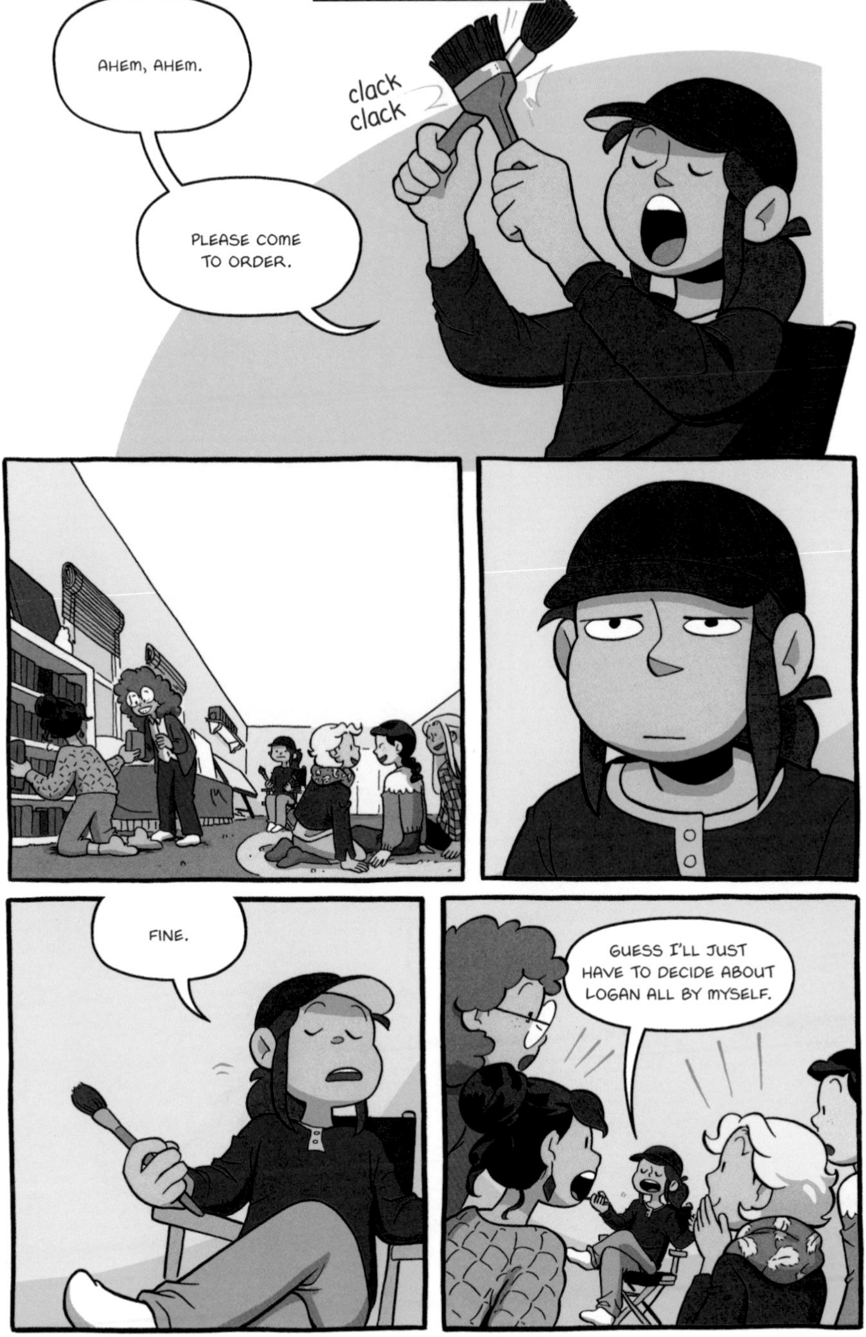

AHEM, AHEM.
clack clack
PLEASE COME TO ORDER.
FINE.
GUESS I'LL JUST HAVE TO DECIDE ABOUT LOGAN ALL BY MYSELF.

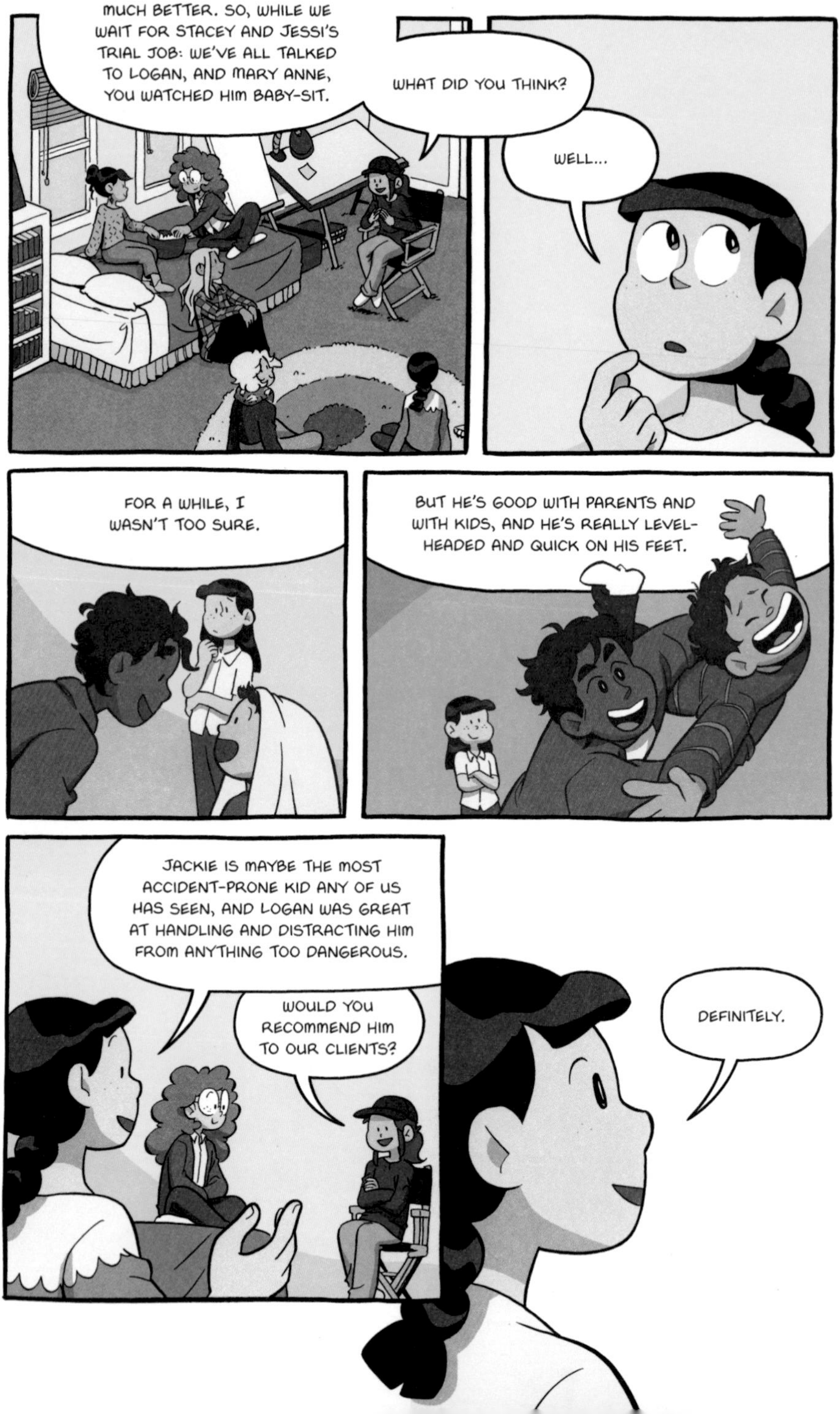
MUCH BETTER. SO, WHILE WE WAIT FOR STACEY AND JESSI'S TRIAL JOB: WE'VE ALL TALKED TO LOGAN, AND MARY ANNE, YOU WATCHED HIM BABY-SIT.
WHAT DID YOU THINK?
WELL...
FOR A WHILE, I WASN'T TOO SURE.
BUT HE'S GOOD WITH PARENTS AND WITH KIDS, AND HE'S REALLY LEVEL-HEADED AND QUICK ON HIS FEET.
JACKIE IS MAYBE THE MOST ACCIDENT-PRONE KID ANY OF US HAS SEEN, AND LOGAN WAS GREAT AT HANDLING AND DISTRACTING HIM FROM ANYTHING TOO DANGEROUS.
WOULD YOU RECOMMEND HIM TO OUR CLIENTS?
DEFINITELY.

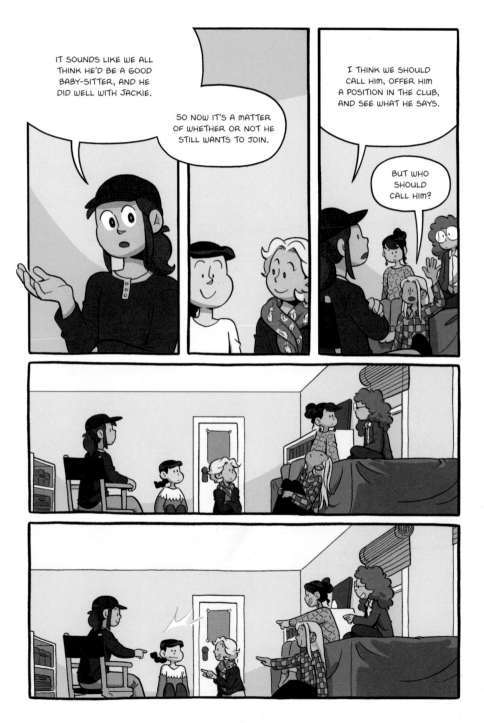

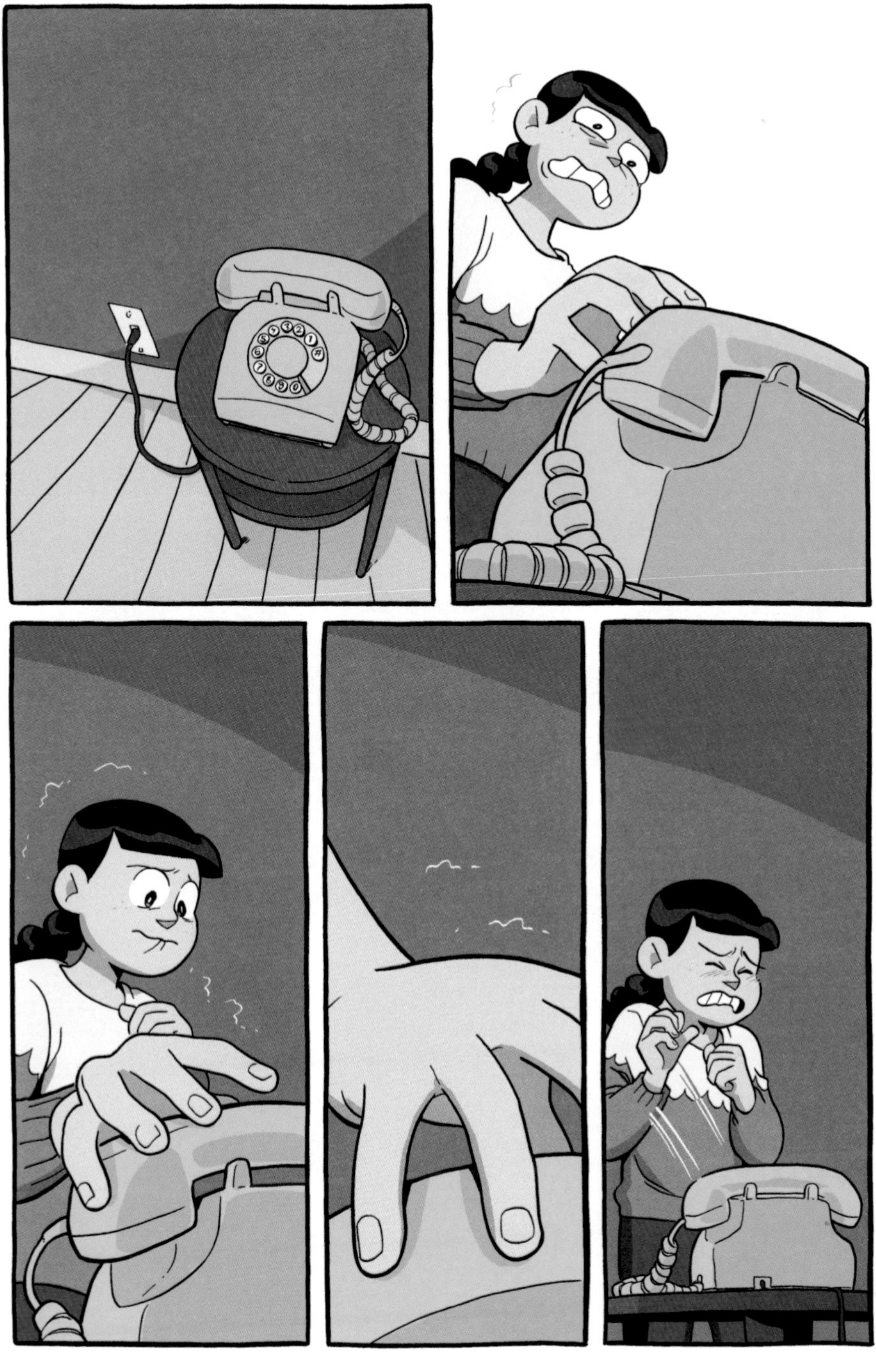

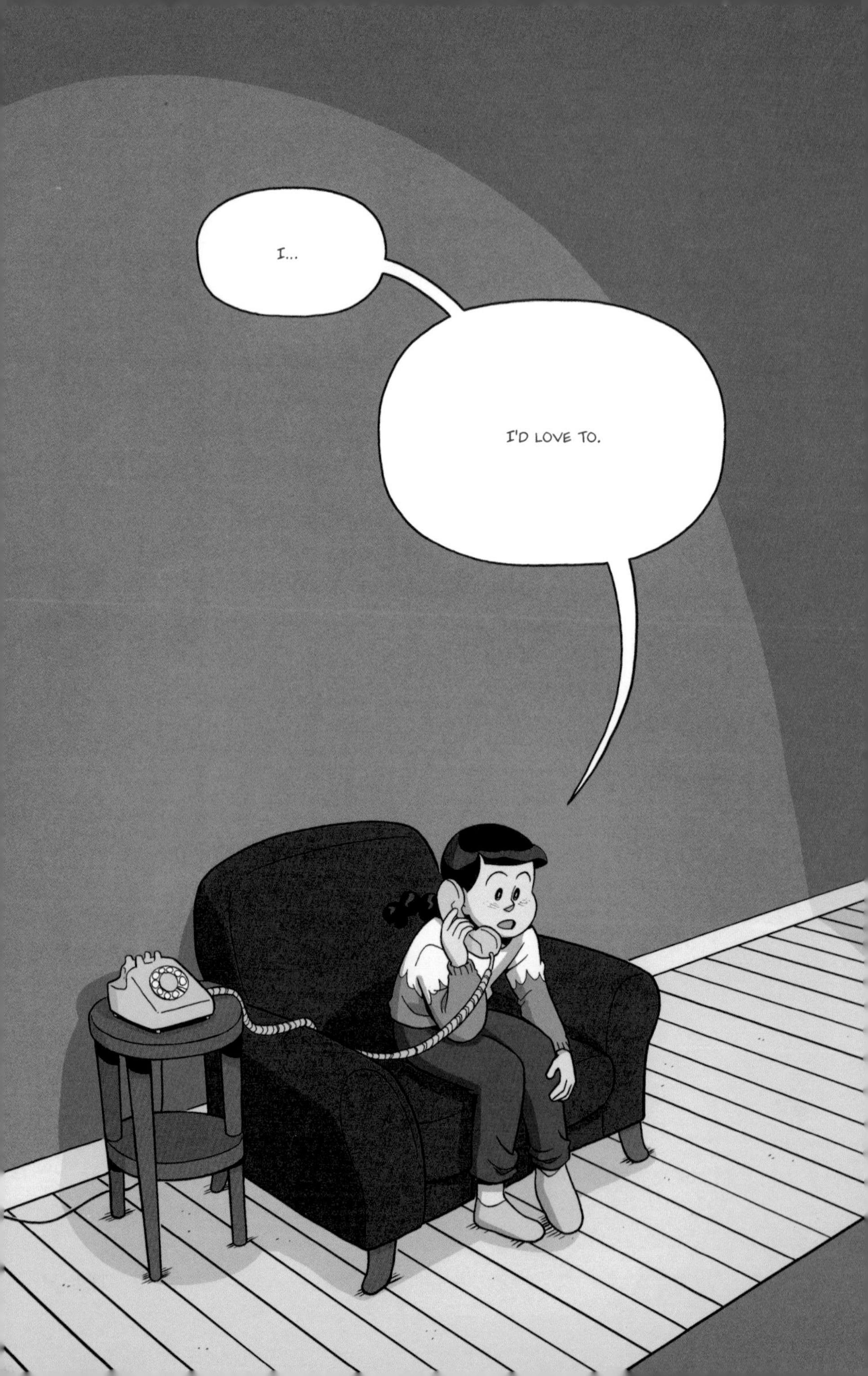
I...
I'D LOVE TO.

Tuesday

Boy, is the Charlotte Johanssen I baby-sat today different from the Charlotte I used to sit for last year. She has grown up so much! Skipping a grade was the right thing to do for her. She's bouncy and happy and full of ideas, and she even has a "best friend" — a girl in her class called Sophie McCann. (Last week her "best friend" was Vanessa Pike. I remember when "best friend" meant nothing — just whoever your current good friend was. Do you guys remember, too?)

Oh, well. I'm way off the subject. Anyway, there's not much to say. Charlotte's easy to sit for and she warmed up to Jessi right away, especially after hearing that Jessi has a sister her age (look out, Sophie McCann!). I brought the Kid-Kit over, and we all had a great afternoon.

Stacey

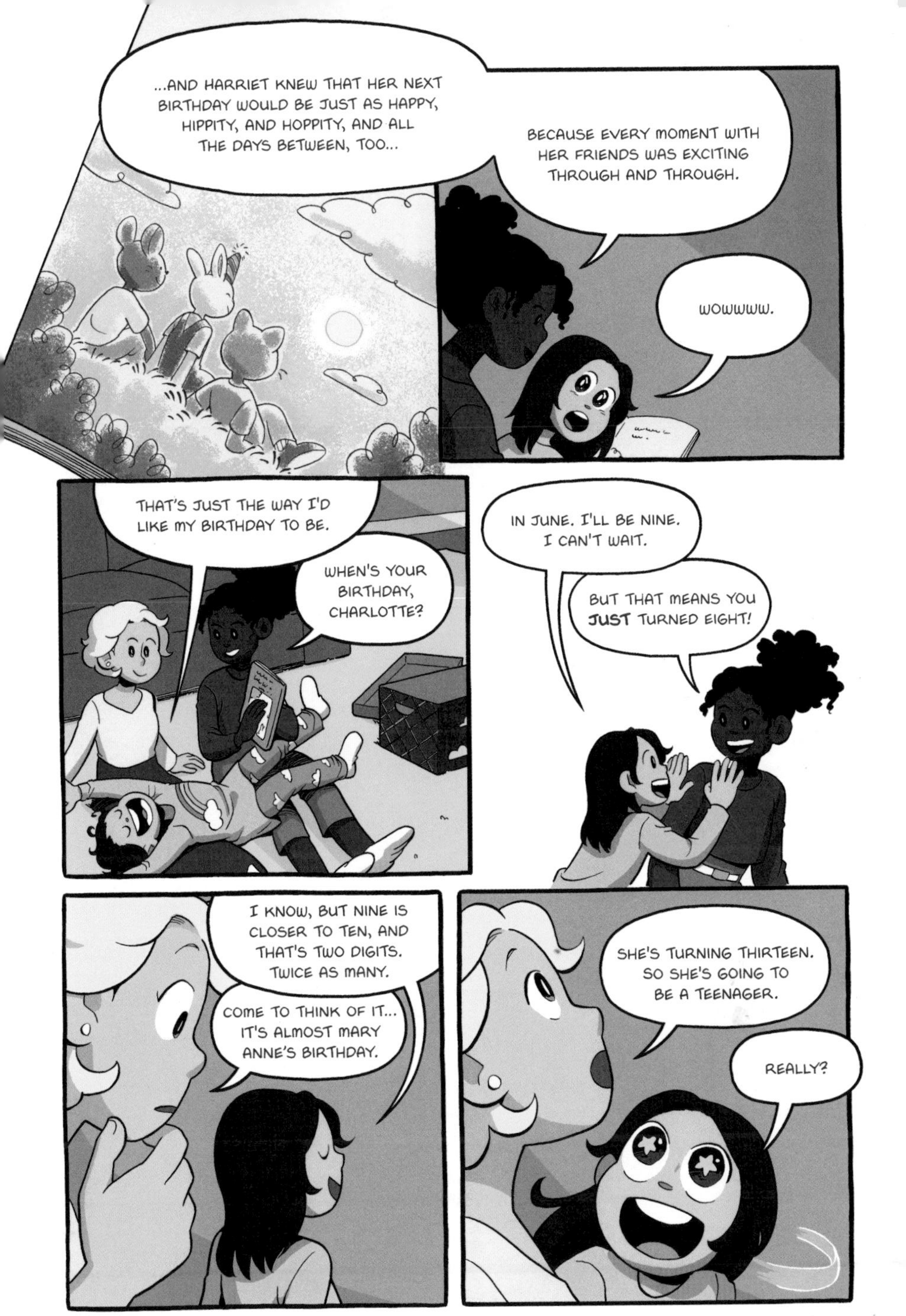
...AND HARRIET KNEW THAT HER NEXT BIRTHDAY WOULD BE JUST AS HAPPY, HIPPITY, AND HOPPITY, AND ALL THE DAYS BETWEEN, TOO...
BECAUSE EVERY MOMENT WITH HER FRIENDS WAS EXCITING THROUGH AND THROUGH.
WOWWWW.
THAT'S JUST THE WAY I'D LIKE MY BIRTHDAY TO BE.
WHEN'S YOUR BIRTHDAY, CHARLOTTE?
IN JUNE. I'LL BE NINE. I CAN'T WAIT.
BUT THAT MEANS YOU **JUST** TURNED EIGHT!
I KNOW, BUT NINE IS CLOSER TO TEN, AND THAT'S TWO DIGITS. TWICE AS MANY.
COME TO THINK OF IT... IT'S ALMOST MARY ANNE'S BIRTHDAY.
SHE'S TURNING THIRTEEN. SO SHE'S GOING TO BE A TEENAGER.
REALLY?

82

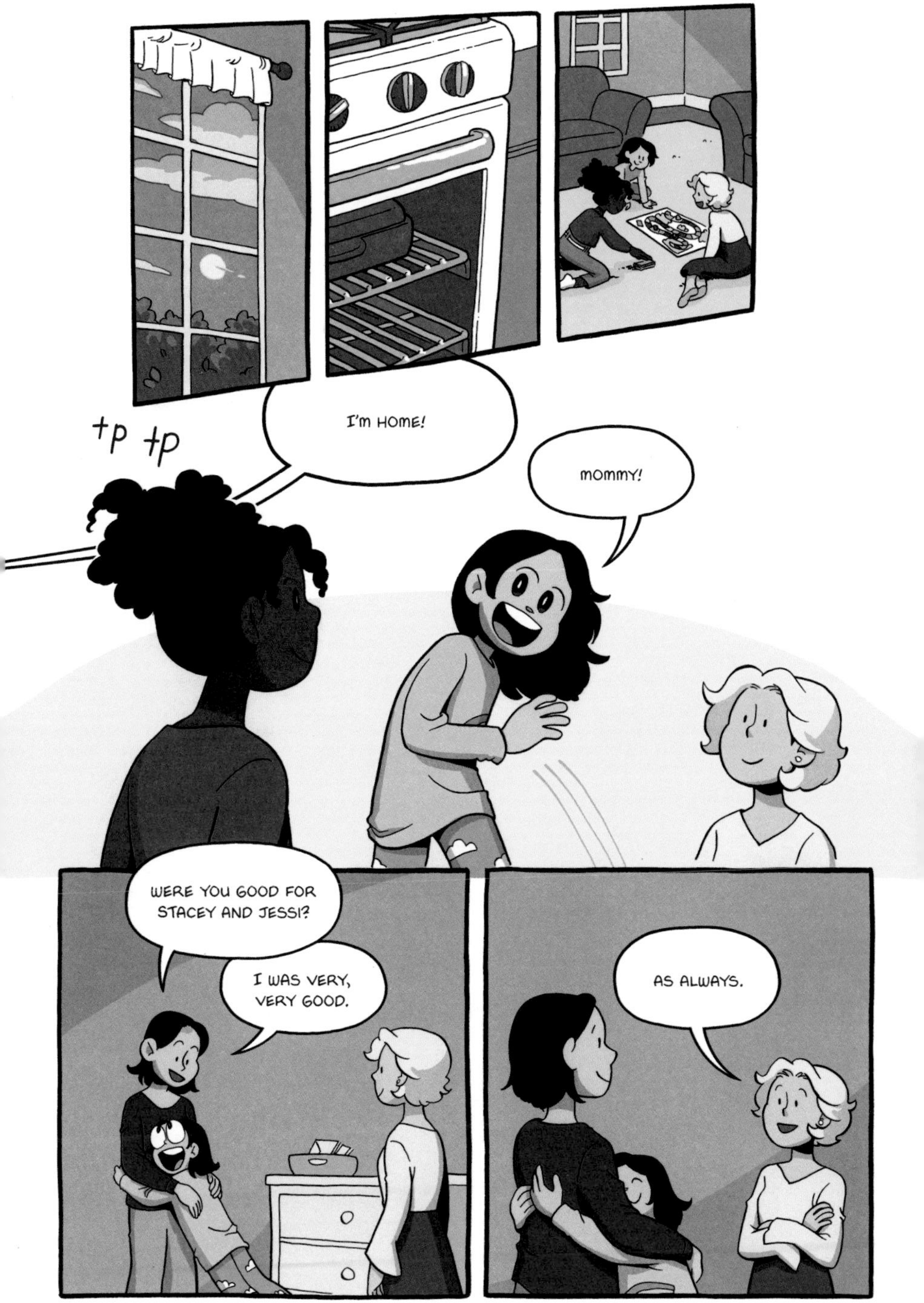
I'M HOME!
tp tp
MOMMY!
WERE YOU GOOD FOR STACEY AND JESSI?
I WAS VERY, VERY GOOD.
AS ALWAYS.

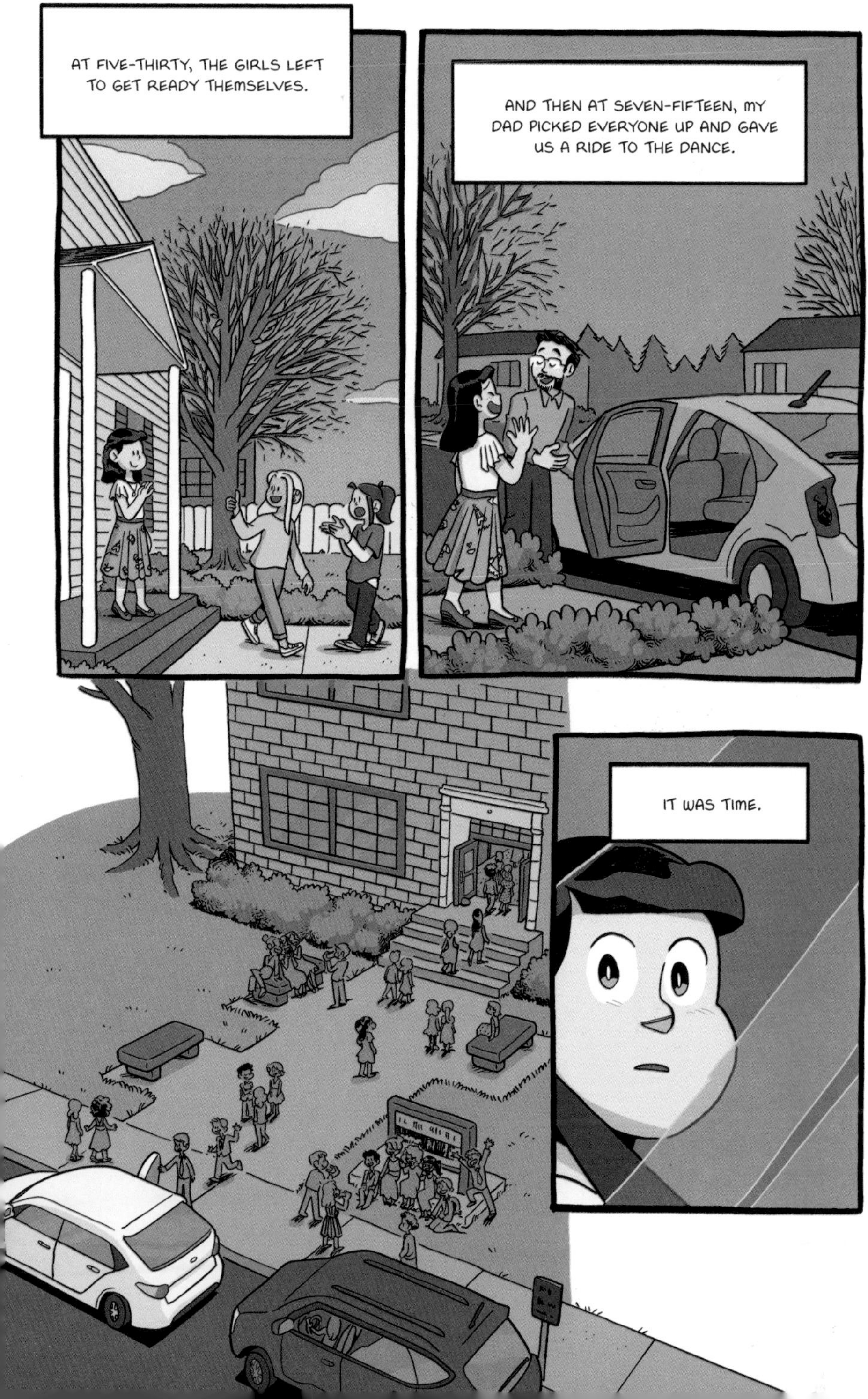
AT FIVE-THIRTY, THE GIRLS LEFT TO GET READY THEMSELVES.
AND THEN AT SEVEN-FIFTEEN, MY DAD PICKED EVERYONE UP AND GAVE US A RIDE TO THE DANCE.
IT WAS TIME.

CHAPTER 10

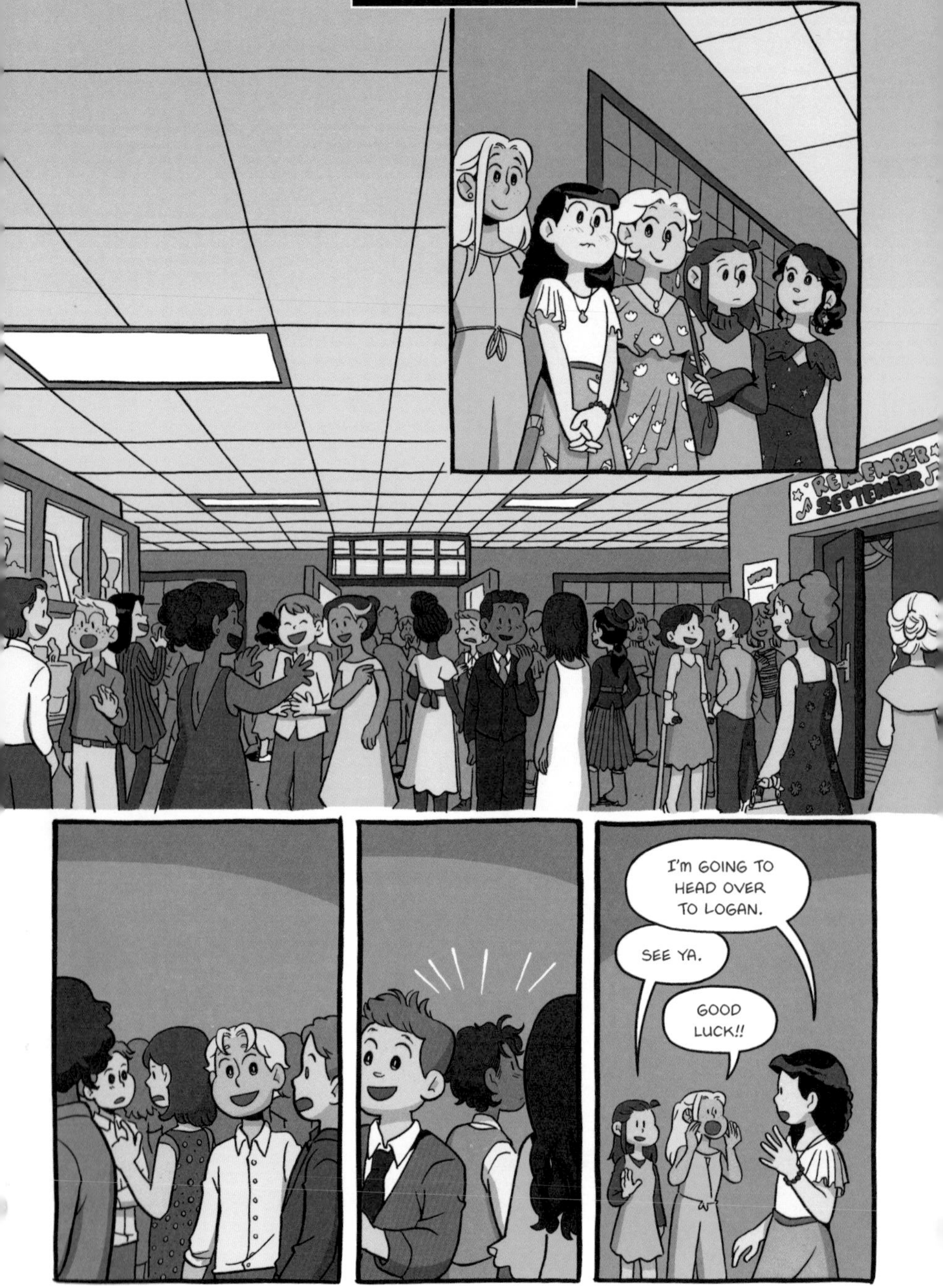
REMEMBER SEPTEMBER
I'M GOING TO HEAD OVER TO LOGAN.
SEE YA.
GOOD LUCK!!

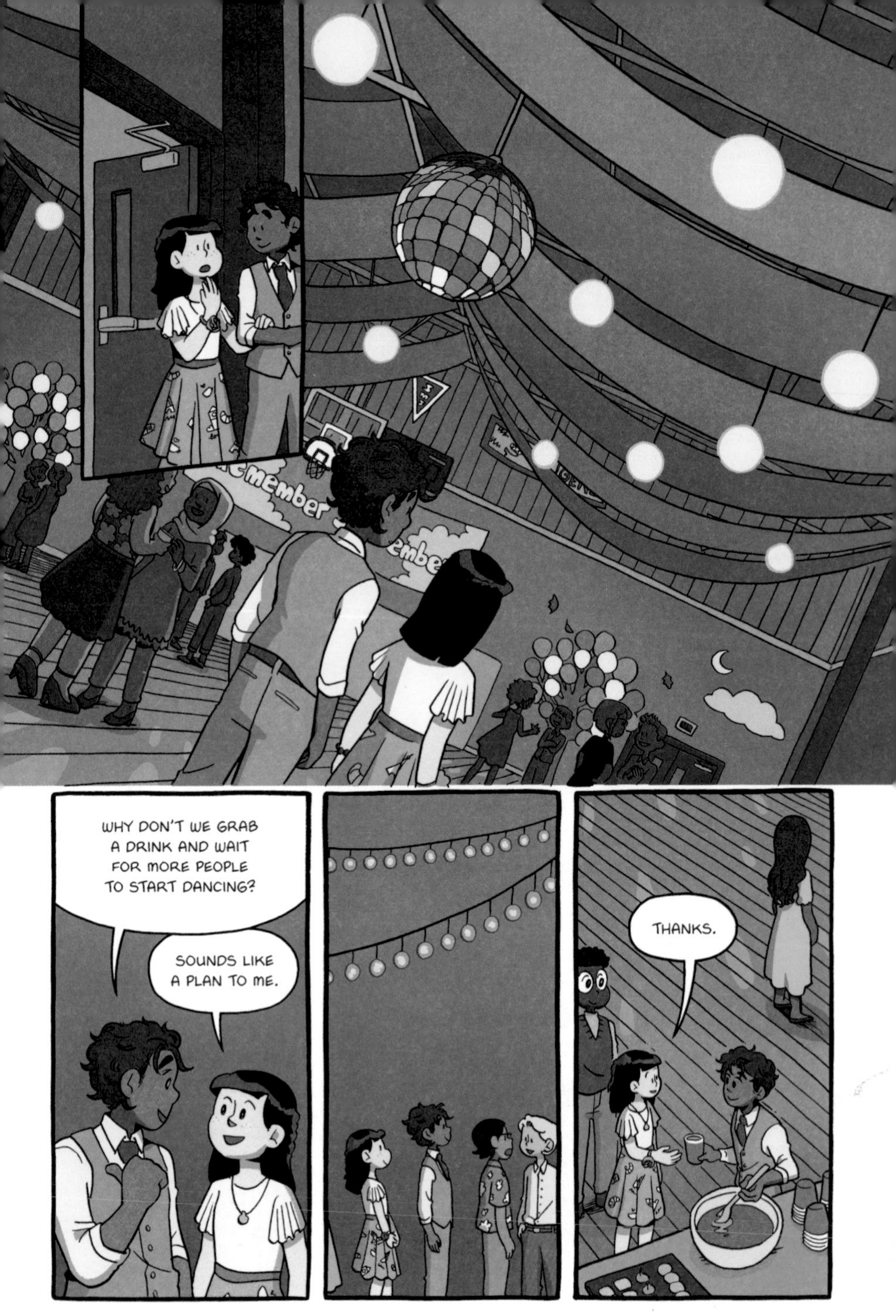
WHY DON'T WE GRAB A DRINK AND WAIT FOR MORE PEOPLE TO START DANCING?
SOUNDS LIKE A PLAN TO ME.
THANKS.

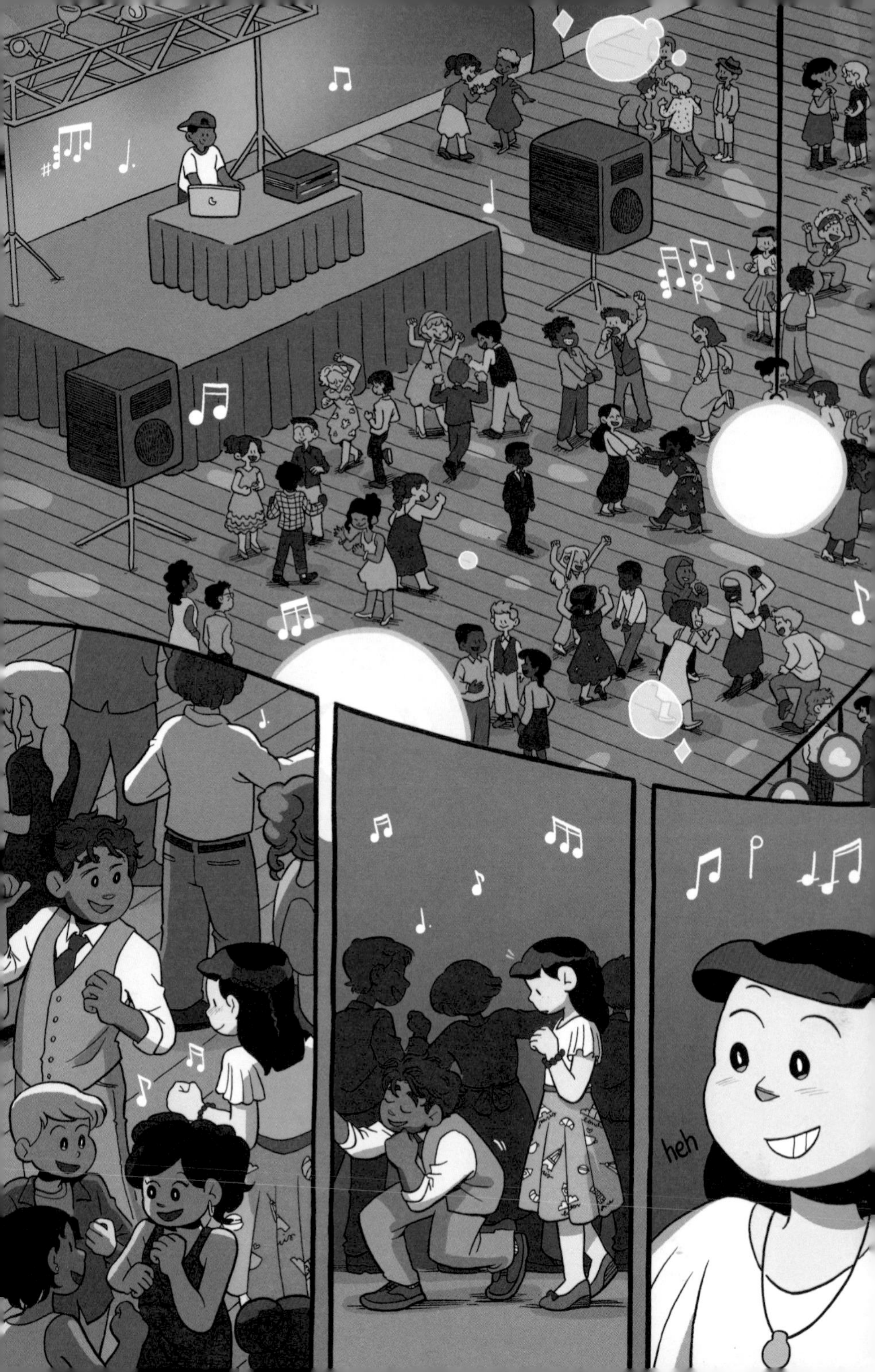
heh

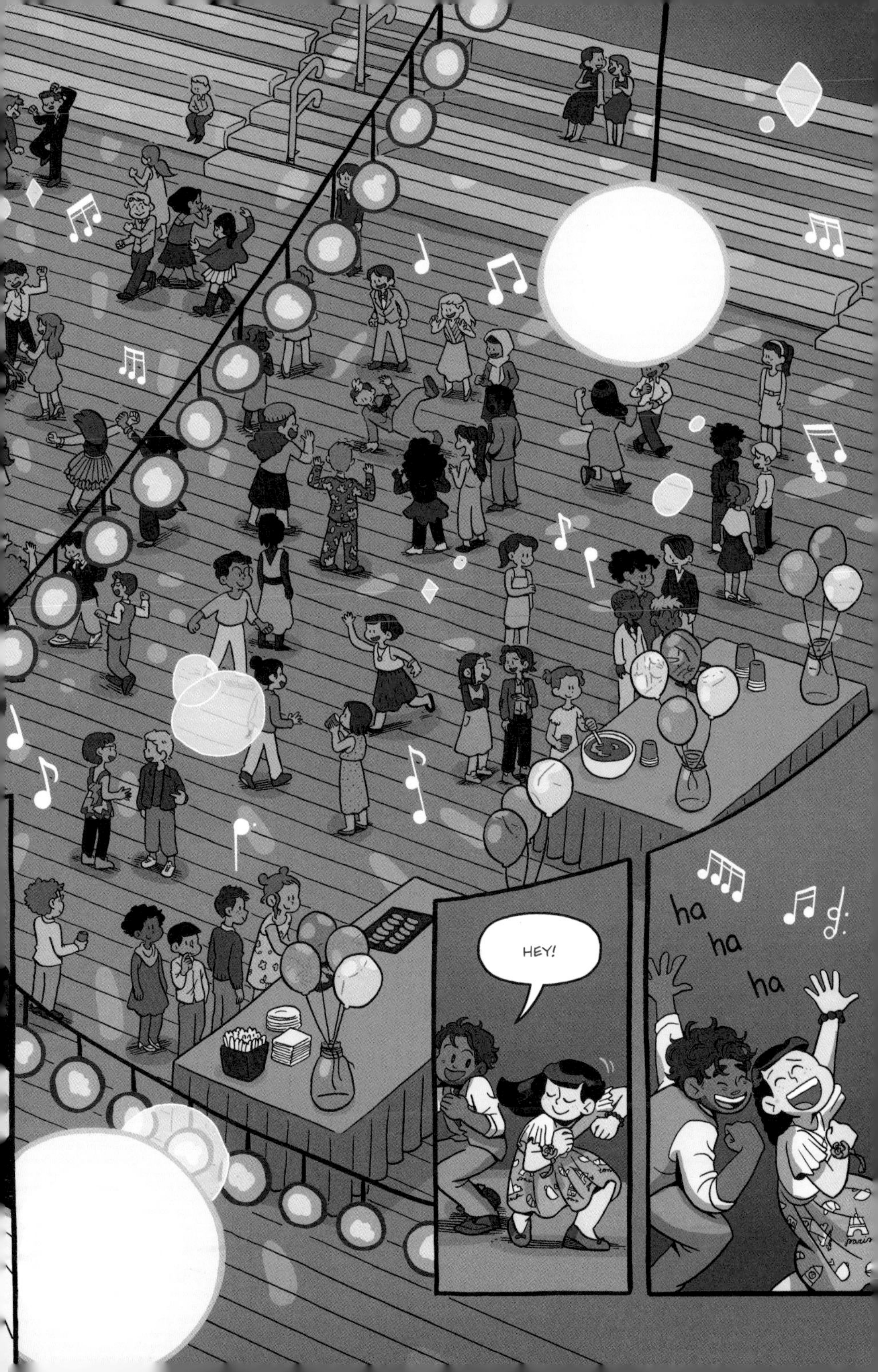
HEY!
ha
ha
ha

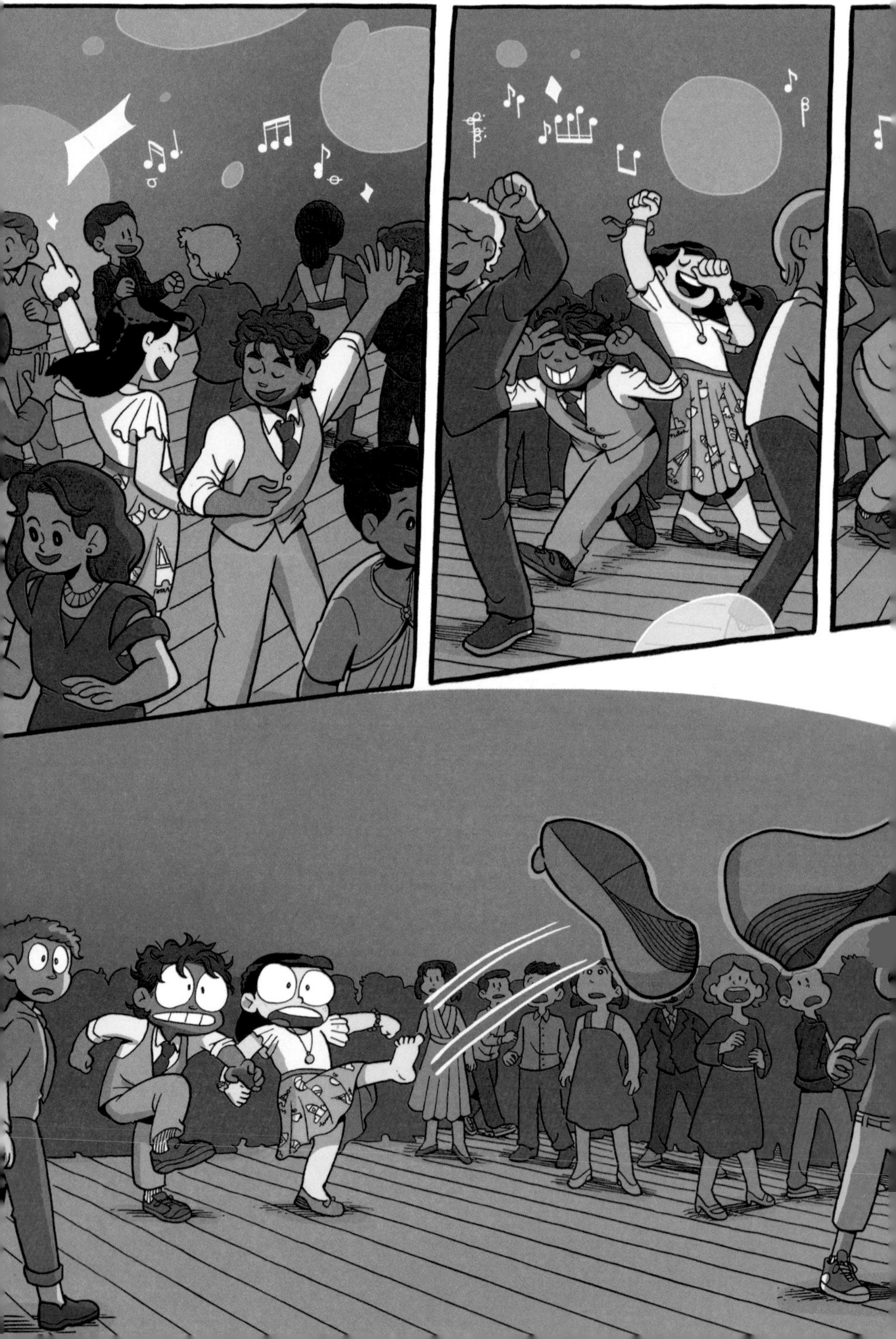

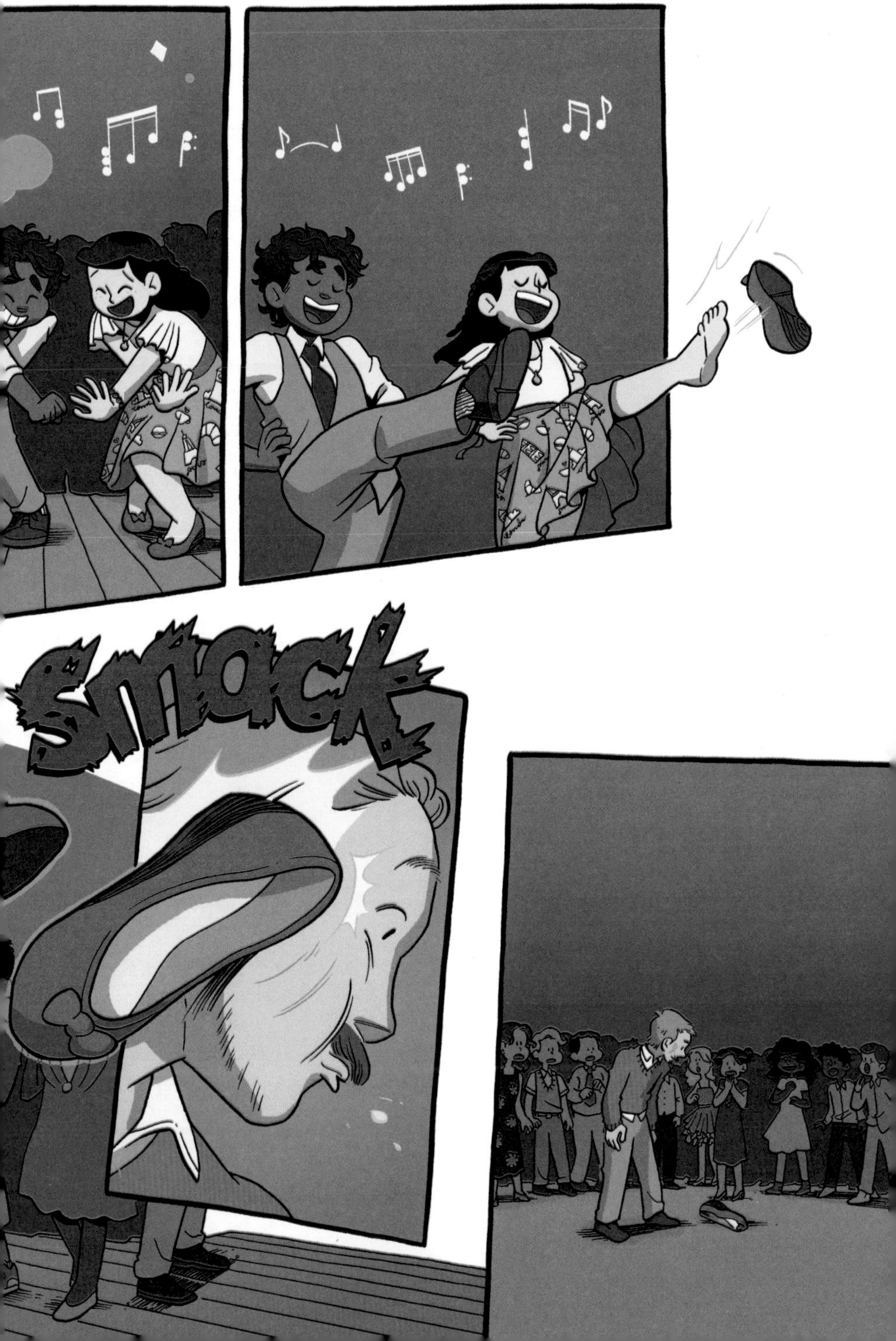

SMACK

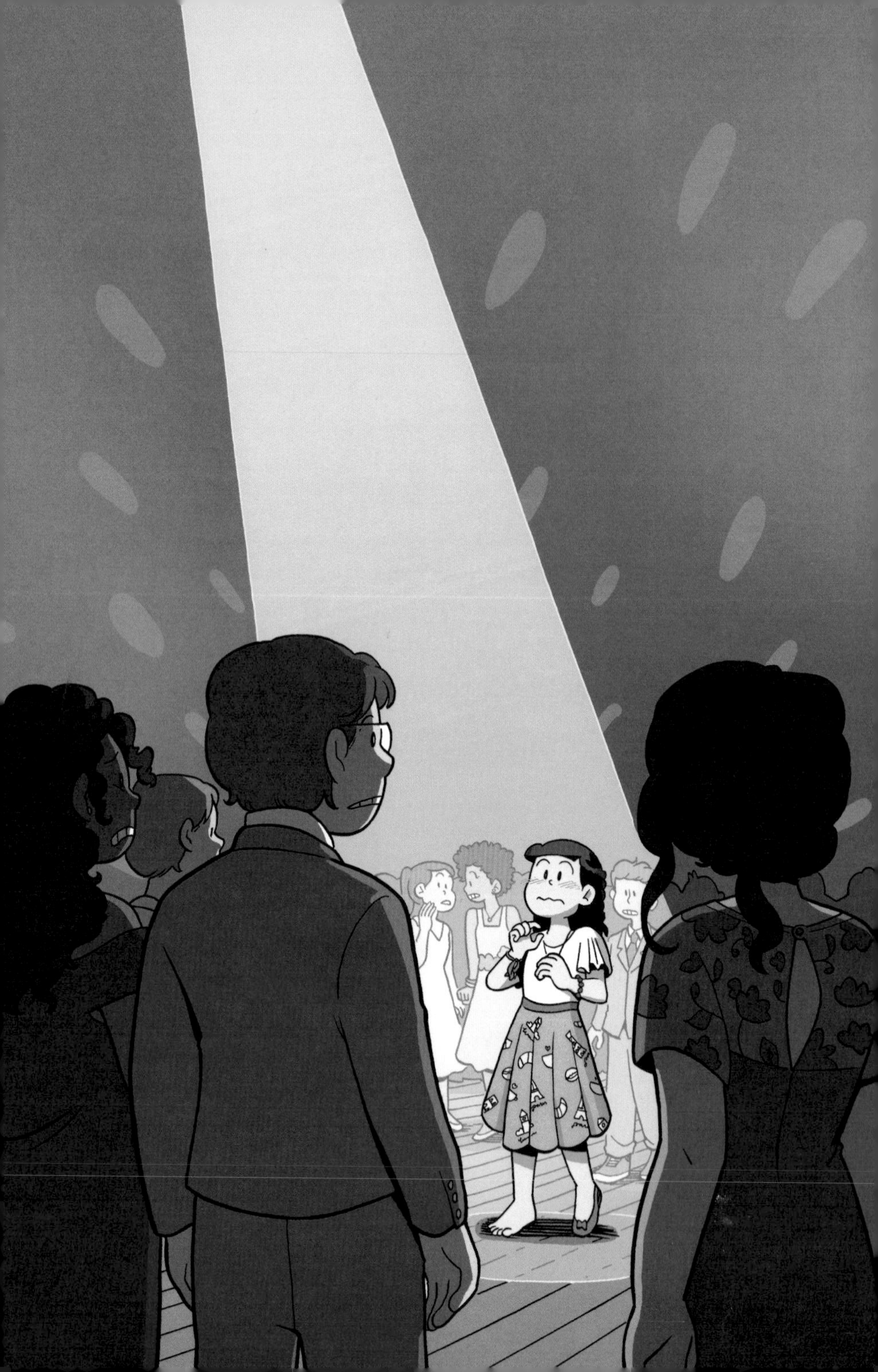

CHAPTER 11

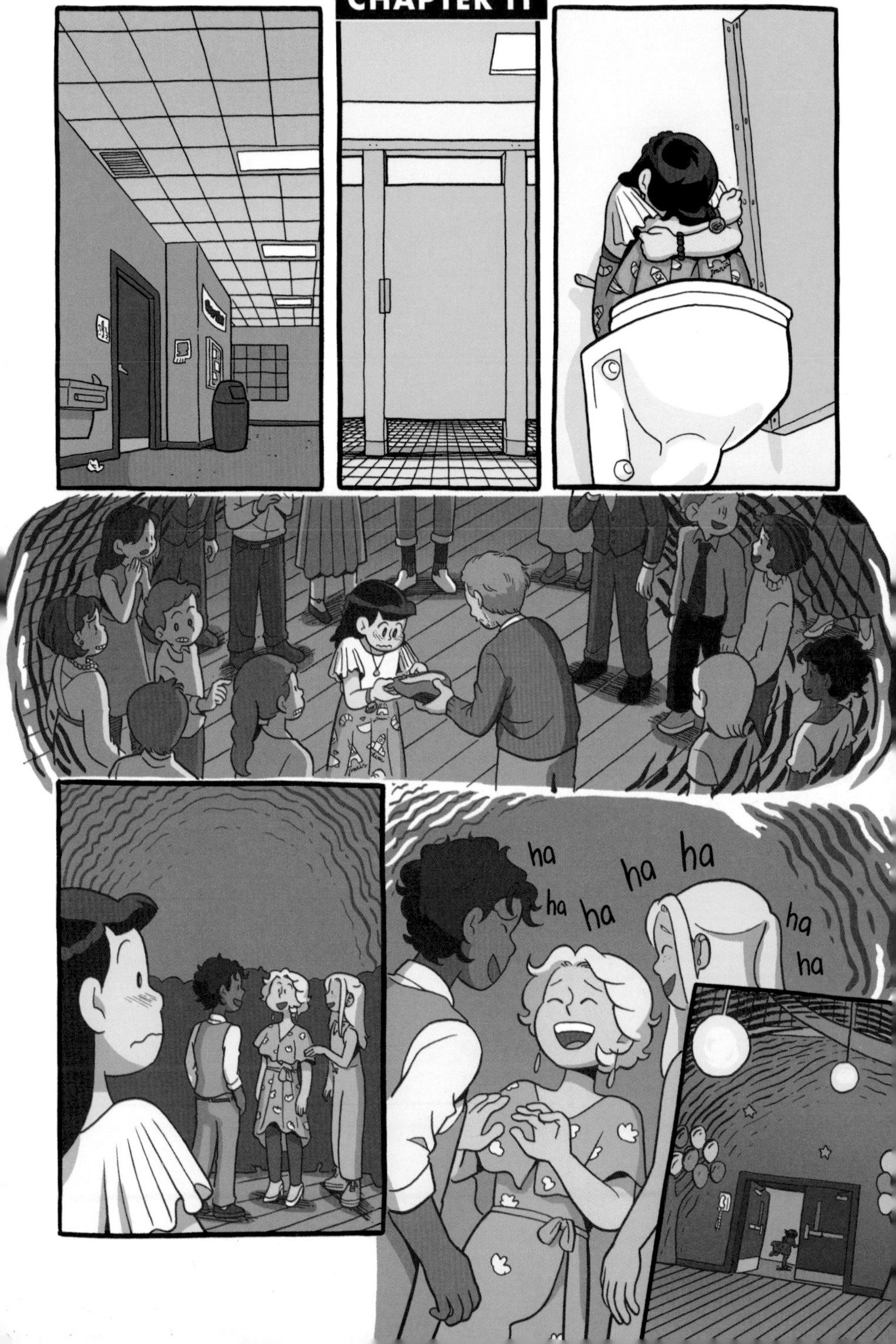
ha
ha
ha
ha
ha
ha
ha

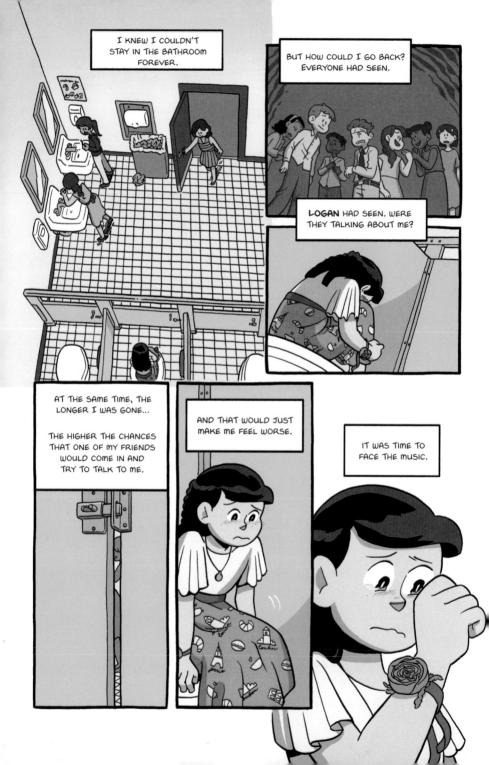

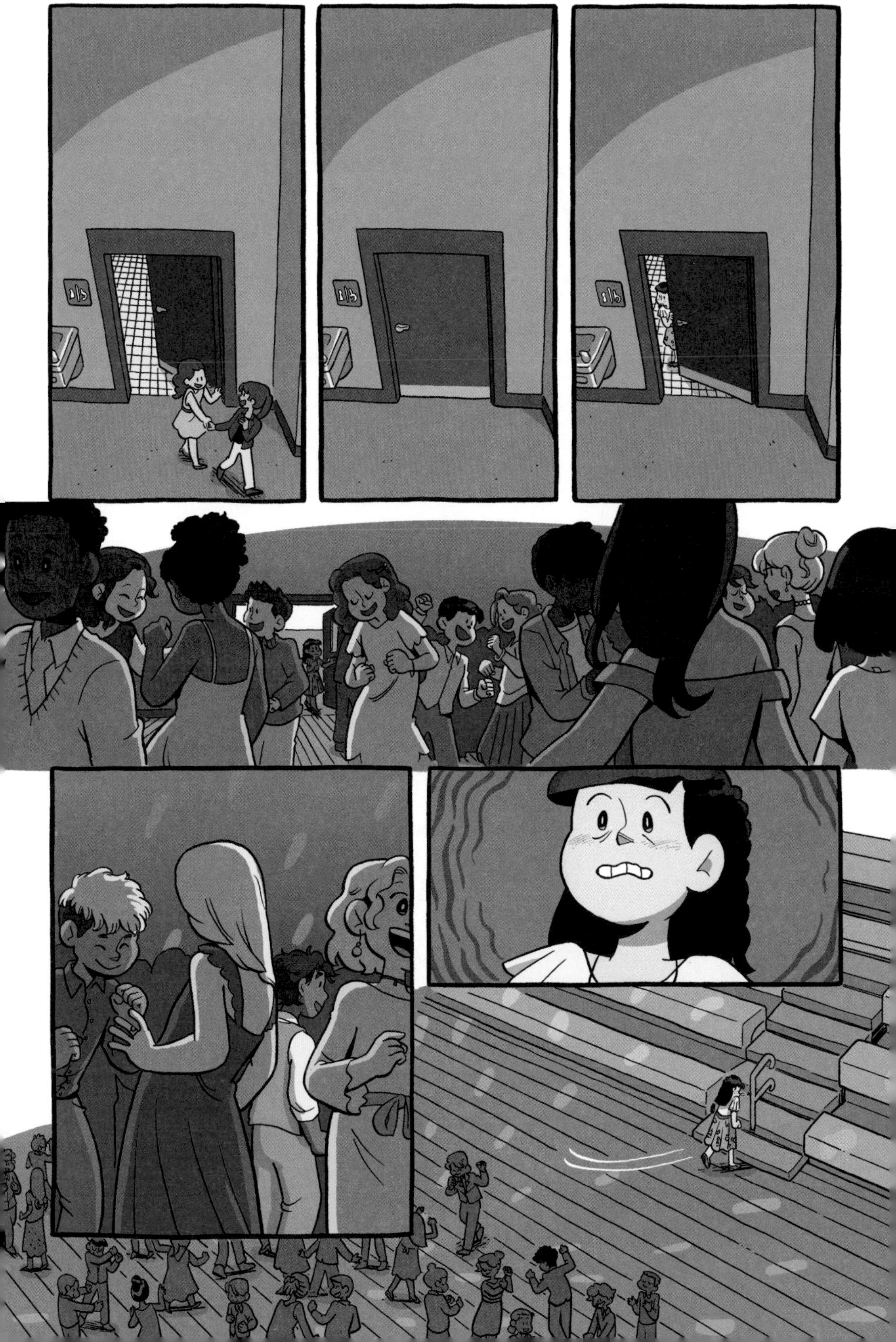

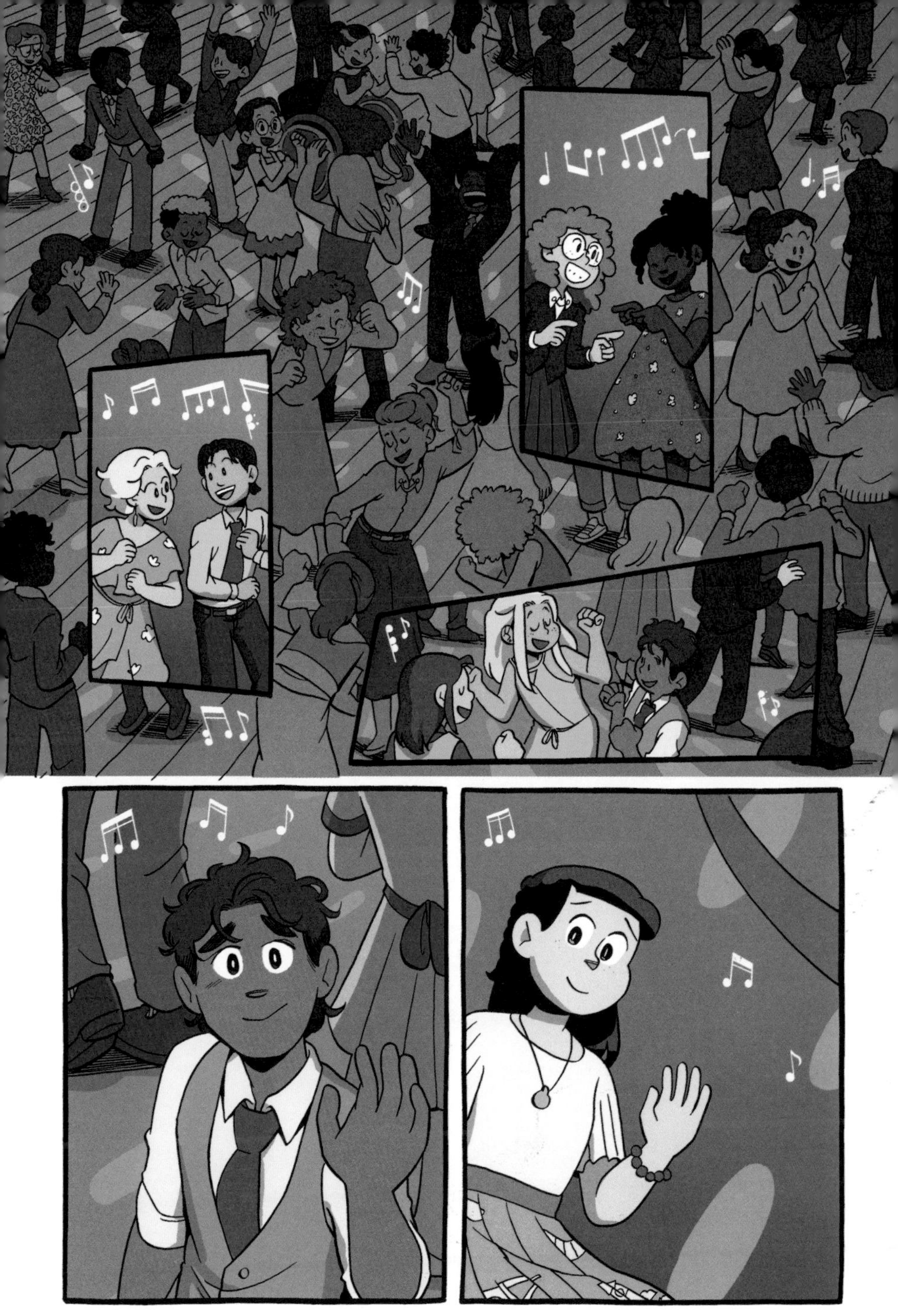

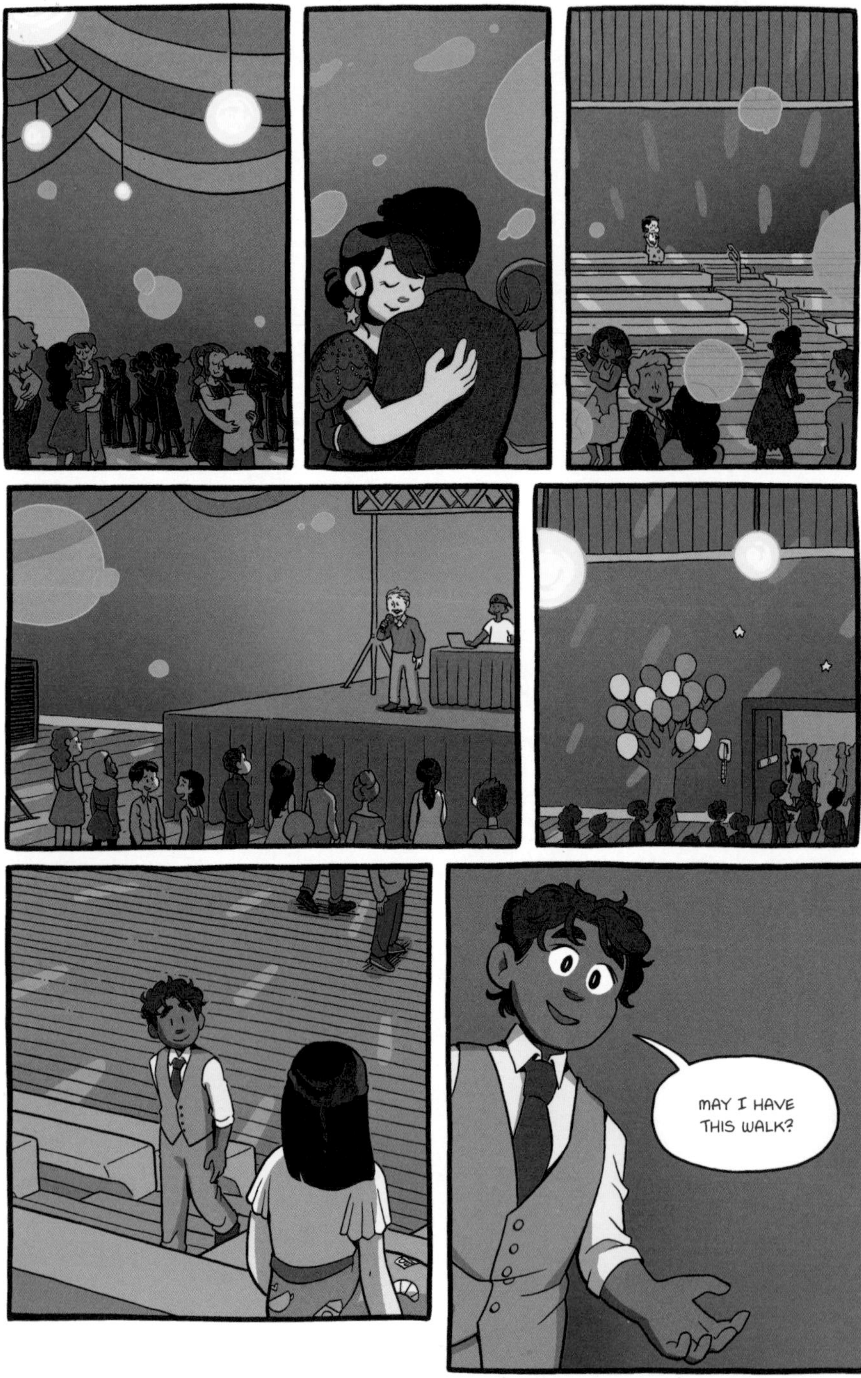
MAY I HAVE THIS WALK?

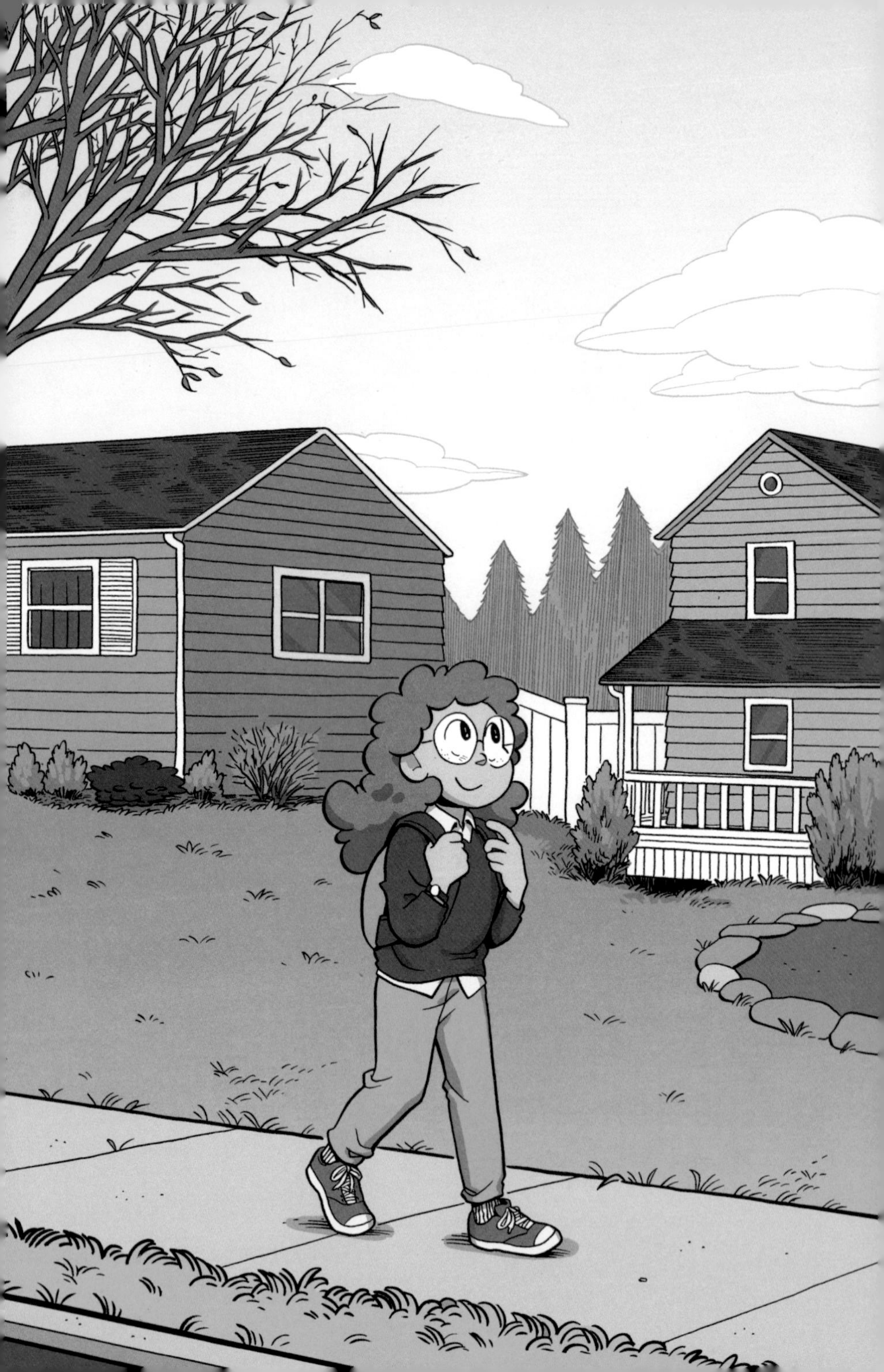

CHAPTER 12

CHAPTER 13

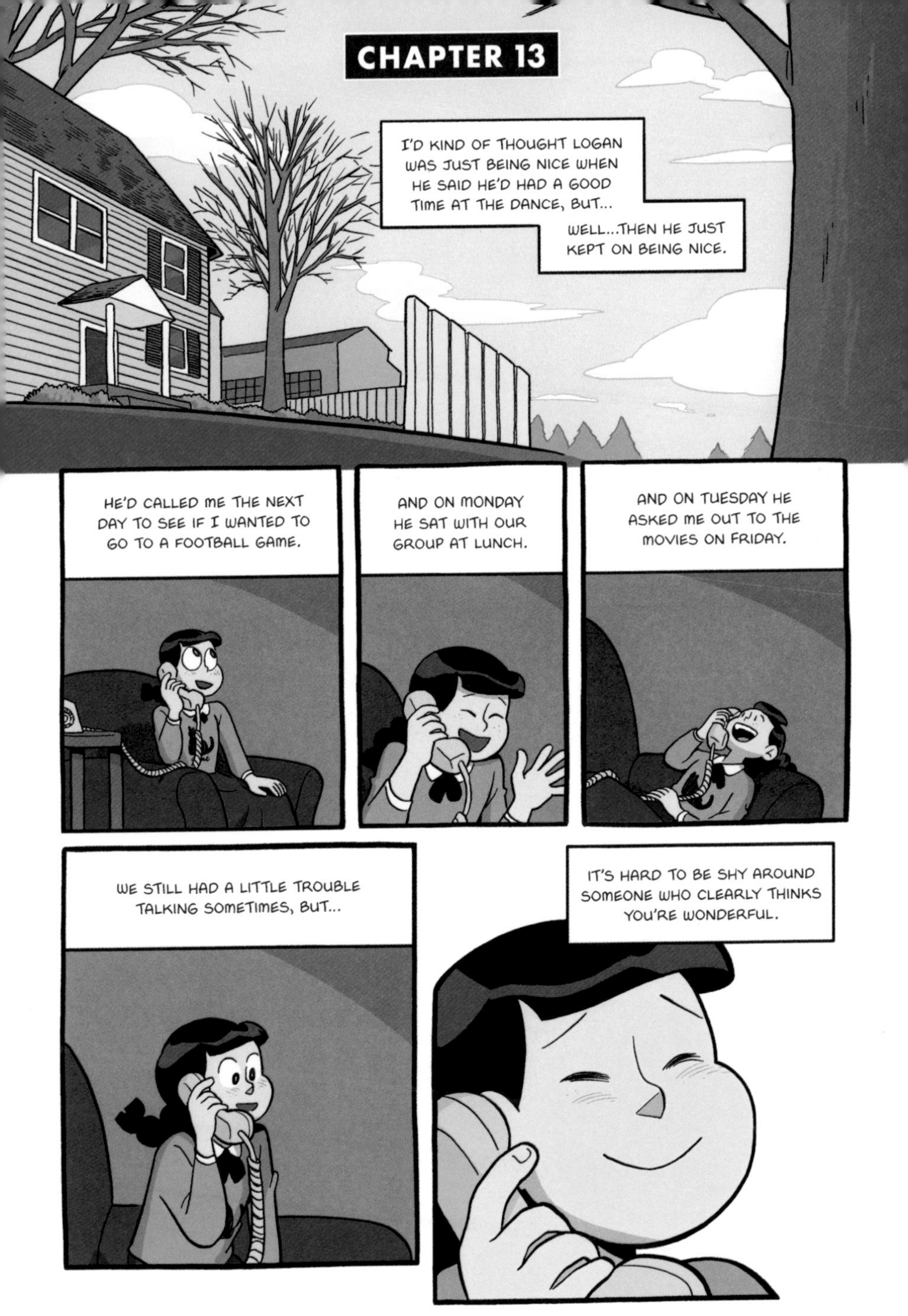
I'D KIND OF THOUGHT LOGAN WAS JUST BEING NICE WHEN HE SAID HE'D HAD A GOOD TIME AT THE DANCE, BUT...
WELL...THEN HE JUST KEPT ON BEING NICE.
HE'D CALLED ME THE NEXT DAY TO SEE IF I WANTED TO GO TO A FOOTBALL GAME.
AND ON MONDAY HE SAT WITH OUR GROUP AT LUNCH.
AND ON TUESDAY HE ASKED ME OUT TO THE MOVIES ON FRIDAY.
WE STILL HAD A LITTLE TROUBLE TALKING SOMETIMES, BUT...
IT'S HARD TO BE SHY AROUND SOMEONE WHO CLEARLY THINKS YOU'RE WONDERFUL.

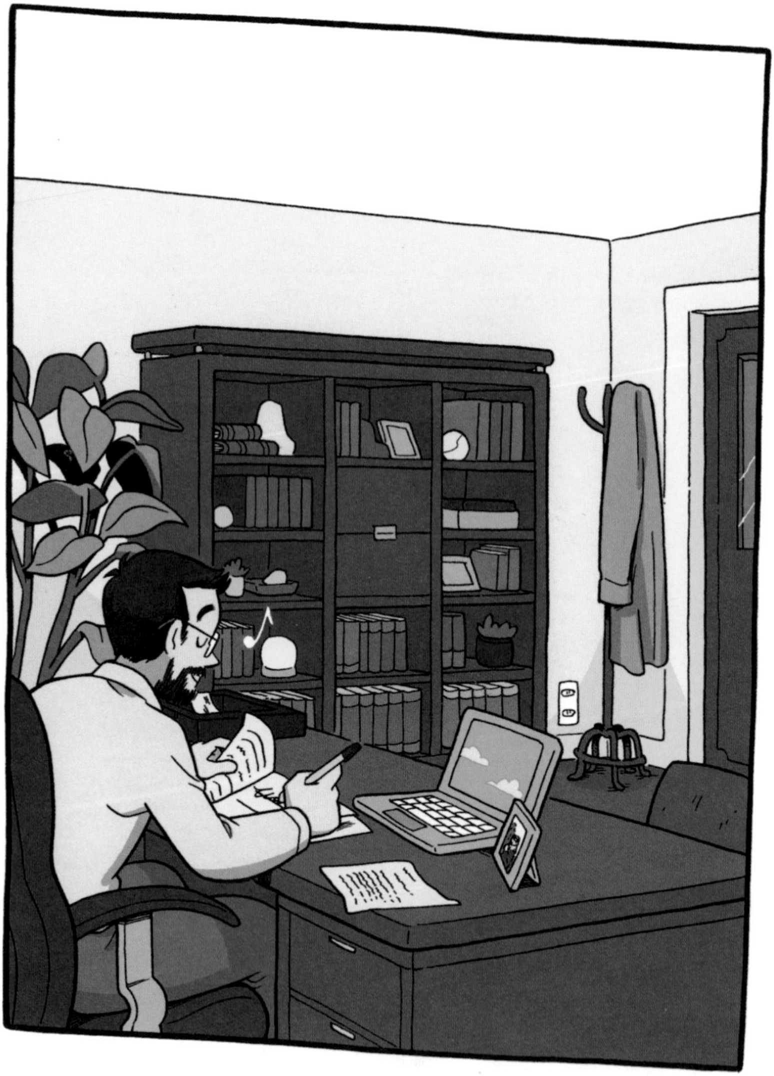

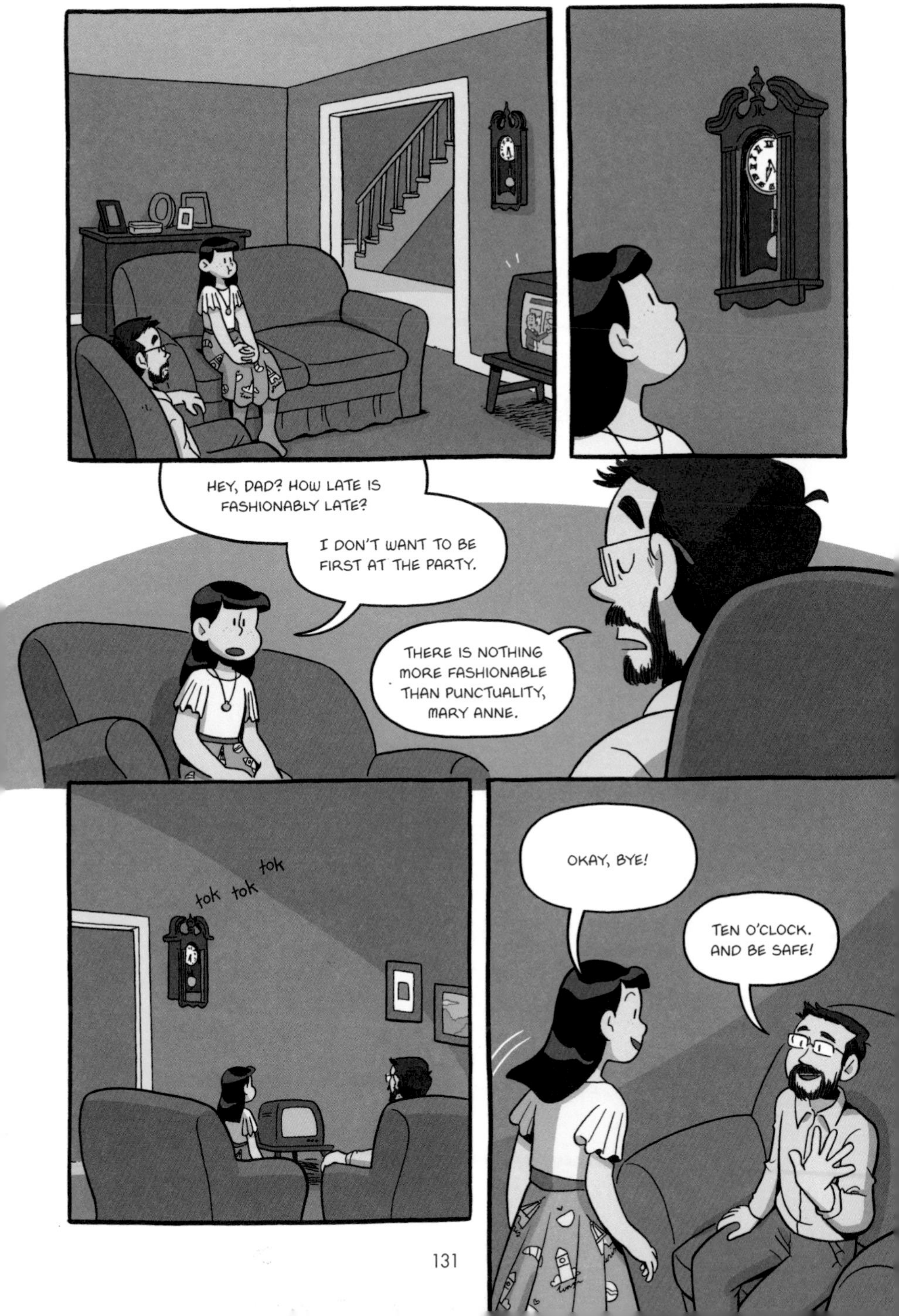
HEY, DAD? HOW LATE IS FASHIONABLY LATE?
I DON'T WANT TO BE FIRST AT THE PARTY.
THERE IS NOTHING MORE FASHIONABLE THAN PUNCTUALITY, MARY ANNE.
tok tok tok
OKAY, BYE!
TEN O'CLOCK. AND BE SAFE!

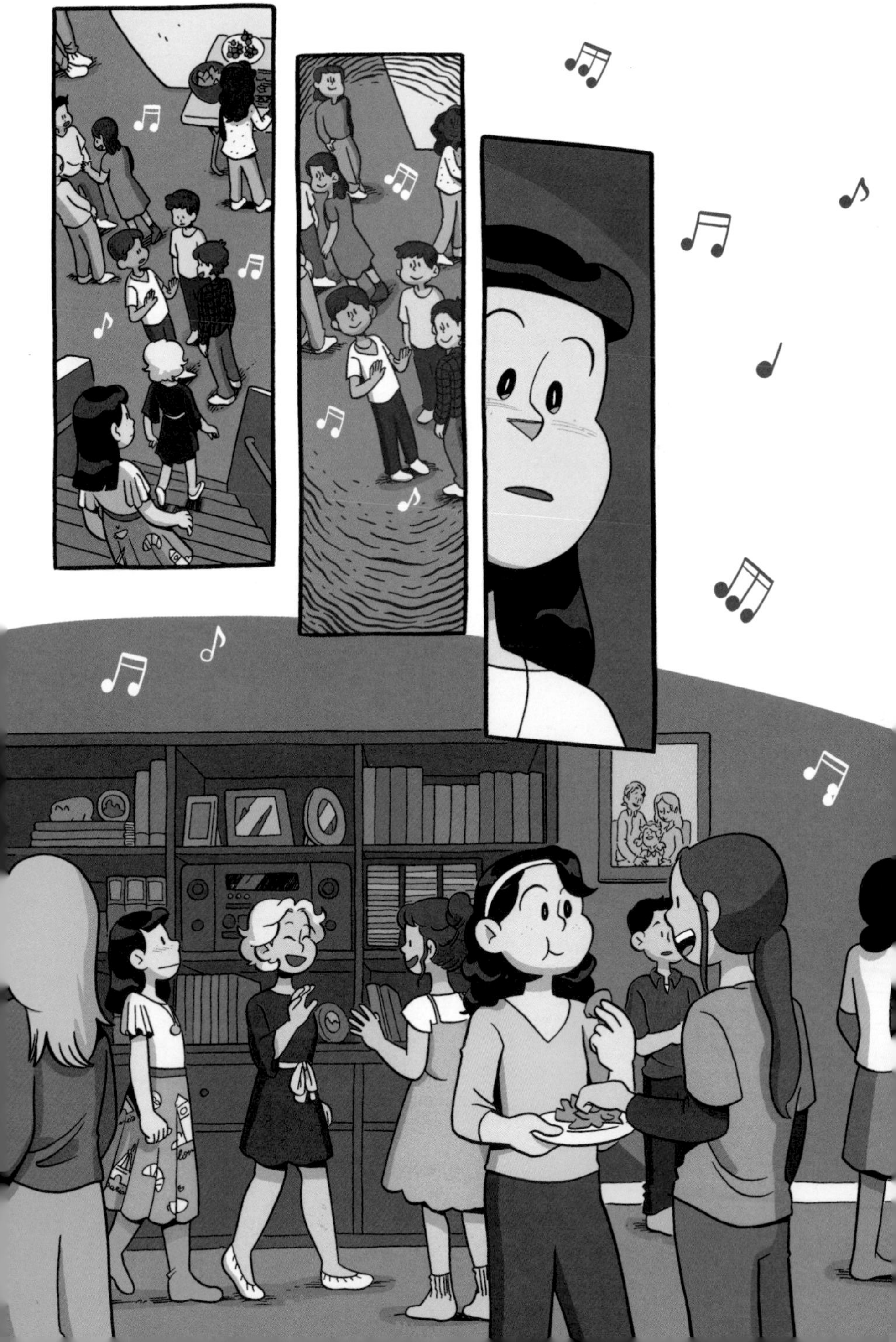

134

click!

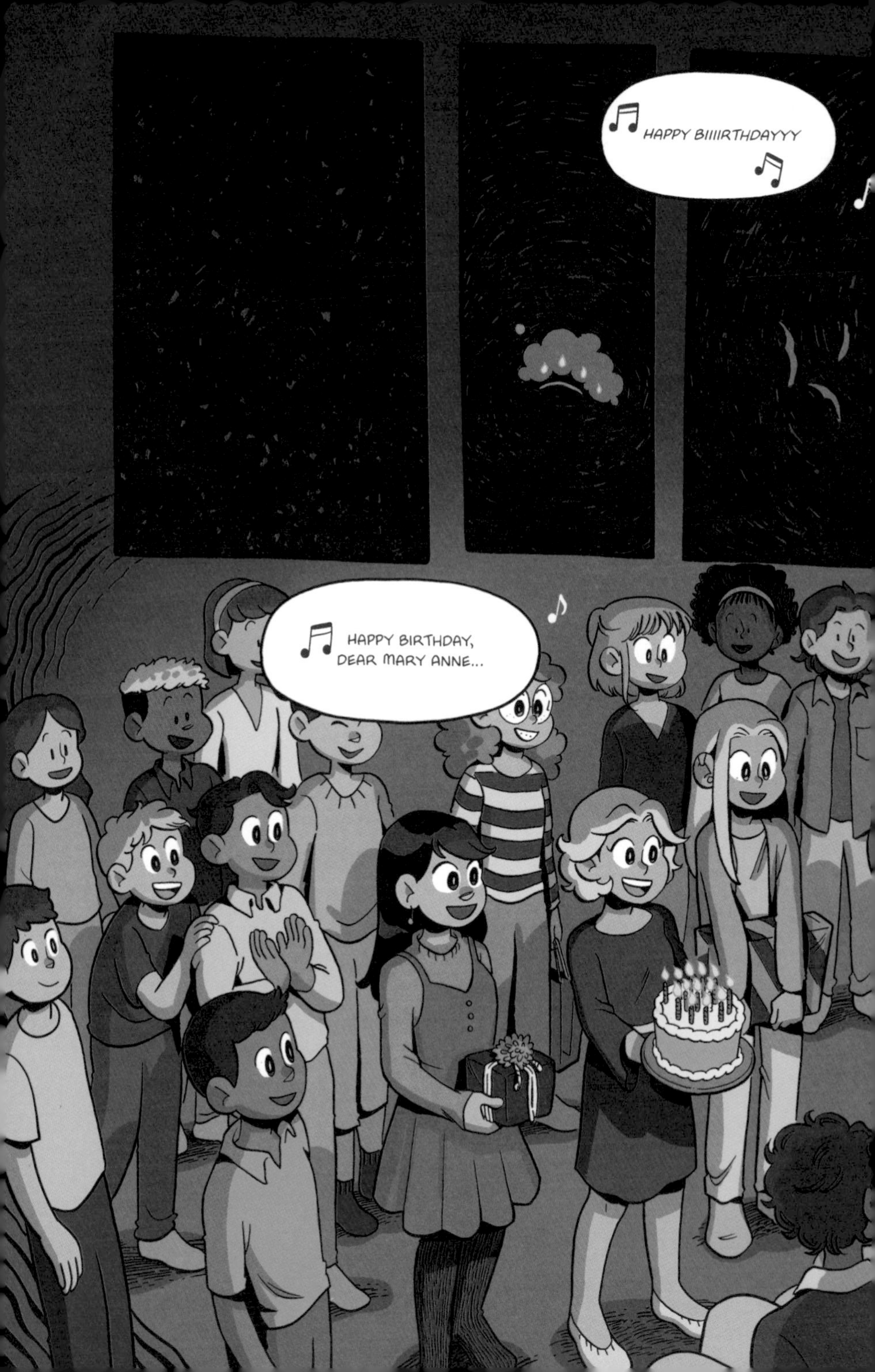
HAPPY BIIIIRTHDAYYY
HAPPY BIRTHDAY, DEAR MARY ANNE...

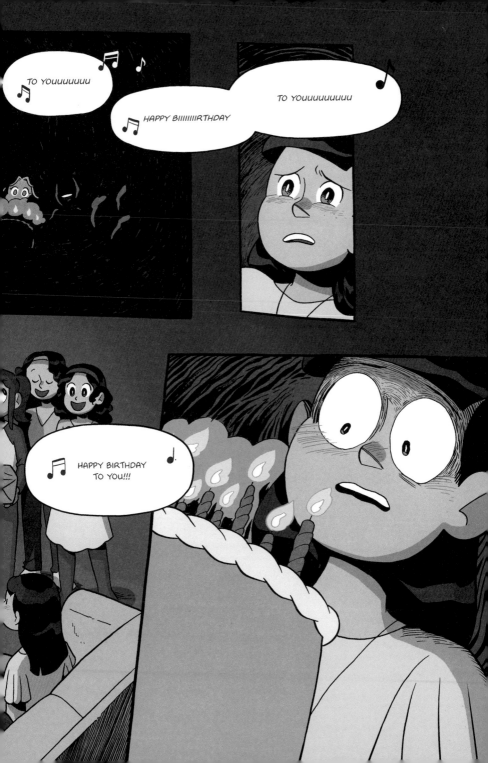

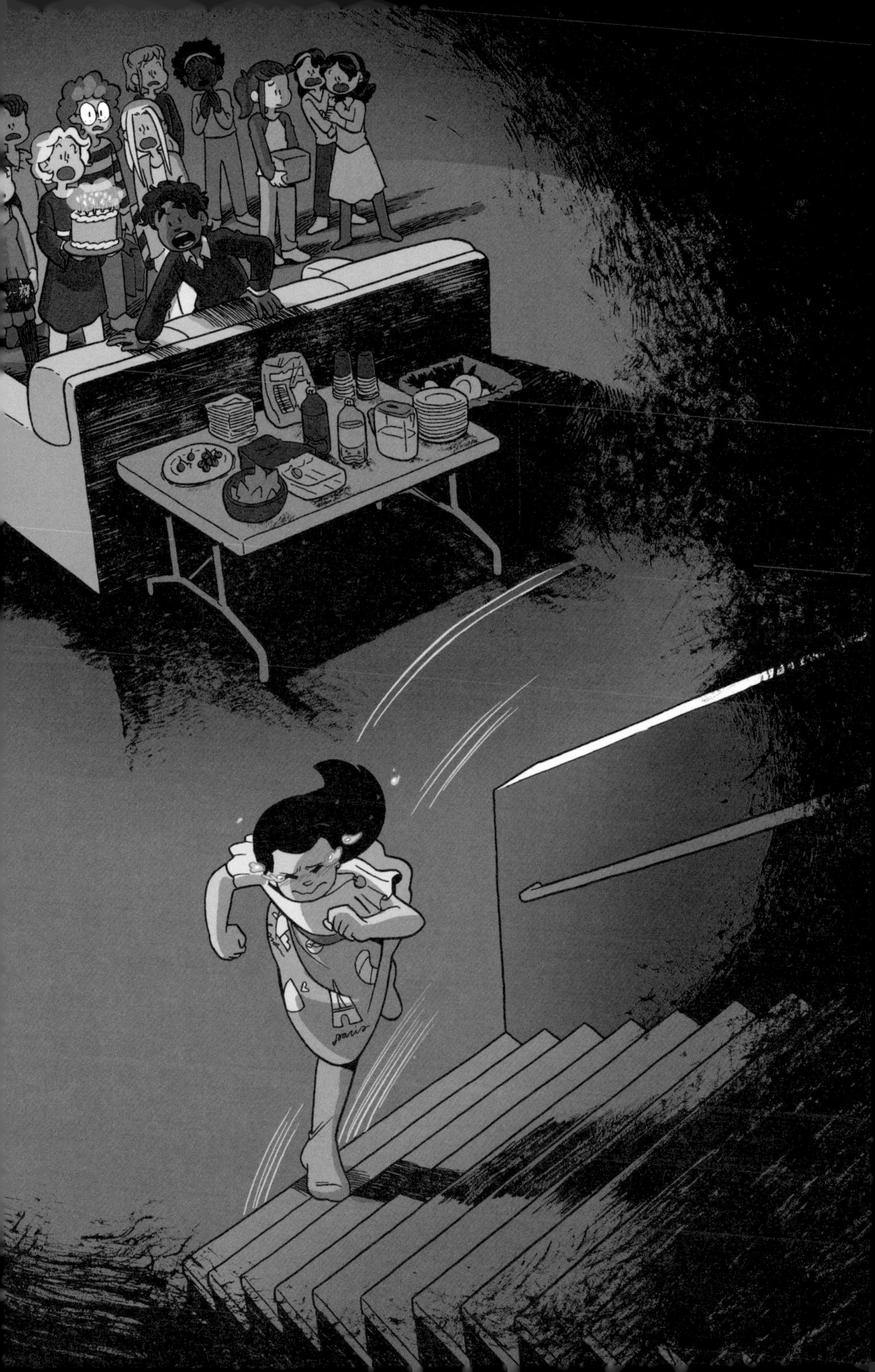

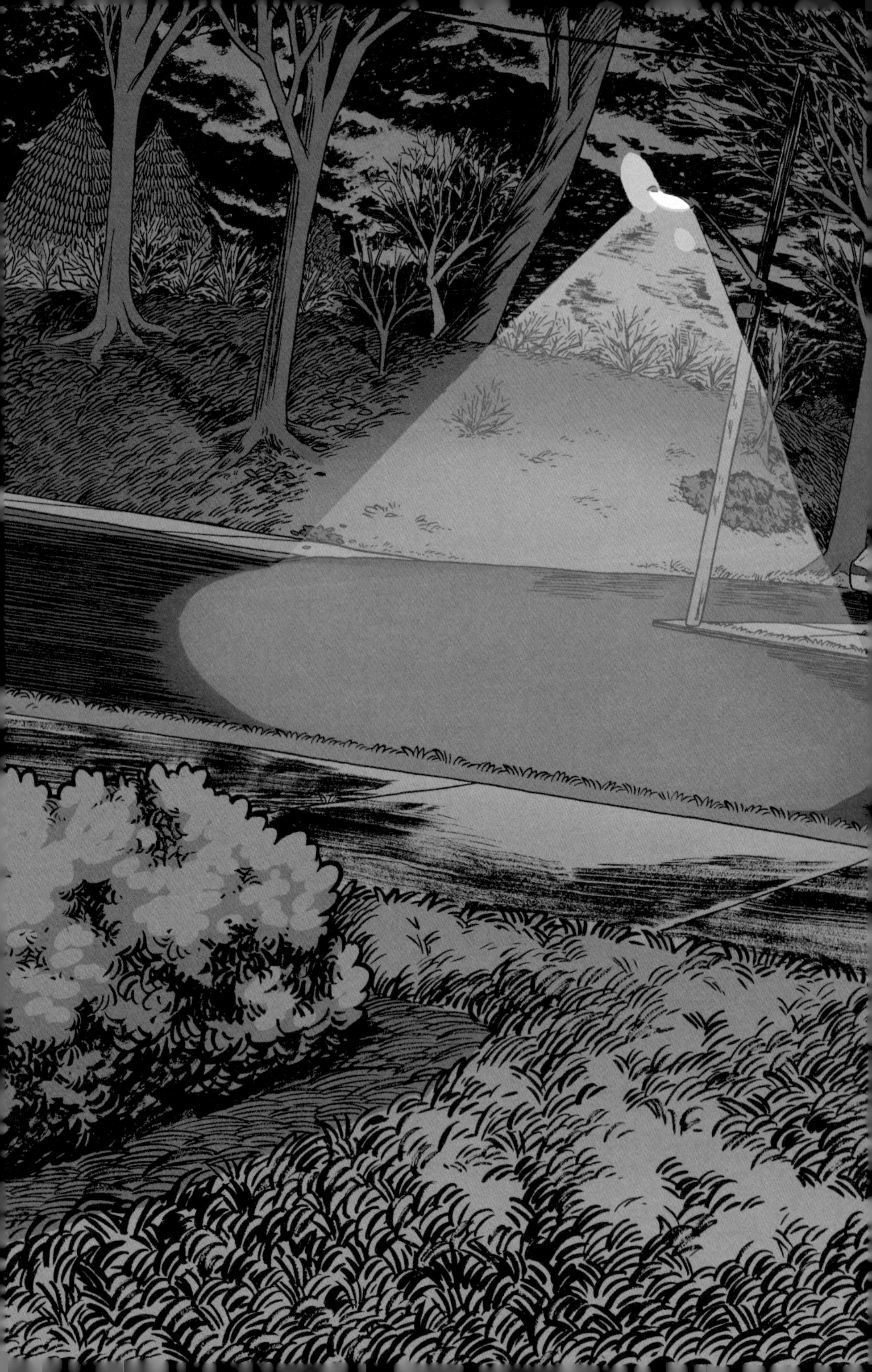

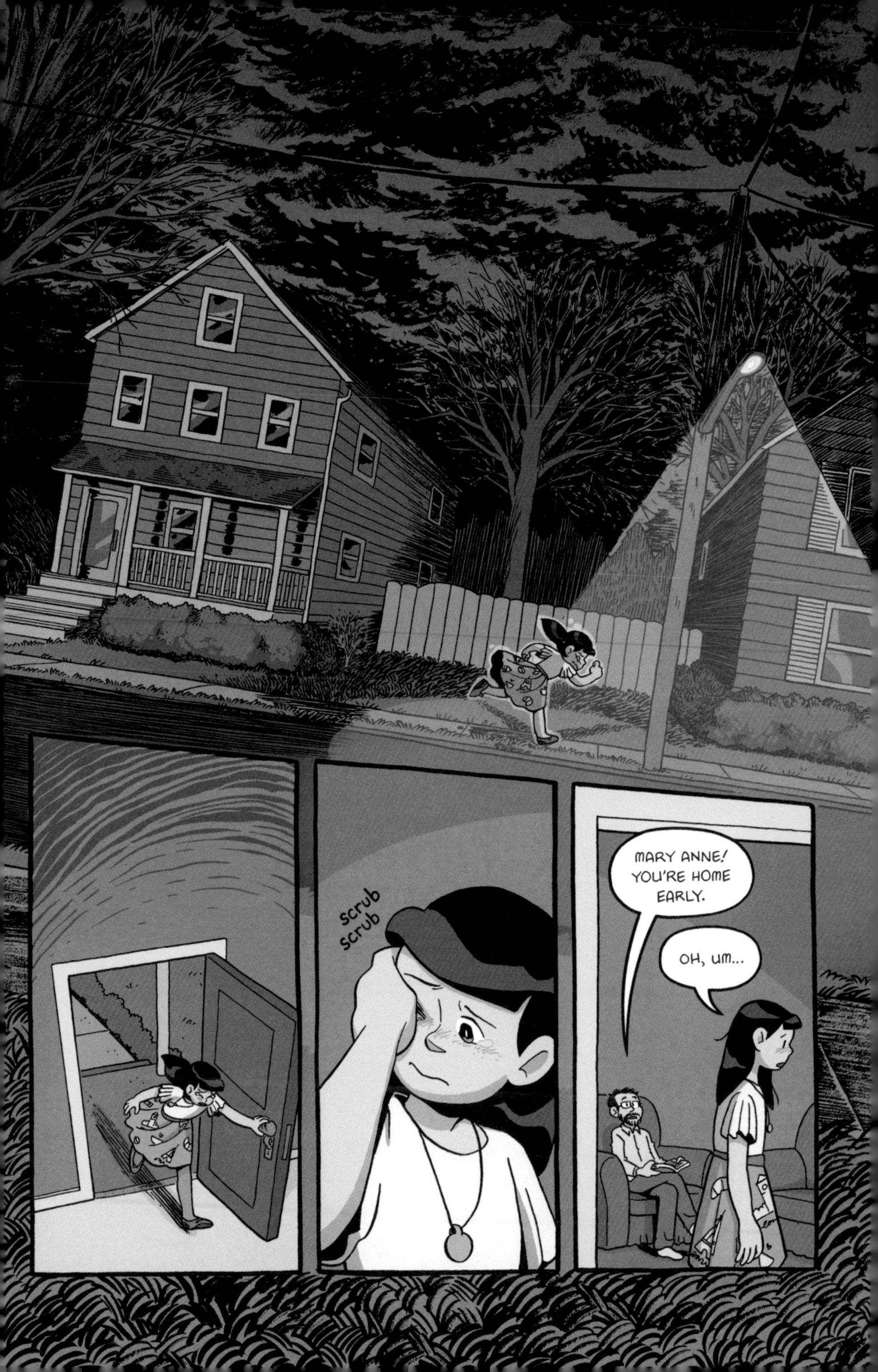
scrub scrub
MARY ANNE! YOU'RE HOME EARLY.
OH, UM...

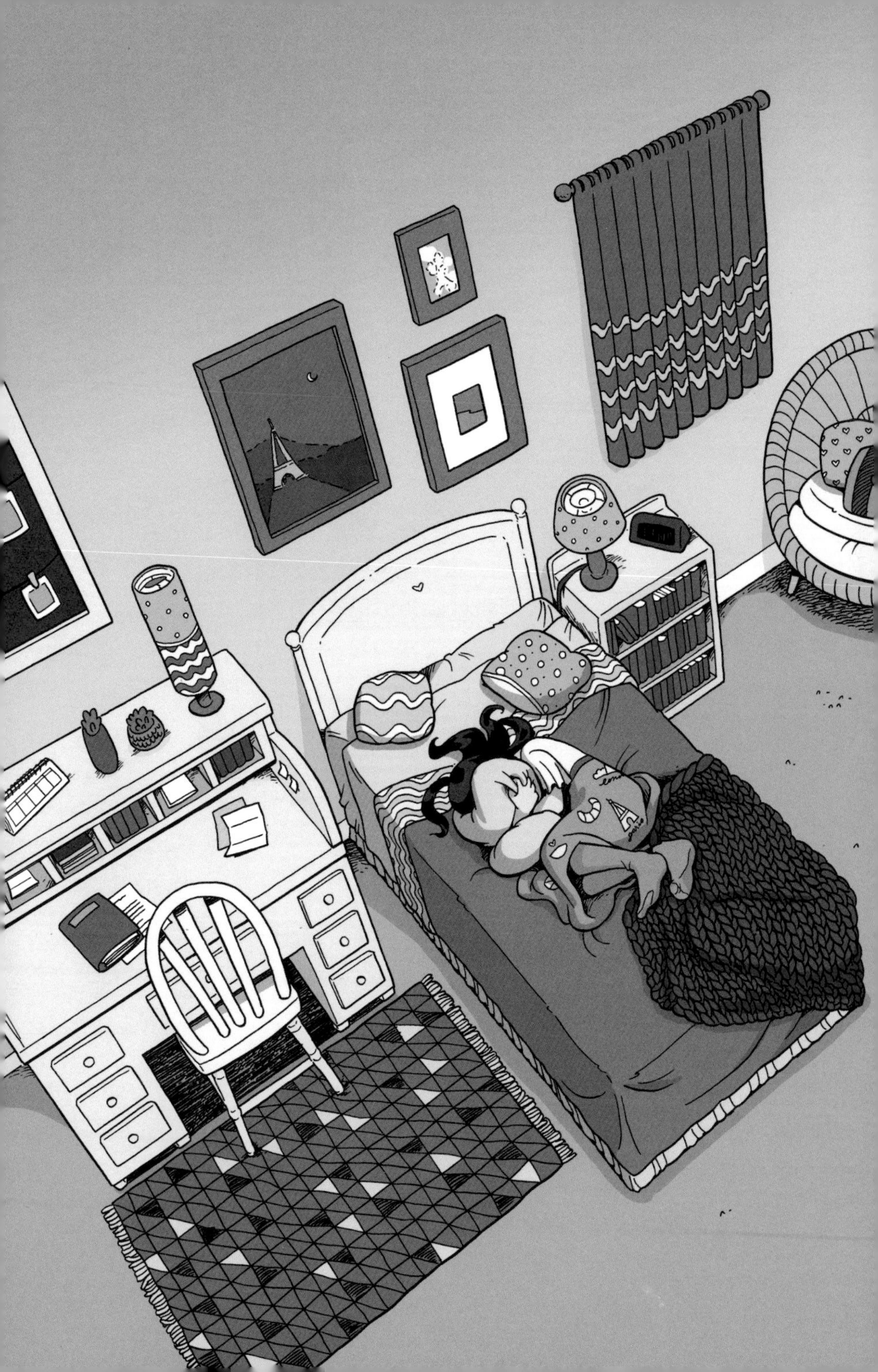
paris

CHAPTER 15

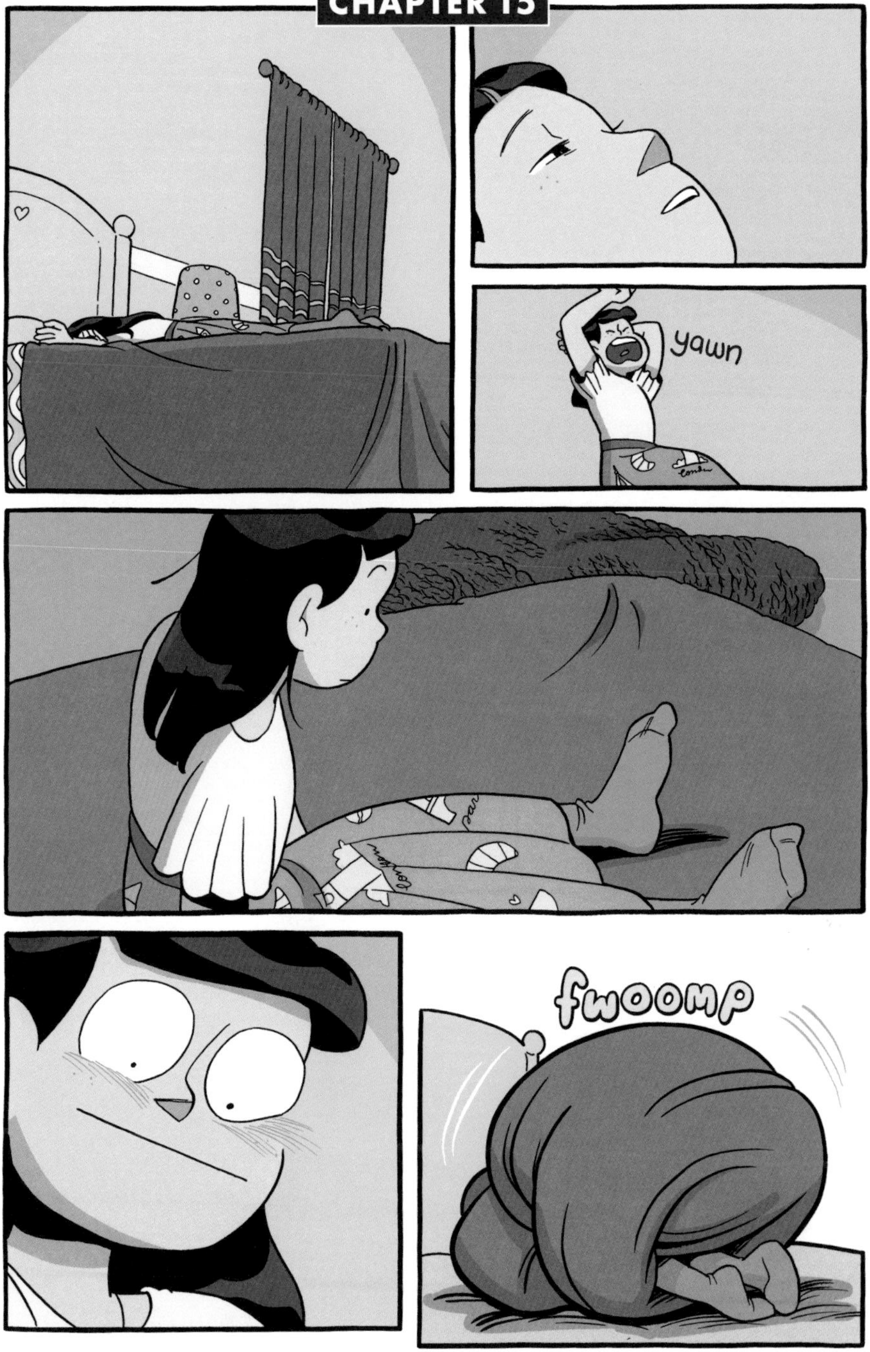
yawn
fwoomp

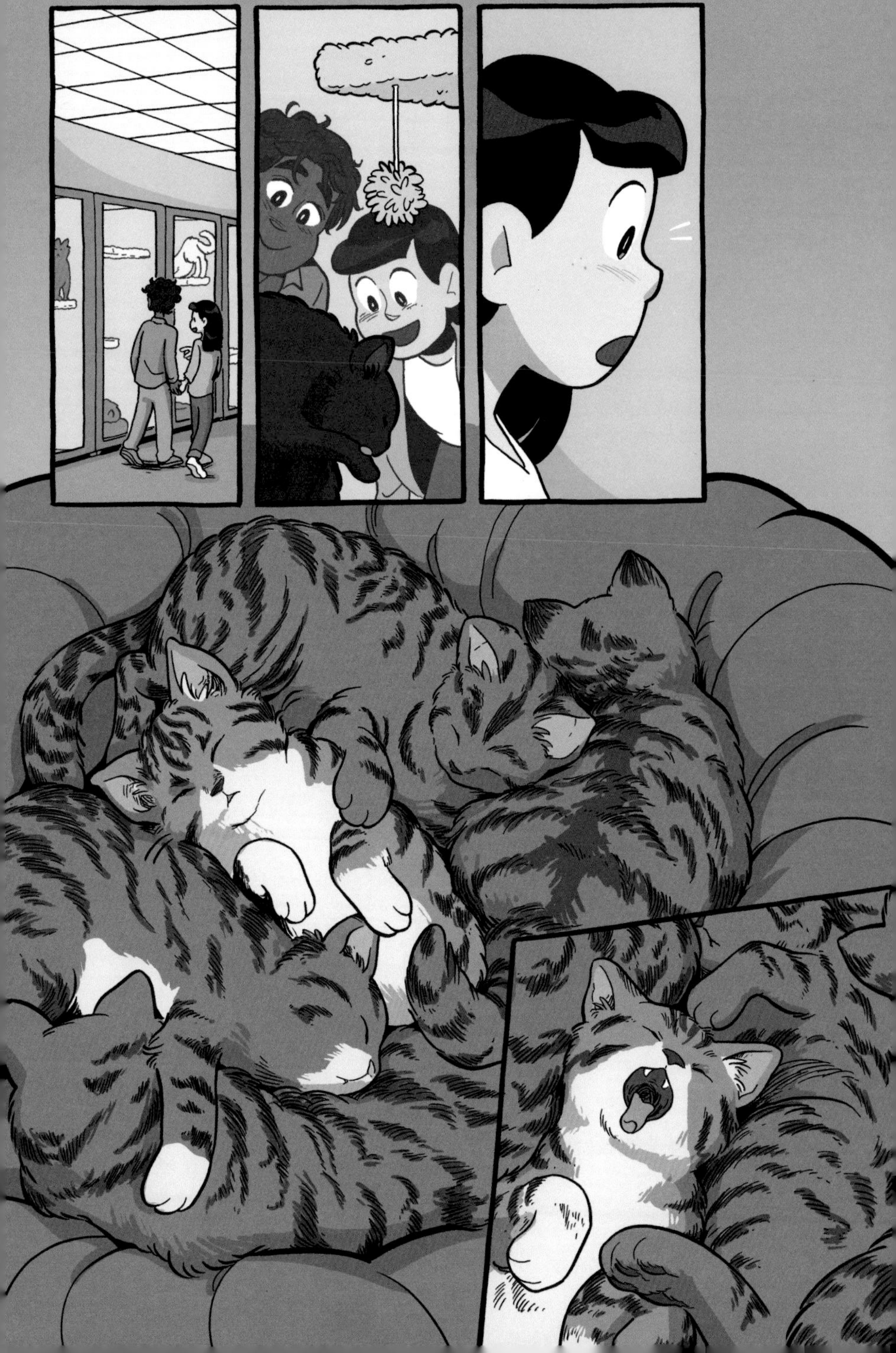

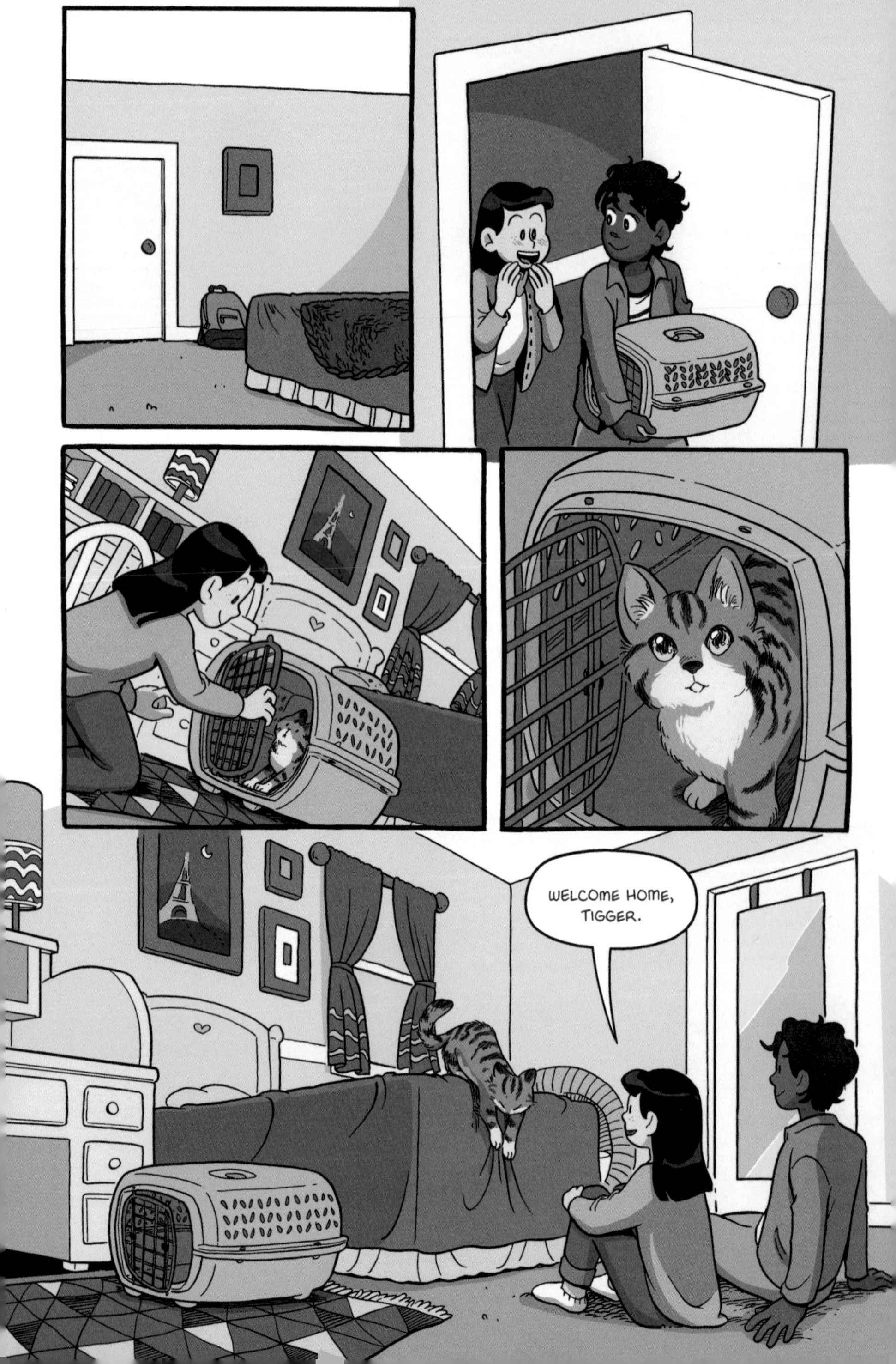
WELCOME HOME, TIGGER.

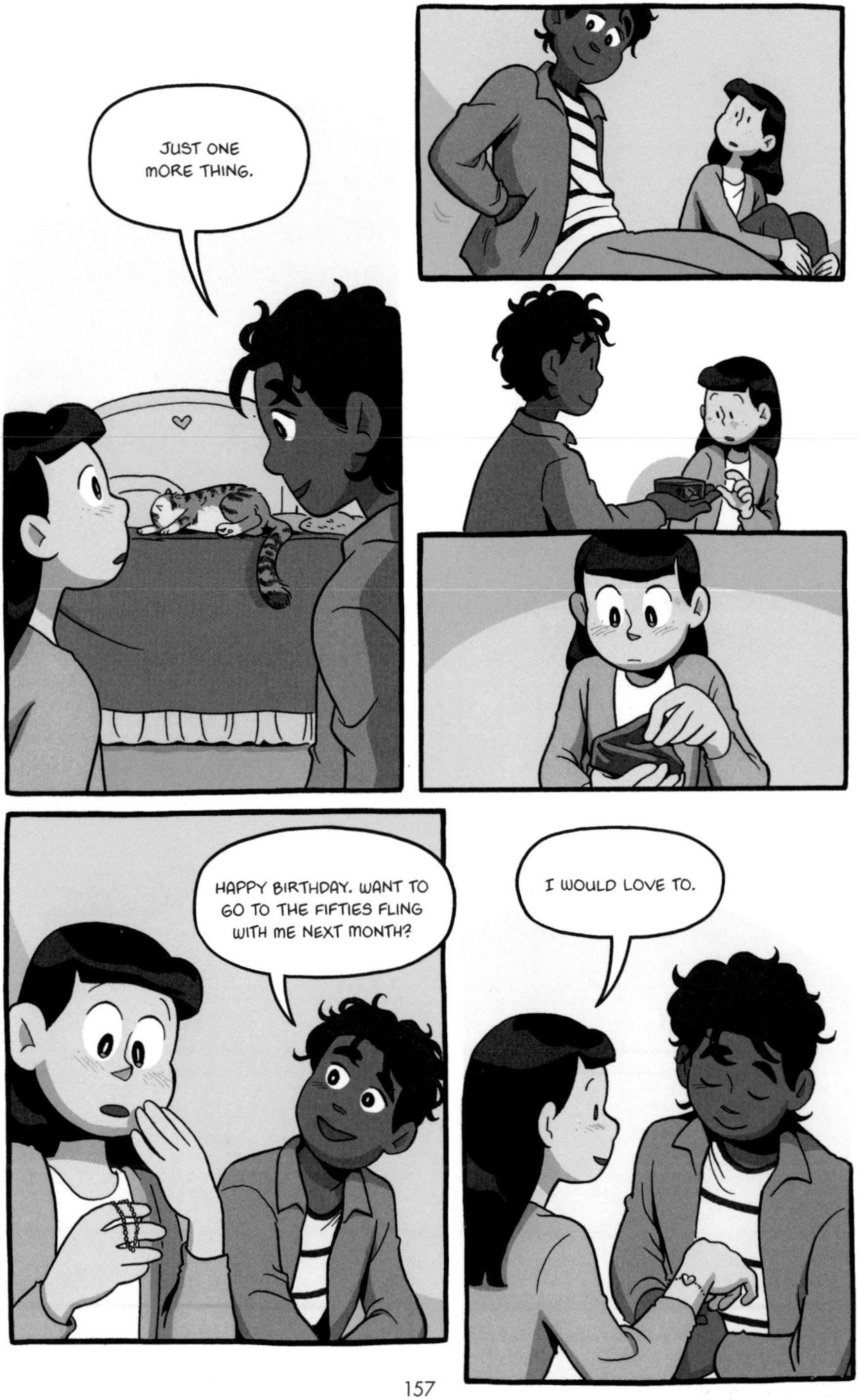
JUST ONE MORE THING.
HAPPY BIRTHDAY. WANT TO GO TO THE FIFTIES FLING WITH ME NEXT MONTH?
I WOULD LOVE TO.

CHAPTER 16

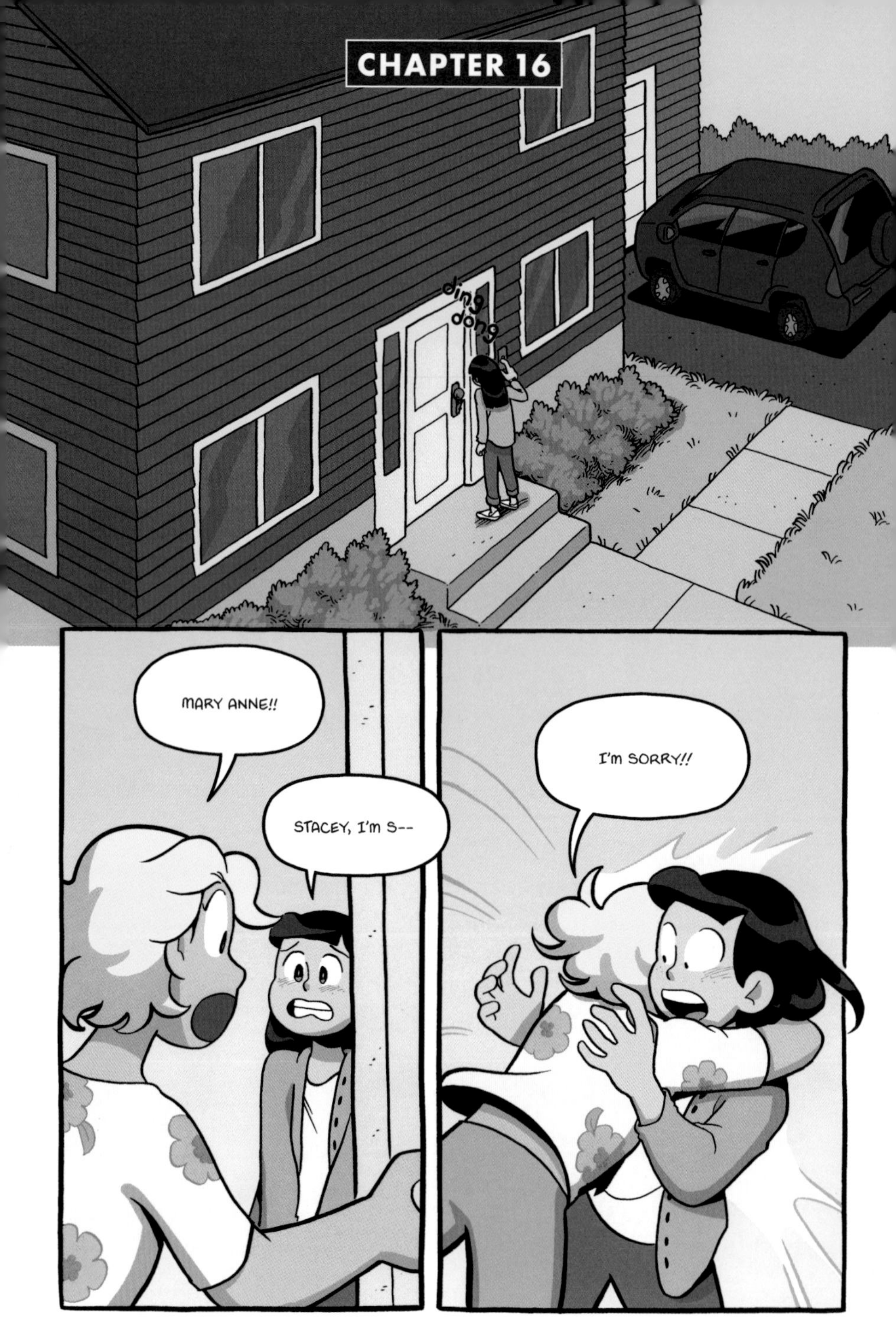
ding
dong
MARY ANNE!!
STACEY, I'm S--
I'm SORRY!!

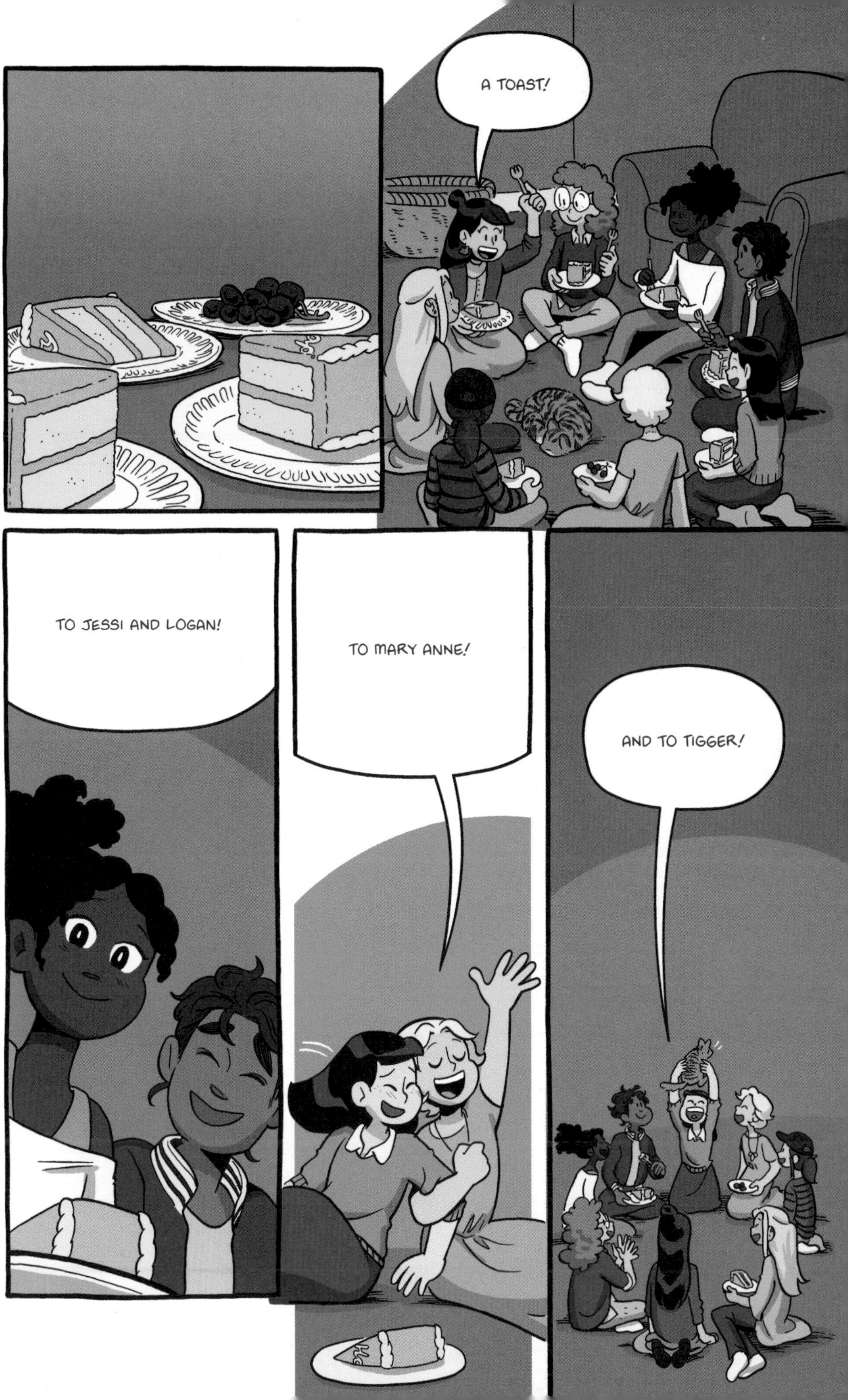
A TOAST!
TO JESSI AND LOGAN!
TO MARY ANNE!
AND TO TIGGER!

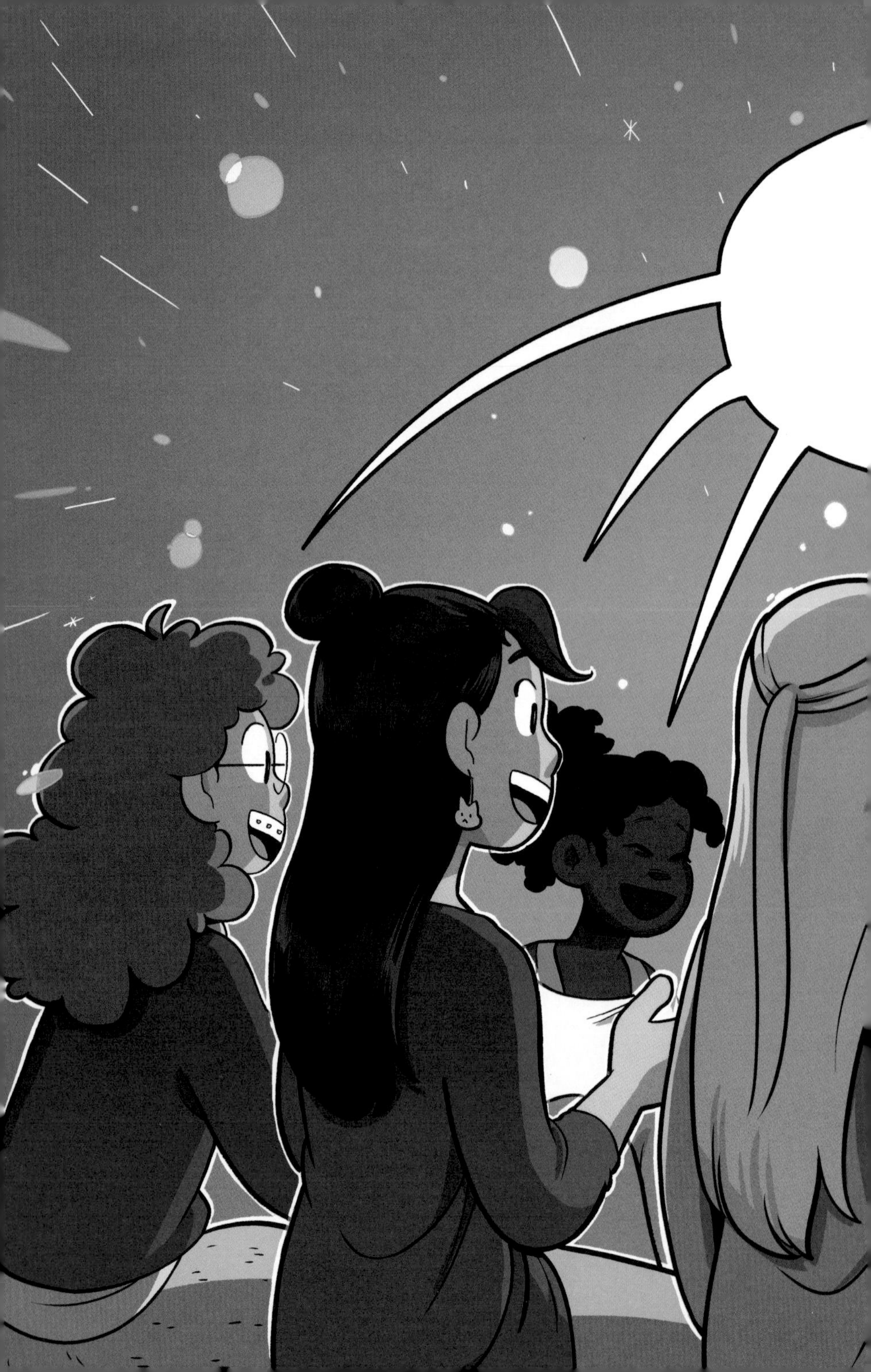

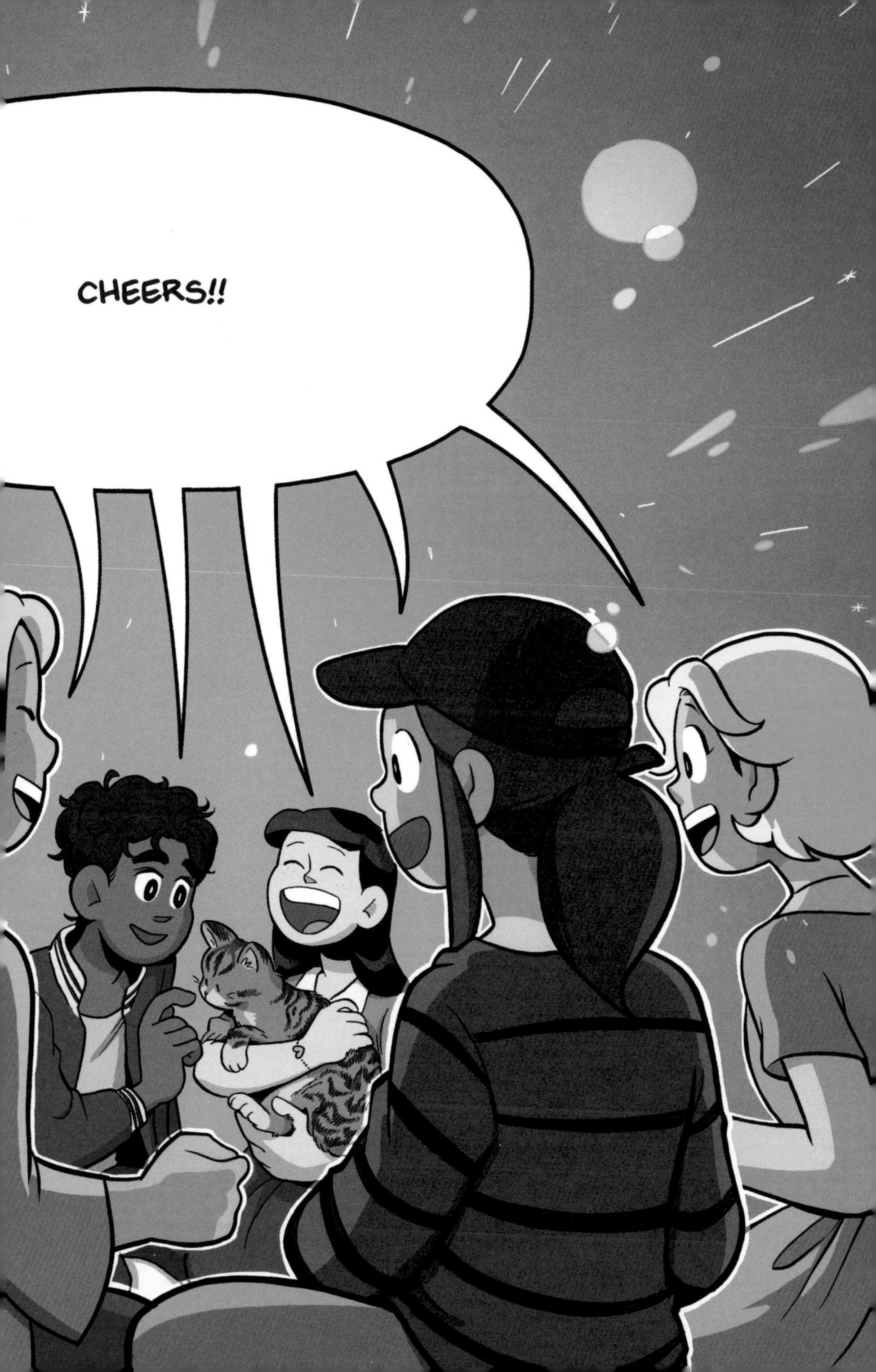
CHEERS!!

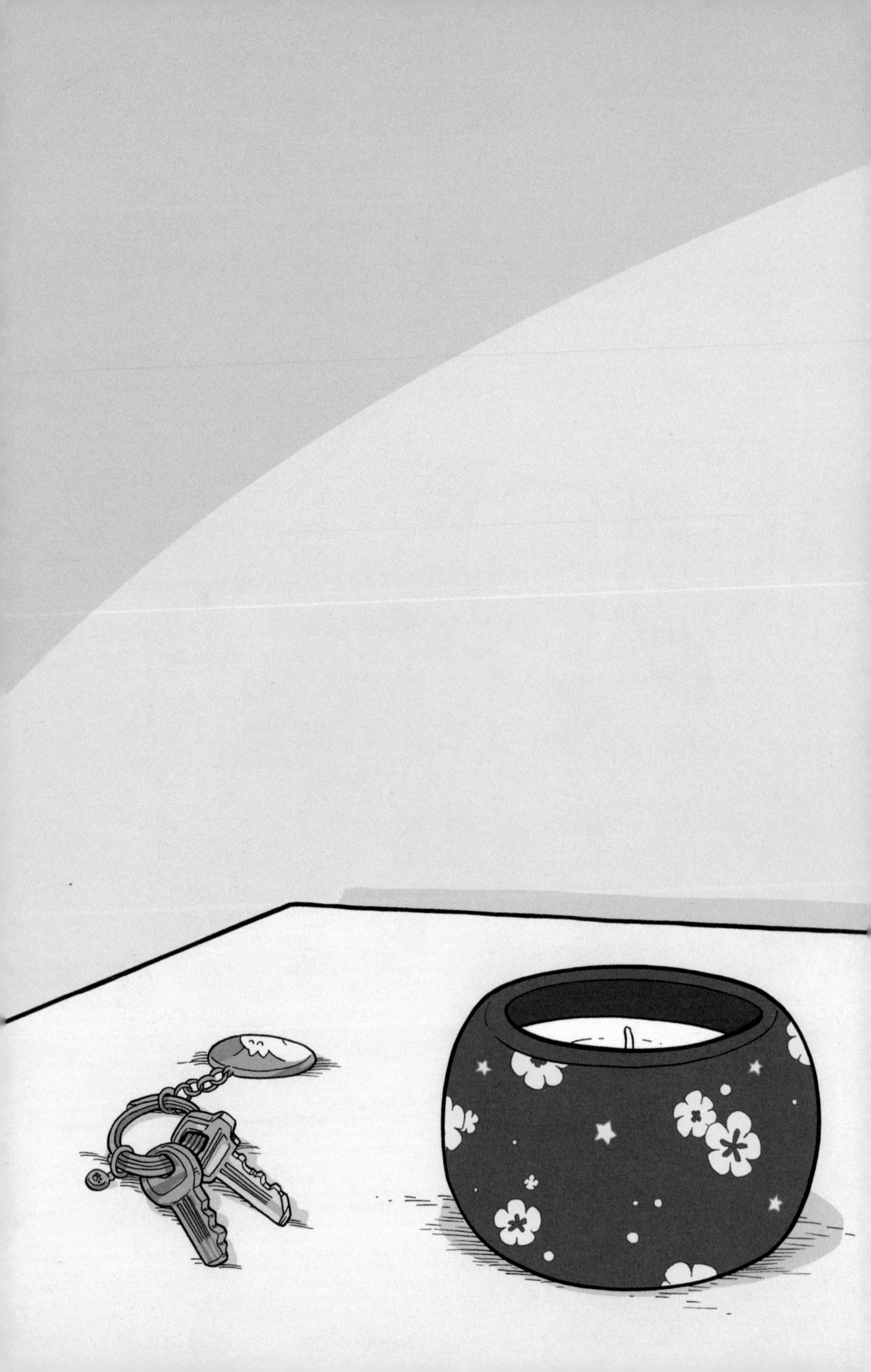

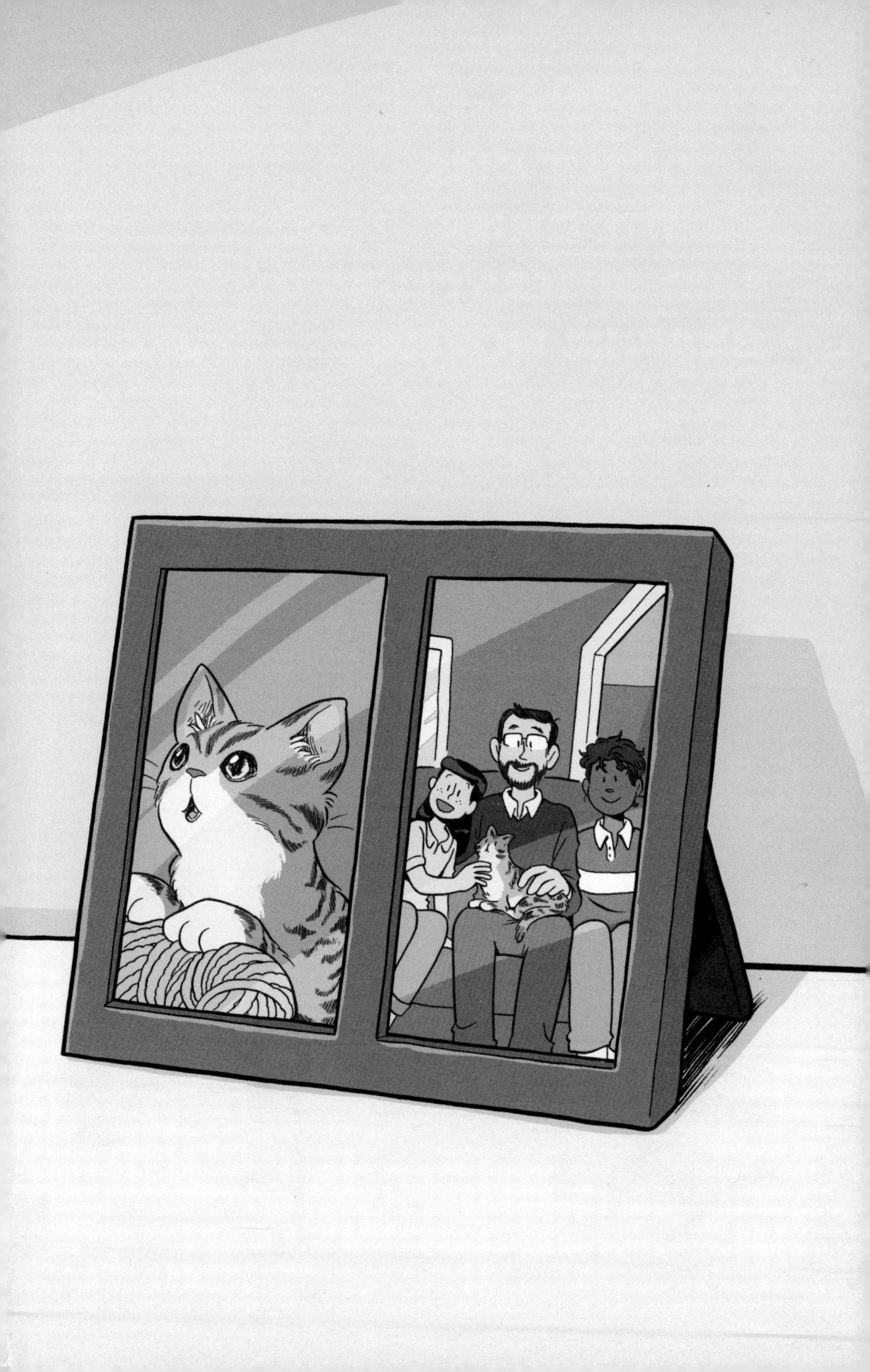

DON'T MISS THE OTHER BABY-SITTERS CLUB GRAPHIC NOVELS!

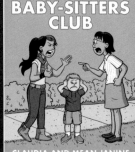

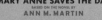